ANGEL'S TARGET

A PARANORMAL ANGEL ROMANCE

ELEMENTAL ANGELS

AIMEE ROBINSON

AMR PUBLISHING LLC

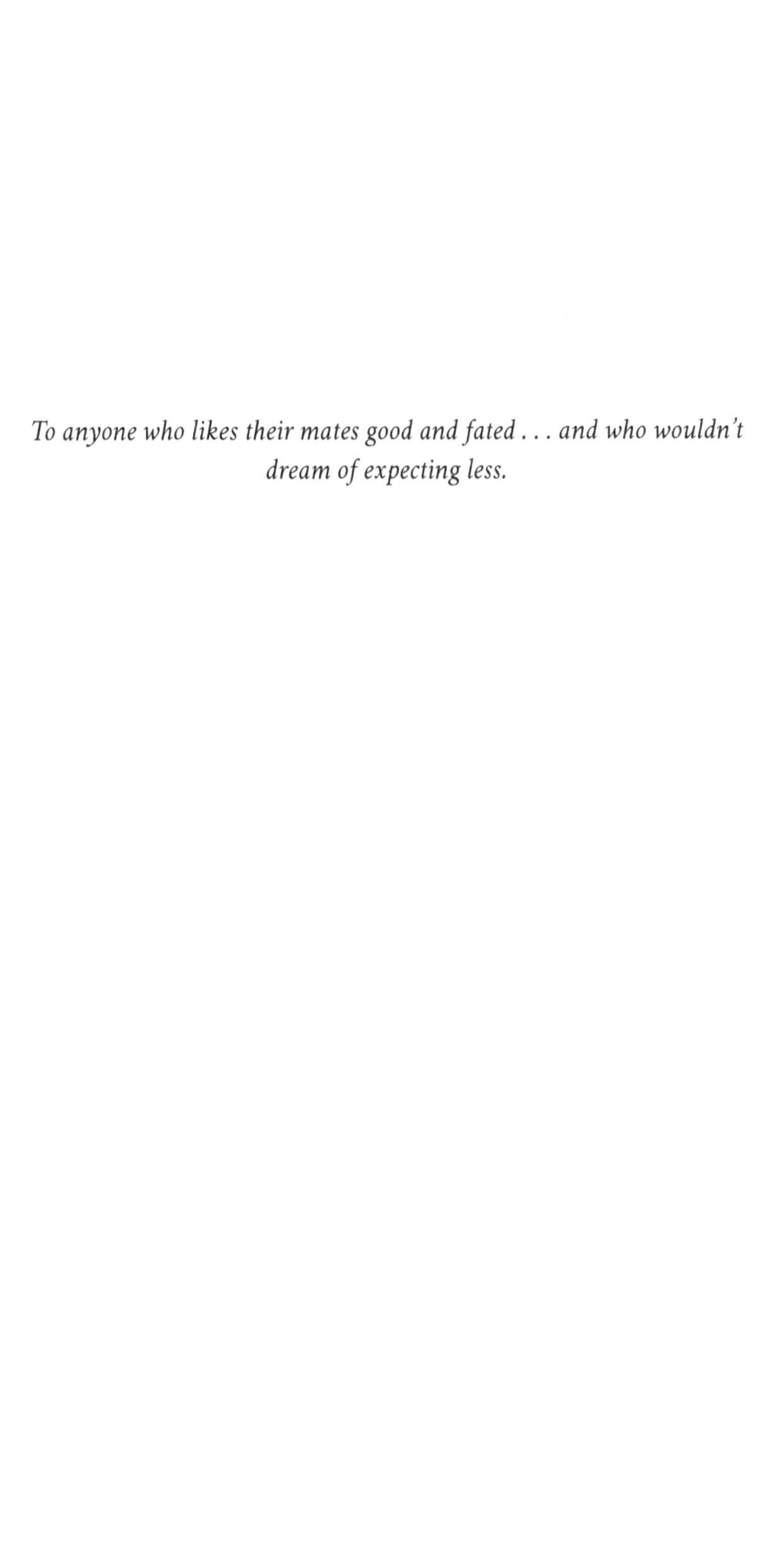

*To anyone who likes their mates good and fated . . . and who wouldn't
dream of expecting less.*

ELEMENTAL ANGELS

Angel's Target

Angel's Duty

Angel's Devotion

Angel's Light

Titan's nose twitched as the unmistakable scent of his enemy's charred flesh hit him square in the face. But it wasn't just the common pig-roasting-on-a-spit aroma that got to him as he took a knee to the pavement and jerked his arrow free from the first body and then his second arrow from the other. Cooked meat he could handle. But the smell of burning blood, with all that copper pummeling his olfactory system, hit a little too close to home.

Always did.

He wiped clean the steaming tips of his arrows across his thigh and sighed in frustration. There was no getting around it. He'd have to torch his favorite pants to remove the stink. A minor inconvenience, he supposed, but that didn't mean he couldn't at least be a little annoyed about it. As he sheathed the last of his arrows, a low whistle rang out behind him. The thud of heavy boots on the blacktop followed.

"I know I'm always giving you shit for all your archery range time, but it's hard to argue with results like that."

Titan peered over his shoulder at the smart-mouthed angel to his rear. Massive wings of gleaming chrome, glinting under the rays of a nearby parking lot light, spread wide from behind the man's immensely broad shoulders. Titan had known the fellow sentinel his entire existence, and still his size never failed to give him brief pause. Chrome's whole body, all bouldered muscles and imposing strength, matched his wings in color and hardness. Everything about the angel, from skin to eyes to hair, shone as brightly as the moon's satellite glow. Yet, as soon as the angel's feet touched down, those condor-length wings retracted into his back and the sheen of his metallic skin followed the retreat. With both feet firmly on the ground, Chrome stood as flesh in front of him once more.

And he wasted no time in pulling out the half-smoked Nicaraguan cigar from his back pocket. Once the tobacco roll was nestled securely between the man's lips, he snapped his large fingers. In an instant, a blue flame sparked to life and danced across the tip of his thumb, as if his nail regularly moon-lighted as a Bunsen burner. Between the cigars he occasionally lit up and the mint gum he always popped in between, the puffing and lip-smacking were pervasive. And annoying. And not something Titan's tense nerves were up for given the body count at their feet.

Rays of blue shimmered against the metallic flecks of silver in Chrome's eyes as he gently brushed the pad of his thumb over the freshly cut end of the cigar. The tobacco heated bright orange and curled in on itself as Chrome inhaled deeply before calling his angel fire back into his body. Titan didn't miss the smug expression that ghosted across the angel's lips.

"It's called discipline," Titan quipped as he stood and turned to face him, ignoring the smoke gathering around them. His chin twitched as the aroma settled into his beard.

Chrome shrugged. "You call it whatever you like," he said through teeth tightly gripping the cigar before he removed it and exhaled a smoke cloud. "I'll stick with my bullets."

Titan sighed as he rested two hands across the wide leather

bow sling that also secured his quiver to his body in the same manner police officers rested their hands at the top of their Kevlar vests. But his type of law enforcement was a wee bit different. Cops were the public enforcers of the criminal justice system but were bound by time clocks and union regulations. Titan and his brothers had no rules, except one: annihilate the demon threat to the Empyrean's eternal light. And that involved a bit more razzle-dazzle than your standard-issue municipal firearm. They were judge, jury, and executioner on a celestial scale, battling an evil mortals couldn't comprehend.

Like the bodies before him.

He stared down at the singed aftermath of his precision and pressed his lips together in frustration. The kills had been easy, welcome, and completely unexpected.

"We haven't heard anything from the charmers for months. Freaking months! And they show up now? In a random loading dock of a home supply center in a suburban New Hampshire strip mall, of all places? Something doesn't make sense." Titan huffed in frustration. The sudden appearance troubled him beyond words, causing his already frazzled nerves to bristle with further tension.

Chrome circled around the bodies like a scavenger sizing up roadkill.

"Well, at least they still look the same. Nothing's changed on that front."

Titan scoffed. "Did you expect the charmers to look different somehow?"

"No. Just grateful for small victories. As you said, it's been a hot minute since we've come across one. Who the hell knows what sick magic the demons are now capable of? For all I know, they could have figured out how to masquerade as little old ladies who wear sweaters in eighty-degree weather and clip coupons all day." Chrome pointed at Titan and raised a single thick brow. "A win is a win, brother."

Titan dropped his gaze to the ground again, though the stench was more than enough to sting his eyes and then some. The bodies at his feet lay still as the final shimmers of swirling gold and teal tattoos settled into nothing more than etched designs against translucent pale skin and bald scalps. The frames of the demon magic users were tall and fit, and their physiques didn't shy away from the apparent strength of their toned nature.

Chrome kicked the lifeless arm nearest him.

"This one's a mystic charmer. See?" He gestured toward the single gold bands around the body's neck and biceps. "At least you got 'em from afar. If they had been from the elite class, and there were two bands on their bodies instead of one, you would have had to actually work to earn your dinner. Those elite fuckers are nasty in hand-to-hand combat."

"I don't give a shit how many bands they have on their arms. You think I'm checking for a driver's license before I smoke them? I shoot sight unseen, regardless of whether they're elite warriors or mystic conjurers. They burn all the same. Besides, mystics are every bit as menacing once they open their spell-casting mouths."

And also every bit as visible to humans until Chrome cleaned up the mess.

"I won't argue with you on that one."

Despite the failed reconnaissance from him and his brothers, and Chrome's not-so-subtle ribbing, Titan was truly grateful nothing had changed about his technique, at least. An arrow, or any weapon for that matter, laced with angel fire still seemed to do the trick. Extra crispy all around, or at least they would be when Chrome did his cleanup. Good to know, though, that Titan could still kill the fuckers with a little stealth and patience. Easy peasy lemon squeezy.

"Did you catch the other one? A third fled after my first arrow hit. While I reloaded, the charmer got wise and bolted."

"No." Chrome cursed as he tapped out his ashes on one of the smoking bodies below. "Fucker heard me coming. He used his magic to ghost out."

"Shit." Titan dropped his hands to his hips and paced in agitation.

He walked over to a nearby streetlight and gripped the thing so tightly at first, flecks of the column's cast iron nearly jumped out of his way like fleeing sewer rats. His fingers settled into the vertical grooves as the metal provided an excellent grip for one to imagine strangling the life out of his enemy. The cold of the black structure was a comfort as he slowly relaxed his fingers, leaned forward, and settled his forehead against its hard surface. Though the column was predominantly made from cast iron and not the titanium his form commanded, the deep ore of the metal still soothed him. Titan inhaled deeply and let its cold, earthen properties settle his jagged nerves. No, not jagged. More like shredded through a rasp grater before being thrown under a concrete mill with diamond-tipped blades.

That more accurately described his frustration and failure.

A sharp tug on his shoulder had his eyes flying open. Though the evening was cool courtesy of the New England October, his forehead still sported a light sheen of sweat.

But it wasn't Chrome's hand that had jarred him to focus.

"If it's a firm grip on something that you're needing, I can think of better things to hug than a streetlamp."

He'd been too distracted to even hear the angel touch down, let alone walk right up to him and grip him by the shoulder. Such an unacceptable lack of awareness. Damn, he needed to get his head in the game.

Titan relaxed his hands and turned to meet the steel-gray eyes of Tungsten. The man's hand on his shoulder didn't move but, rather, held firm to Titan like a safety harness, as if Tung knew Titan's mind had gone wandering into darker places and their leader needed to throw him a line. Which was ridiculous, really. Because Tung was their prime, the commander of the sentinels, and it was Titan's role as second to serve and advise *him.* Not the other way around.

Then words like gravel, spoken too low for anyone else's ears, penetrated his pity party. "We have a lead."

Titan whipped his head around, nearly knocking over the heavily muscled angel in front of him. Tung's words . . . Surely, Titan had heard wrong.

"What?" Shock and renewed determination flooded his body, all but providing a visible pep in his step. "How? I killed those two, and Chrome said the third got away."

At the mention of the enemy, Titan glanced over at the bodies. Chrome had taken a knee between the two stiffs and gripped the forearm of each charmer. His military-style fade highlighted the sharp angles of his face and body, which were more than menacing in their precision. But as he settled the stogy between his lips, it was the bluish tint of his smoke under the moonlight that completed the picture. The angel almost looked like a bizarre rendition of the Thinker. If said Thinker could incinerate hellions with a touch of his finger and then chain light his next cigar off the flames.

As if Titan's mere thought had summoned the stuff, blue flames emerged from Chrome's palms and slowly snaked up the charmers' bodies. There were no loud pops of superheated fat or water, no raucous licks or sizzles of hair incinerating in the fire. Just a silent simmer and low flame barely worth heating up a science lab beaker or a backyard barbecue weenie. But it got the job done, and when Chrome raised his head to call back his angel fire and inevitably admire his handiwork, all that remained were ashes. The angel would hardly have to recharge his fire at all after expending such little effort.

"There were two more charmers. Mystics also." Tung's eyes flashed pewter as he crossed his arms across the bulk of his chest. A rare sly smile inched over his face. Titan's curiosity was piqued. Tung rarely exhibited such outward displays of confidence. He had always marked their victories with solemn celebrations, never losing sight of the larger picture. There was always another battle to be won, always another course to take beyond the immediate safeguard. For the leader of the sentinels to allow his silent boasting to be visible spoke volumes. Hope, that thorny devil of an emotion, tickled Titan's senses and made his fingers itch to reach for his bow.

"Tell me," Titan demanded.

"I saw them advancing to meet up with their buddies. But they were late to the rendezvous. By the time they arrived, your arrows had already flown and Chrome was giving chase to the third."

"If you saw them, why didn't you—"

Tung's hand flew up. "Aurora. That's where they're going to search for the light. The town's not far from here, and it's their next mark."

Titan initially bristled at Tung's abrupt gesture but didn't take true offense. He was being impetuous. It was a quality ill-suited for the prime's second, and even worse when the stakes were so high. But then Tung's words truly sank in.

"The guiding light from the Empyrean? You think they've finally found it in the mortal realm after all this time?"

A solemn nod was all the confirmation Tung offered.

"I can't believe we finally have a lead on the light. An actual lead! Do you realize what this means?" The words flew fast and fierce now. Damn, desperation wasn't a good look on him.

"Be still, Titan. This agitation does not serve you. Or us."

Titan swallowed down his unspent words and exhaled. It was as if the breath that left him had been lodged in his lungs since he and his brothers had first fallen from the Empyrean— the highest realm of heaven. A shaky nod was all he could offer in place of composure.

"We think it's a woman, Titan. They're going after another woman."

Tung's firm grip settled along the column of Titan's neck, and he was gently pulled closer to the angel. The multifaceted gesture was meant to impress importance and urgency to any onlookers but also impart comfort and understanding into his uncharacteristically distracted second.

Stern pewter eyes shot daggers at Titan and offered a solemn reminder of the second's tragedy six months ago, the last time they had learned of the charmers' intentions to go after the light.

The last time a woman had been the target.

And the last time—no, the *only* time—Titan had failed to protect a human from the charmers. An abduction, of all things. Not the charmers' usual style, but devastating nonetheless.

Resolve bloomed white-hot behind his ribs. His arm tensed and sprang up to enact a similar grasp on the side of Tung's neck.

"When?" he bit out with a ferocity he had no qualms displaying to his prime. "Tell me when."

"We go now. To Aurora. The town is not large, and the sun has only been down for an hour or so. The charmers can't move in daylight, so that brief window is more than enough time for them to get ahead of us."

"They won't. Not this time. Not ever." Titan dropped his hand, secured his bow to his back beneath his quiver in the bow sling he'd designed, and closed his eyes.

The transformation started, as it always did, at the tips of Titan's fingers. Tanned, smooth skin rippled and then hardened into smoky, charcoal-gray metal. Solid titanium coated his body in slick, hard armor. Everything on his person, from his casual jeans to razor-sharp arrowheads to the very wisps of his neatly trimmed beard, engaged in the transformation, until he was nothing but a solid, massive column of extremely motivated and highly vengeful titanium sentinel.

And that was before he released his wings.

With a roll of his metal shoulders to settle his weapons between his shoulder blades, he snapped his eyes open and unfurled gleaming metallic wings. At first, they took on a sheer appearance, almost like a ripple of current forming a nondescript shape in the air. The current had no solid state, no physical limitations, and would slither through any obstacle, such as clothing, until it was free to harden into wings.

And harden they did. Massive sheets of feathered titanium shimmered into place, with a final wave of an iridescent rainbow skating down the length of them from the farthest tips to the deeply nested roots at his back. The kaleidoscope of colors, a natural hallmark of titanium once heated, shimmered out of sight and left gleaming sheets of silver wings in its wake.

A brief chill skittered down Titan's spine, as it always did when entering his metal state. It was both a warning and an embrace. A reminder that he, like his brothers, no longer possessed the celestial powers they had once commanded when they served in the Empyrean. But that did not mean they were without power of their own.

Titan flapped his wings once in impatient agitation. The bite of the autumn wind couldn't touch him in his solid titanium state as he leaped into the air. To his left, the high-polished flash of Chrome's silver wing alerted him that his brothers had followed. But before he could make a beeline for Aurora, the dark gray form of his leader settled abruptly in front of his flight path.

"Chrome and I will head back to the den to gather the others."

Smart. Even smarter that Tung didn't insist Titan accompany them. He was far too wired, far too intent on preventing another woman from falling prey to a threat she had no hope of fighting off.

"Titan."

His name was clipped and firm on Tung's lips. A command. Tung's steely gaze brooked no bullshit, and his not-so-gentle tone was all the warning Titan would receive that night.

In other words, don't be foolish. Don't be rash.

"We'll join you in Aurora in one hour." Tung nodded his order, which they all knew had zero room for interpretation.

And that was just fine with him. Because if he had his way, which he would, Titan would be heels up in a lawn chair roasting marshmallows over smoldering charmer ashes forty-five minutes before his fellow angels even had a chance to join him.

CHAPTER 2

Rose Meyer engaged the after-hours emergency contact sequence on the phone system and settled back in her office chair. The old leather groaned as she leaned back as far as the dinosaur piece of furniture would allow, kicked her feet up on her desk—silently wishing for a more ergonomic office chair with a mesh back—and closed her eyes.

One minute. She'd allow herself one minute of quiet, one minute for the work conversations to clear out and the scheduling needs to scatter before she'd let her evening duties take over.

Her evening duties that no one knew she'd started six months ago when her sister, Tammy, went missing.

The phone in front of her beeped. An indication that someone had called the after-hours number for the small HVAC company she managed. Rose cracked one eye and peered at the phone, but she let out a grateful sigh when no message had been left. Even though the automatic dialer would go to Rob's cell phone, she didn't wish that kind of stress on the grizzled company owner. Rob and his wife, Carla, had their hands full this time of year, when all their technicians were running ragged, turning on the heating systems for the season. New England could have some pretty abrupt cold snaps early on, and even though many of their customers proudly boasted about running to Dunkin Donuts in their flip-flops and hoodies, the majority of their customers were sensible, though still conservative.

They'd wait as long as possible to turn their heat on, but that didn't mean they wanted to leave things to chance either. When they finally did turn it on, they needed it to *work*. Hence all the early season welfare checks on those ancient oil heaters. And the incredibly grueling day that occupied the poor owners, who were as much a family to Rose and Tammy as their own parents.

Rose loosened her trademark messy bun and shook out her long hair. The instant relief on her scalp was always a blessing and one of her most-looked-forward-to moments of the day. While the blood returned to parts of her neglected noggin, she settled her palms low on her back and pushed. A soft groan rumbled out of her as she allowed herself to tend to her soreness and discomfort. The self-courtesy didn't happen often. Beyond tending to the bare necessities of her well-being, she rarely paid much attention to herself. So the little back stretch was a welcome treat. She closed her eyes again briefly, arching into the maneuver a little more deeply before settling back into the chair. When she opened her eyes, despite her best attempt at prevention, they quickly fell to the photo on her desk.

And that was all the reminder Rose needed to get her ass in gear. Rest time was over.

She didn't need the ever-present gazes and permanent smiles of her mother, father, and sister bearing down on her from within a mahogany frame, group-hugging it out for a photo op that would turn out to be the last time they were all together as a family. Oh, she was in the picture, too, but she never focused on herself. Everything about her was eclipsed by Tammy, her twin sister. Sheets of Tammy's long, sleek hair radiated a rich chestnut, while Rose's hair tended toward a mousier brown. Tammy's complexion was alabaster and youthful, with rosy hues dusting the apples of her cheeks and tops of her shoulders courtesy of their very sunny Fourth of July barbecue. Rose, however, was ashen to Tammy's radiance, a byproduct of her preference for the indoors, and she hated tank tops with a passion. No sun-kissed shoulders over there.

For all that the sisters were different, however, they couldn't have been more alike. Rose didn't know whether that was the way with all identical twins, but it had been for her and Tammy. Her sister was four minutes older, and damn if Rose wasn't constantly reminded of that fact. But for all the wisdom that came with being the older sister, no matter how many minutes, their bond and connection had never suffered for it.

In fact, it was Tammy's wisdom and nurturing that Rose had leaned on the most during their parents' divorce.

Rose exhaled an uneasy breath as she recalled her sister's solid arms around her, rocking her back and forth in her twin bed upstairs in their parents' old house. Downstairs, their mom and dad had been yelling. Again. That time, it had been about—surprise!—money. Specifically, college admission fees. She and her sister had been in their senior year in high school when the true financial burden of having twins reared its ugly head for their household.

But the week before that, the yelling had been about their minivan being left in the garage when the gas tank was on E. Before that, it had been a scheduling mix-up that escalated as a result of poor communication. Then there had been the unexpected work trip, or too many late nights out with friends watching sports at a bar downtown, or the accusations of who put what where. Their parents had always been at it, and the household tension sat heavily on Rose's heart like a stack of cinder blocks.

But Tammy had been by her side the whole time, a fellow soldier on the front lines.

"They're good people, Rose," Tammy had whispered against Rose's temple. The words had floated through the thuds and bangs resonating through the floorboards from the fight downstairs. "Always remember that. Our parents are good people. They're absolutely wonderful humans." Rose's breath had hitched as she sobbed into Tammy's shoulder. "They're wonderful humans . . . who don't belong together."

Those were the wisest freaking words Rose had ever heard.

And that was why that stupid photo on her desk was there. To serve as a giant reminder of where she'd been, what had happened since, and where she needed to go. That photo had been taken when she and her sister were sixteen, two years before the divorce proceedings started. By the time they were in college, the deal had been finalized. The house had been sold, both of her parents had moved into apartments, and she and Tammy had officially been on their own. After college, they got an apartment together and resumed life post-divorce. Tammy had worked at a marketing agency in town, while Rose stayed working part-time hours in the office at Rob and Carla's HVAC company, which had been her first job after school and had become a second home to her. Her loyalty and the owners' devotion were a boon for both, eventually earning her a promotion to office manager in the years to follow. All had been as well as could be.

Until her sister disappeared six months ago.

Rose checked the time on her phone quickly before throwing her water bottle in her bag and hiking it up on her shoulder. It was seven thirty and her need-to-work-late excuses that she'd throw her bosses' ways had officially dried up. Her stomach seized and fluttered with the same nervous energy that always overtook her whenever she'd psych herself up to head out on her sister's trail. There was no amount of antacids in the world to quell the uneasiness in her gut when she thought back over the long months without Tammy. Back when Rose had first called the police because Tammy hadn't come home after work that night. Back when, a month after diligent searches by law enforcement and endless shed tears by her parents, the trail had gone cold.

It had all stopped. The searches, the concern from neighbors and coworkers. Everything. If anyone ever needed to know the over/under on a small town doling out compassion on a missing person case, it was one month.

The police had to focus their resources elsewhere, and despite their assurances to the contrary, Tammy's disappearance would no doubt be relegated to the stack of cold cases in a dusty basement. In the days that followed, her mother had shut down, becoming nearly catatonic, and when she refused to discuss Tammy again, the woman had turned to comfort in the arms of her new husband and his family. Her father, for all his directness and compassion, couldn't even look at Rose. It broke his heart, he said, to see one twin without the other. To see Rose's face and hear Rose's voice, exact replicas of Tammy's, and yet not have both his girls in his arms. Even Rob and Carla, who loved her like their own daughter, had to detach in their way. Conversations with Rose that used to be happy and jovial often turned to strictly business.

It hurt like hell. And Rose had freaking had it.

She peered down at her phone one final time and swiped through her latest notes. Notes that originated where the police had left off. Five months' worth of interviews, GPS logs, social media tracking, and—with the help of a former college friend who had an on-paper interest in computer science but a very off-paper interest in computer hacking—security camera footage with timestamps.

Specifically, the footage of the night Tammy had gone missing.

Oh, the police had acquired all the camera footage local businesses had available that night. They had absolutely done their due diligence. But they were working with limited resources. Aurora was a small town, with even smaller businesses to boot. With the exception of your long-standing mom-and-pop shops, many of the local corporations employed remote workers and no longer saw the benefit in maintaining corporate campuses with all the bells and whistles.

This included security cameras. Ain't no reason to pay to secure a building when most of the people and things in it were either off-site or vacant offices. So, what footage that had been available didn't cut the mustard.

Except for the unopened jewelry store across the street from Tammy's firm.

Rose leaned her nose closer to her phone screen as she pinched her fingers wide to expand the view of the footage her friend had procured. A grainy image of Tammy filled her view. The last image she had of her sister. And she'd almost missed out on it because the police had been told by the jewelry establishment that, though the cameras were installed, they hadn't been operational yet.

To Rose's great relief, there was a big difference between a camera not being operational and a camera being operational, yet being unequipped with login credentials for the jewelry store to access. Apparently, the jewelry store owners hadn't been aware of the precise difference. And thank God for it.

That hunk of glass, metal, and wires was the best lead, the only lead, Rose had on her sister's disappearance. And all it cost her was a Marvel movie binge weekend with her college friend courtesy of her credit card to cover the streaming service, pizza, and *good* beer, whatever that meant.

"OK, Tam . . . what happened to you? Where'd you go?" Rose's soft, determined words carried an air of intimidation as she played back the camera footage. Her hand gripped the phone tighter as her sister's image casually walked across the screen, heedless of whatever impending event was about to rip her from Rose's life. Tammy had on her black slacks and leopard-print ballet flats she always wore to work, coupled with a light blue button-down blouse. Her handbag was slung casually over her shoulder as she walked out the front door of the firm and toward the parking lot. Nothing special. Nothing doing. Rose had memorized this scene long ago.

But it was what came next that Rose needed to study and make sure she saw as clearly as possible. She squinted closer so that the phone screen was mere inches from her nose.

The pale bottoms of Tammy's flats were clearly visible as she walked across a parking lot toward her sedan. Though it had been April at the time and normally would have had plenty of sunlight flooding the parking lot at the end of the workday, Tammy had stayed late to help with a project launch. It had been dark when she'd left.

Rose stared intently as Tammy reached her car and walked around the back to put her work bag and laptop in the trunk. But right as she slammed the trunk door closed, a lurking presence appeared behind her, though Rose couldn't be completely sure because of the camera angle and the shadows of the parking lot. When Tammy abruptly whirled around, her hands seemed to land on pale bare forearms. Very pale. Almost blindingly so, like a brand-new piece of chalk or printer paper. Similar pale hands settled on Tammy's waist, which Rose could barely make out against her light blue blouse.

But what she could make out were the glinting flashes of gold poking out under the sleeves of a black hoodie. A cuff or bracelet of some sort. Unfortunately, Tammy's position blocked a clearer view of the attacker, for that's what he was. Rose leaned into the footage and swallowed back the unsettling truth of the abduction as her sister punched, bit, and kicked her assailant. A sense of helplessness, fierce worry, and big mad anger bloomed in her chest, but she had to stay focused and get through the assault. For Tammy's sake.

"There." Rose paused the scene right before the feed abruptly cut out. During Tammy's fight, her sister had let her ferocity fly. Though the video had no sound, Tammy's mouth was open wide with presumptive screams. She had curled her fingers and raked them down the large arms holding her. But when her right hand reached the gold cuff, her fingers caught hold and she gripped it—and pulled.

The cuff detached and flew wildly from Tammy's grip during the struggle. Where it landed exactly Rose couldn't tell. The scene had become a jumbled mass of shadows, limbs, and general poor visibility. Then the video cut out for good, the cause of which her computer hacker friend was never able to determine.

But that was what tonight was for. To see if she could pick up the trail the police insisted had run cold.

Because if that gold cuff was still on the premises some-where, Rose would damn sure find it, along with her sister.

CHAPTER 3

The cold roof shingles of the Aurora Public Library rasped against the soles of Titan's boots. The municipal parking lot below was quiet. Titan crouched low to ensure the bulk of his body was concealed by the peak of the roof and silently appreciated the human forethought to *not* build flat roofs on the New Hampshire town's public buildings. He scooted over to the edge and dug his fingers into the smooth well where the roof ended and the gutter began.

Titan didn't need to look over the edge to gather his bearings. His mind recalled every square inch of pavement, all thirty parking spaces, and the dimensions of every slab of granite curbing that snaked alongside the library's property line. Aurora wasn't a large town, and the library was as centrally located to the town's main drag as it was to the thicket of suburban cookie-cutter housing developments.

Perhaps that was why he had been drawn to this place six months ago. Drawn to her.

Titan rolled his shoulders and pressed the muscles surrounding his shoulder blades closer together. It was an innate reflex, an automatic maneuver to ensure his weapons sat secure and centered down his back. His eyes flashed to the corner of the parking lot nearest the sidewalk, the one that led to the main thoroughfare in town.

The one she had walked down.

It had been her hair that had first grabbed his attention. The straight sheet of chestnut that was so long, it barely grazed her hips as she ambled to her car. The sway of her hair had been a welcome distraction to the otherwise uneventful patrol he and two of his sentinel brothers, Iron and Steel, had been out performing.

The sun had just gone down, but it was still well past the end-of-day punch out for the regular nine-to-fivers. The lot should have been empty. And it was . . . except for a single red sedan parked nice and close to the copse of trees separating the park and the lot near the library. But it was way too far away from any sensible amount of light.

The grunt and firm jerk of Iron's full-bearded chin had Titan turning to his right, away from the woman. And that had been when the dashes of shadows between the trees registered, followed by brief glints of gold.

Charmers. Four of them. Their eerie pallor was easy to identify, even under the waning moon's glow. The ghostly exposed skin of their arms was reminiscent of the translucent flesh of many deep-sea creatures relegated to the abysmal zone of the ocean's depths, completely untouched by the sun's rays.

Steel and Iron leaped before he did, their great wings unfurling and their honed bodies morphing into their metallic forms. Titan had risen to join them. With his bow unleashed, he commanded his titanium forth, but a cry diverted him from his targets.

The woman. A fifth charmer, of elite class based on the double gold bands around its neck, had grabbed her and hauled her close as he lifted his bone knife to start the bleeding process

—one that wouldn't leak out her blood, but instead bleed out the light of her soul.

Like a shot, Titan flew off the roof and barreled into the charmer with all the force of an asteroid. Between one second and the next, Titan reached for an arrow, infused his angel fire into the head, and jammed it into the charmer's throat. Not exactly galant, but no less effective.

But when he turned to the woman, a sixth charmer, a mystic, had her by the throat. All it took was one vile whisper from the bastard's lips and swirling black magic appeared, so thick it nearly had mass of its own. The blackness engulfed the charmer and the woman, then they were gone. All in seconds, before Titan even had time to rise from his kill.

The memory was still a ravaging haunt on his conscience.

"C'mon, asshole. Where the fuck are you? I know you're here." Titan's words hissed out through clenched teeth as his body thrummed on a razor's edge of adrenaline. He had allowed the memory of that night to invade his thoughts for only a moment. More so out of respect and reverence for the woman he hadn't been able to save. And for pure blood-soaked revenge.

Because charmers never abducted mortals. That just wasn't their MO. Their tactics had always been more of a cat-and-mouse game. They preyed on sources of pure light and energy, the goodest of the good and most innocent of the innocent. Anything to snuff out potential sources of the Empyrean's eternal light. The better the soul, the brighter that soul's light. Their methods weren't to maim or kidnap, but to drain. Bone knives imbued with tainted magic were used to slice open victims and draw out their light, slowly disentangling each strand of a human's soul and dissolving them like acid.

Yet she had been abducted. Not drained, but taken. On his watch.

Fuck.

Titan shook his head free of the painful memories. Tung had

sent him here and given him a strategic head start before his brothers arrived. Alone time for him to assess and get his head in the game. For him to set thoughts of that woman aside and lean into the hunt.

A low hum vibrated in Titan's ears. He quirked his head to the side. It was barely audible, more of a depressed whine than an easily registered sound. But it was there. And it was a telltale indicator of a black magic portal.

Titan unclipped his bow and gripped an arrow. He had another thirty minutes before backup arrived, but he was resolved not to need it. Stubbornness was a lovely byproduct of his metal, after all, what with titanium being one of the strongest metals on earth and, therefore, not easily changed once its course was set.

He braced his feet against the pitch of the roof. His thighs strained with the balancing act as he knocked his arrow. The sharp bite of his bowstring pinched his cheek as his eyes danced over every pebble, bush, and shadow in the vicinity.

Quick shuffles against the pavement drew his aim to the left. A person wearing a black hoodie and jeans had just come down the sidewalk leading from town. And judging by their fast pace and sensible sneakers, they were in a hurry to go somewhere. But there were no cars in the parking lot, and at nearly eight o'clock at night, most of the main businesses were closed, hence the vacant lot.

Titan's arrow tracked the mortal as it reached the bushes and trees lining the parking lot. He'd never let loose his weapon on an innocent. No. Rather, he used his arrow as a tracking tool, a guide to follow and attune himself to, rather than a target to take down.

The person's behavior was more than curious as they dropped to their knees in front of a bush and jerkily rummaged through the branches. Another second went by before the person got wise to the darkness and pulled a flashlight from their backpack. It made no sense, though. If this little mortal, perhaps a teenager given the slight build and baggy clothing, had lost an item, why the hell would they go looking for it at night? Titan rolled his eyes as he reached the most likely conclusion: a teenager had lost their phone and wasn't willing to incur the wrath of their parents, who would most likely just get them a new one anyway. Lovely.

A quick scan of the mortal's perimeter didn't signal any warning bells until a flash of gold caught his eye. The gold of a charmer cuff. In the mortal's hands.

This night just keeps getting better and better.

The teenager remained squatting on the ground as they examined the jewelry, then they threw off their hood and revealed mahogany strands tied tight in a messy bun. A brief sliver of a pale, slender neck glowed in the moonlight as the mortal turned the cuff over in their hands.

It was a woman. The woman Tung had mentioned was no doubt the target of the next attack.

At least he was in the right place at the right time.

But as he stared curiously at the mortal, nearby grass and stones crunched, and ominous footfalls ate up the earth. They were heavy, yet lithe and charged with purposeful intent. To the right of the woman, at the far end of the tree line rimming the park, was a charmer. An elite charmer, warrior class, was charging with a gleaming bone knife in hand straight at the woman.

Solid metal took over Titan's form as he bolted up the sloped shingles and leaped off the roof. By the time his rear foot had become airborne, titanium wings had burst free of his back. He dove like a bird of prey descending on its next meal. A high-pitched whine filled the air as his titanium wings cut through the wind. His bow arm was cocked a second later. The iridescent rainbow of his angel fire infused the arrow in his hand before it turned into solid blue flames.

Baleful growling rumbled up from the charmer as the elite glanced at Titan, who had expected the smirk and wink his enemy threw his way. The elite charmer was much larger than the mystic class. And though their magical abilities were limited, their skill set was just as deadly, if not more so. The muscled warrior barreled through the grass toward the woman, heedless of its disturbance or the righteously pissed-off attacking angel. The charmer's cutoff hoodie and cargo pants whipped and rustled with his effort. The bastard had speed, that was for sure, even in human clothes.

The woman stood up and turned as the charmer stampeded toward her.

Titan loosed his arrow. The bolt found its home in the charmer's shoulder just as Titan touched down in front of the woman and quickly returned to his human appearance. Yes, staying in his metal form would have been smarter, but he had already made enough of a scene. He wouldn't risk further questions.

The night was otherwise quiet. There was no screaming. Not from the woman, nor the charmer. He suspected she was in shock, which was just fine with him. His sole attention needed to be on the enemy in front of him.

Then the guttural groans started.

Ah. There we go.

The charmer had absorbed the shock of the hit well but would never be able to put off the inevitable. The warrior went to his knees, grasped the arrow, and yanked it out of the meat of his shoulder. The damage had been done, however. Angel fire was lethal to charmers. All it took was one hit of the stuff, and they'd fall eventually. The fire would eat away at the healthy tissue, char the bone, and dry up the vital fluids in the demon's body.

But it was the eventually part that was the worry.

That shoulder hit hadn't pierced anything vital, which meant the warrior no doubt had a fair amount of fight left in him and still would until the fire spread and Titan was able to torch him properly.

"Stay behind me," Titan ordered the woman as he stowed his bow and reached for the knives on his weapons belt. He hunched down low in a fighting stance, bracing his right leg behind the left, and palmed his knives. No, they weren't solid titanium, as that would make the blades too brittle and less likely to hold an edge. But the custom steel blend was just as deadly and highly effective in Titan's proficient hands.

"What is that thing?" The woman's voice quivered behind him, but she had the good sense not to question his command.

"What am I, indeed?" the charmer hissed out as he calmly rose to one knee. If there was pain, and Titan knew there was plenty of it, the pissant didn't let it show on his face. The warrior merely sneered, as if a face full of ugly was the last thing this bastard wanted to be remembered for.

"I'm more interested in what *you* are." The words came out clean and crisp and were directed toward the woman.

Titan gripped the hilts of his blades more tightly. *Throw them. Throw them and end this.* Titan's nostrils flared with a frustrated breath. Something in the charmer's words gave him pause.

A tempered whine resonated beyond the copse of trees. More portals. More charmers.

"Less talking. More dying, please."

Titan reared back and heaved one heated blade after the other. The first sliced the side of the charmer's neck, just above the second gold band. Black blood was freed from its jugular confines and poured down the muscular expanse of the charmer's shoulder and chest. The demon's hand flew to its throat, doing a poor job of wound compression and an even poorer job of giving a shit that it was about to die. Which annoyed Titan to no end.

Because before Titan's second blade hit its mark, the charmer summoned its remaining strength and heaved its bone knife straight for the woman.

Titan was in mid-throw when he saw the offensive attack. Once his knife left his hand, he pivoted and turned toward the woman. All thoughts of his marksmanship left his head as he gave the really-needed-to-die-soon charmer his back—a big no-no in the fighting world, but desperate times and all that. With no other choice left to him, he called forth his titanium wings and leaped toward the woman. He collided with her before he tackled her to the ground. The angel waited and even prayed —*ha!*—for the telltale *ping* of a knife hitting his metallic wing. Nothing.

Nothing but the sharp wince and a soft curse from the woman beneath him.

He had managed to grab her to his body before she hit the ground. Slowly, he inched her away from the cocoon of his chest. As he did so, he slid his wide palms up and down her back, assessing for any sign that the dagger had penetrated. But he came away with nothing. Nothing but strong—albeit tense— shoulders, a rapid heartbeat, and the deep slink of her lower back.

Titan leaned back to look at her—and stared into the face of the woman he had lost to the charmers six months ago.

He froze. Literally could not move a muscle, despite the imposing threat of more enemies that were no doubt coming through the portals.

He took in her face. Wide, frantic green eyes that were sunk far too low into her face for his liking stared back at him. Her lips were pressed together as if she was holding back a cry of pain, and her ashen complexion in the moon's glow mimicked a combination of shock, fear, and agony.

Her pained expression kicked his systems back online real

quick. There would be time for questions later. But only if he made sure there was a later.

"Where? Where are you hurt?" He freed one hand, still gripping her tightly with the other, and delicately hovered his fingers over every available inch within reach.

"My arm." Her words were stilted and strained.

Titan lifted the hand cupping her right bicep and gingerly peeled her tight fingers back, revealing a large gash of bright celestial light. The light of her soul. Perfect catnip for the charmers and the very thing he was duty-bound to protect.

He turned his ear toward the rush of advancing footsteps behind him. No doubt the first charmer was well on his way to becoming a pig roast, but the others behind him were worrisome.

"We've got to go. Now."

Without hesitation, he covered his hand over her exposed upper arm and lifted her with him, never letting her out of the cradle of his arms. He could fly them out of there. But only if they left right the hell now. She'd see his angel form. But then again, she'd already seen his wings. None of it could be helped.

But the moment his palm made contact with her bare skin, a jarring vibration began to thrum in his chest, like the beginning rumblings of an earthquake before Mother Nature took it up to full speed. Heavy breaths shot out of him as the vibrations increased, becoming hot in their intensity, until every inch of his skin trembled with heat that rivaled the sun.

Titan instinctually dropped the woman and backed away. It was only when she was well out of reach that the burning got too hot, too volatile. As if his body automatically knew to hold back on whatever was happening until she was out of range.

And then fire, so bright blue it was nearly white, engulfed his body, from the top of his head to the tips of his wings. It was a force he had not known since before he fell.

His angel fire. His full and menacing celestial force. Without earthbound limitations. Summoned on its own.

Titan didn't know the hows and whys of it. Didn't know why his full fire had come to him, instead of the limited amounts he had access to in the mortal plane and the need to recharge nightly. All he knew was that his body thrummed with a long-gone weapon his makeup craved, as if his sight had returned after being blind for so long.

With a glance at the woman to ensure she was safe, Titan turned to the charmers advancing toward them. And with a movement that was as instinctual as blinking, he released his full angel fire on the mob.

But he wasn't foolish. Titan had no idea how long this would last or how this even came to be. He could have just shot his only load, for all he knew. So, he wasn't about to wait around and further test out his trigger finger.

He recalled his fire—and damn, did it feel good to be at full bore again—ignored the pained screams at his back, and turned to the woman. Without asking for permission, he took her hand, placed it back on her bicep, and snaked her other one around his neck. The weight was slight, yet oddly comforting.

"We're leaving."

"But . . . but . . . how did you—"

"We'll talk when you're safe. Right now, I'm getting you out of here."

Titan clutched the woman tightly to his chest, tucking her head securely under his chin, and leaped off the ground.

CHAPTER 4

Cold, furious wind whipped around Rose as she clung to the man holding her. Hundreds of feet above the freaking ground. Her body had as much tension as an iron spring with absolutely no hope of release in sight. As her brain warred between self-preservation and its need for answers to the inexplicable, Rose focused instead on what she could control.

Her arm.

Whatever that thing was that threw a knife her way had excellent aim. In the confusion of it all, she hadn't even seen the weapon hurtling toward her. Oh, but she felt it. Kind of hard to ignore the deep slice that definitely penetrated more than just her epidermis. But just how much more she had no clue yet. The closed fingers of her left hand pressed more firmly over her cut. She pursed her lips and prepared to breathe out the pain. The pangs were still there, but they had dulled to a mellow throbbing. She closed her eyes for a moment and offered up a silent word of thanks to Carla for the new company hoodie she'd had made for the employees. The woman had gone with the extra-plush fleece liner, and Rose couldn't help but be grateful for the added layer of padding.

And that was about the last of the immediate circumstances she could control, unfortunately. She had tried once to open her eyes and look down, but that had turned out to be an exercise in dumbassery. If she'd forgotten how bad her vertigo had been the last time she went to the amusement park, seeing the tips of her sneakers dangle well above where solid ground should be sent her all the reminder she needed that heights weren't for her.

But one thing she didn't mind? The only things that were giving her any sense of security amid the chaos of the last few minutes? The strong bands of muscle wrapped unforgivably tight around her waist and torso. She had no idea who the man was and had no explanation for anything she had seen, but his arms were definitely real and hadn't moved even an inch since he'd lifted her off the ground. She had never felt anything so solid and unmoving, even with some of the dips and dives they'd taken in the air.

The air. Gosh, were they really flying? And did he really have *wings?*

She should have been more afraid of him holding her, of everything about him. But her fear and panic at being sliced open, then carried hundreds of feet above the treetops, lessened slightly as normal human sensations began poking through. His beard, for instance. Even as she lay crushed against his chest while they were airborne, she had a hard time ignoring the tickle of his beard on her forehead every time he opened his mouth or swallowed. The dark hairs that grazed her skin were lush, though still trimmed. Full, but neat. It was a contradiction, but an innately human one.

Because if he took such care with his appearance, surely he was capable of taking the same care with her. Maybe?

And why the hell was she even thinking that? It was the fear, she thought. Fear played some scary tricks on the mind.

Because the reality of her situation, if she could even call it that, was preposterous. Laughable. The stuff of Hollywood movies and live-action character events. Certainly not real life. Men didn't fly in real life.

Right?

"So . . . cold . . ." Rose's chattering teeth betrayed her stalwart determination to keep silent. She had no idea who this man holding her was, but he seemed to be on her side. So, she dearly hoped to keep quiet lest her need to ask incessant questions derail his no doubt much more important need to keep them from falling out of the sky.

One of his strong arms, the one with the large hand cradling her head to his chest, pulled away. For a moment, her breath hitched at the loss of security. If all she had were his two arms to keep her from plummeting to her death, surely cutting her supports by half wouldn't bode well for her not eating a face full of branches.

But it was just the opposite. Even with only one arm solidly around her waist, she had no loss of certainty in her safety.

Soft fleece caressed her ears as their frozen tips gave way to tingling blood flow. The man had used his free hand to pull up the hoodie of her sweatshirt, taking extra care to unhook one of the garment's edges that had been snagged on the tip of her ear. Both the warmth and the gesture were comforting.

"We'll be there soon."

It was the first time he had spoken since they left the ground, and his voice surprised her. Yes, she had heard it when they were in the parking lot, but she had been a little distracted by the whole knife-wielding guy and her new savior's metallic wings. It hadn't registered until now how lovely his voice was.

Despite his neatly trimmed beard, which, even in the darkness, boasted saturated hues of black coffee, his voice was light. Crisp and bright, like a tenor's tone. Not the gruff and gravelly harshness she perhaps incorrectly associated with bearded men.

It was oddly refreshing and took the intimidation factor of her rescuer down by a degree or two.

"Where is 'there'?" She spoke softly into his chest but soon realized he was able to hear her just fine.

"I have a cabin near North Conway at the edge of Mount Washington Valley. It's secluded from the tourists. It's safe, and it'll buy us some time until we can get things sorted out."

It's safe.

Those were words Rose had never had to think about until this evening. "Safe from what?"

The man returned his arm around her torso, held her more tightly to his chest, and said nothing. She had asked a question he clearly didn't want to address. Perhaps it wasn't safe to discuss, open and exposed as they were? Perhaps more of those bald pale things with knives were around and he could see them but she couldn't? Or maybe, like any stubborn man, he had used up his word quota for the day and if he didn't deem it important, he wouldn't address it?

But she wasn't being fair then, was she?

Rose sighed and relaxed her shoulders as best she could. He was probably just being incredibly sensible, which grated against her emotionally upheaved state. They could hardly carry on a lengthy conversation as they were, and she sure as heck knew how tired she was. She could only imagine how much energy he was burning off.

But still . . . there were two things she needed to know now.

"Are we really flying?" she whispered.

He hesitated. "Yes."

Great. Not sure that helped matters, but great. At least it was an answer.

"And . . . you know my face."

She didn't want to blow her wad just yet. Didn't want to give more information about Tammy than she needed to. Not until she had more information about what the hell was going on.

"Yes." The word was clipped and resolute.

And that right there sealed the deal. Whatever happened next, she was all in. Because this man, who miraculously sported wings on his back and carried her above the treetops, had information about her sister.

She would bury all her fear and anxiety and press on. The answers would come later.

And she would have her answers.

———

She's alive.

That thought hammered against Titan's cranium over and over again as he glided them away from Aurora. The other thought he had, the one that wasn't merely focused on a guilty memory, was far more sensory in its makeup.

Soft.

Every inch of the woman in his arms from the waist up was hugged tightly to his body as he let his wings do their thing up above. Even through the layers of clothing, through her over-stuffed-though-New-England-appropriate hoodie and the wide leather strap of his bow sling, her softness resonated. At first, when he got them airborne, his sole focus had been on getting the hell out of there. But as time went on and he had no awareness they were being followed, he opened his senses and allowed them to feed him whatever information they could.

Chief among them was her softness. Not that of her hair, which, though still richly brown, lacked the luster he recalled months ago, nor that of her skin, which he had touched ever so briefly. No, the softness he was referring to was a mixture of soul-deep malleability and slinky curves. As if every part of her, inside and out, had no qualms about giving in to the flight and relaxing completely in his arms.

Well, except for her teeth chattering. But he would fix that momentarily.

"Hang on. I'm going to land."

The telltale tips of red spruce trees bloomed before Titan as he made their descent. The cabin he was taking them to was tucked deep into the side of the valley and abutted Mount Washington in the rear. There were no trails or footpaths to speak of. And as he had built the thing to be as close to the mountain's rock face as possible on one side, with the rest nestled among the spruce trees, they were completely protected from nosy travelers and tourists.

The soles of Titan's boots touched down on the small patch of gravel he used as a landing pad in front of the door. His wings quickly shimmered into translucence before retreating altogether. Though he had no qualms about his makeup, and, yeah, he had some serious explaining to do about the whole flying thing, he wished to prolong that talk a little while longer.

First, he needed to get her warm.

The mountain was known for some bizarre and dangerous weather, never mind the extreme dips in temperature, compared to the rest of the area. All things that a hoodie and blue jeans were no match for.

"Let's get you inside."

Titan settled the woman a few inches away from his chest, but he wasn't yet prepared to let her go entirely. Because how could this be real?

It had to be her. The only woman he'd failed to protect in his endless earthbound existence and the only object of his constant nightmares. She was alive! But how? And even though she was technically not dead, her visage told a different story. She had changed . . . and not for the better. Titan's angelic vision took in every detail. The night's dim light was of little consequence to his sight. Her skin carried a pallor he hadn't recalled. Yes, her frame was still slender, albeit more so, but her gait was also more resigned. As if an exuberance, as well as pounds, had been shed over the past few months.

Titan tried not to dwell on his observations as he shuttled them inside his cabin. He was, however, grateful she even allowed him to do so. But he was no fool. When he finally slammed the metal bolt home in the door lock, he lingered for a moment longer than necessary and then braced himself for whatever manner of terrified miracle was about to come his way.

"Where did they go?"

The question confused him at first. But then he gathered her meaning. Ah. His wings. That would be the first interrogation item on the list.

Not exactly what he would have prioritized in his line of questioning, but his preferences, aside from those pertaining to her immediate safety, could show themselves later. Especially his curiosity at how *she* had managed to manifest *his* angel fire when he touched her.

Titan curled his fingers around the cool metal of the lock, allowing the elements to feed him strength. It had been a habit of his before he geared up for any difficult conversation. The properties of the metal both soothed and energized him, as it did for all his brothers.

And he would need all the help he could get. May the mages help him.

Titan still faced the door as he unstrapped his bow sling. He wanted her to get as clear a view of his back as possible. Wanted her to know that his wings, and him for that matter, were not these evil things to be feared. Best if he removed the threat. So he kept his wings retracted and, thus, appeared like any other man.

Titan lifted his bow and quiver over his head and, keeping his weapons in one hand, raised both hands and slowly turned around. He allowed her to take in every inch of him, from his boots to his cargo pants to his weapons belt. He was a big man by human standards, but nothing so egregiously beyond the physique of a well-trained athlete. If the charmers had abducted her and held her prisoner all these months, he highly doubted they had given her the same courtesy of sizing up her opponent before they descended on her.

Not that he was her opponent. The concept was as acrid to his senses as the smell of boiling charmer blood.

He completed his about-face and stared at her. "I'm happy to answer any questions you have. Any at all." His words came out calm and resolute, a byproduct of his experience leading the sentinels, but inside, he was anything but. It was all he could do not to run to her, inspect every inch of her for damage . . .

Or worse.

He swallowed back the thought as he returned his focus to her original question. "Before we get to that, I want you to know that you're safe here with me." He shook the straps of his bow and quiver in emphasis, though he wasn't sure his intended message could be well received until he turned the lights on. "Let me see to your wound, and then I'll make you some tea while you ask me—"

"Never mind the wings. Where is my sister?"

Titan's brow furrowed in confusion as he lowered his arms. "Sister?"

The woman dropped her left hand from the cut on her arm and clenched her fists at her sides. "Yes, my twin sister, Tammy. You said you've seen my face before, but I've never seen yours. That must mean you've seen my sister and know where she is."

Silence stretched on in the little stone cabin until the woman again threw words at him that nearly knocked him off his feet.

"She went missing six months ago. And I need to find her."

CHAPTER 5

Adrenaline was a nasty beast. It robbed one of all good sense, like it did for Rose as she stood stock still in front of this man. It robbed her of knowing she was in the presence of a most likely lethal man she didn't know and who, oh yeah, could fly. Of paying attention to her body's basic needs, like her lack of warmth or familiar shelter, or, at the very least, tending to her arm.

Nope. None of that took top billing at that moment. And instead, she stood feet away from some sort of pseudo-winged warrior, who could present any amount of unknown threats to her, and demanded information from him.

Rose took a deep breath, held it for a two-count, and let it slowly flutter out between her dry lips. And then she waited.

"Did you say sister?"

Great. He was going to play dumb.

"Yes, my sister. You said you've seen her."

The man shook his head, scratched the tip of his bearded chin, and threw his weapons on the leather sofa next to the door. They landed in a huff, as if they, too, took affront to his reaction. Then he busied himself with firing up two battery-powered lanterns on opposite sides of the small living room.

"No. That's not what I said." The old wood floor groaned as he paced in agitation across the small living room, positioning the lanterns for optimal lighting. "You asked if I recognized your face. Which I did." He paused in his musings and stared at her again. He pressed his lips together and settled his hands on his belt. The action softened Rose's steely intent a bit as her eyes fell to the bunched shoulder muscles beneath his pale green Henley shirt. Shoulders, she recalled quite well, that had helped hold her imperceptibly still through the night air.

"You have a twin. A twin who went missing."

"Yes," she clipped out. "You seem to be a little slow on the uptake. Of the two people in this room, I don't see how you have an excuse for mass confusion."

The man dropped his head and cursed. "I need a drink." He pointed to the couch. "Sit. I'll be right back. And don't touch the arrows."

Rose crossed her arms over her chest. "I don't need to sit, and I don't need to be told not to fiddle with pointy things. What I need is answers."

"Fine. Sit. Don't sit. It makes no difference to me. But I sure as hell need a minute." He gave her his back as he stormed off toward what she assumed was the kitchen. The familiar ticking of a gas stove's pilot light engaging mixed with the delicate clanging of glass and porcelain. After a few minutes, the man returned with a tumbler of amber liquid dangling from his fingertips and a steaming ceramic mug nestled in the other. He handed her the mug.

Rose eyed the thing like she was a second-grader and the mug had a serious case of cooties. But despite herself, she still accepted it. Which was infuriating. She was supposed to be steely and focused on finding her sister. Not playing placated houseguest to a Hawkeye wannabe.

But the heat radiating from the ceramic was so enticing in its seduction. So much so that she was willing to put the interrogation aside. Just for a moment.

Rose cupped her frigid hands around the mug, opened herself to the onslaught of heat, and dipped her face down into the herbal tea before he could even remove his hands from the mug. Peppermint. He'd brought her peppermint tea.

Aw, hell. How could she possibly dislike someone who did that?

When she gripped the mug more tightly, the tips of her short nails bumped into his hand. She immediately went to jerk back, but then the rough pads of his calloused fingers retreated just as quickly.

But not before his eyes changed color. At least, she thought they did. It was so brief. A literal blink before she missed it. His irises, which had been deep brown a second before, shimmered with a sheen of an iridescent rainbow. The reds, oranges, yellows . . . all the colors had been present and accounted for as they quickly made the rounds through his eyes, like a rainbow conga line. But before she could study them further, the colors were gone, and his eyes flashed silvery charcoal before returning to brown once more.

"What the . . . ?" Rose nabbed the mug from him lest she drop it completely and stumbled back a few steps. Like a character in a sitcom, she backed herself right into the couch and parked it when she couldn't back up any farther.

Maybe I should sit for this. No . . . definitely. I should definitely sit for this.

"Up until ten seconds ago, I had no idea you had a sister." He paused to sip from his drink.

Was it her imagination or did she smell apples? Was his drink a brandy of some kind? And why the hell was she interested in what his drink preferences were?

"And up until thirty minutes ago, your face was the one I

thought I was seeing on the backs of my eyelids right before I woke from my nightmares." He walked over to a small table in the corner and set his drink down. Then he took a chair tucked into the table, swung it around, and straddled the back of it. It wasn't lost on Rose how his thighs flexed within his cargo pants and hung over the edges of the seat. "So, no. I did not know you had a twin. When I saw you tonight, I thought *you* were the one I failed to protect six months ago."

"Failed to protect . . . Tammy? From what? And your eyes . . . how did they—"

Oh, some great interrogator she was turning out to be. Yup. Truly intimidating. Why had this man not given up all his secrets to her yet? Surely, he couldn't resist her hard-ass line of questioning and take-no-shit attitude. It was about as effective as using a two-pound kitten to intimidate people to stay off one's lawn.

Just sip your tea and shut up. At least that much you know how to do.

Rose silently drank her tea and didn't even bristle when the hot drink scalded the tip of her tongue.

"Tammy—your sister," he added for what she suspected was more his clarification than her own, "was abducted by an enemy that my brothers and I are charged with hunting down. She was the first woman, and the only mortal ever, who I was not able to save from an attack."

Wait . . . did she hear that right?

"You said . . . mortal."

The man rested his forearms on the back of the chair and leaned forward as he nodded slightly at her assertion. His presence was neither intimidating nor aggressive, however; just merely expressing the importance of his words.

"My eyes." He paused to make sure he had her full attention.

What? Did you think I'd lose interest and pull out my phone to start clipping digital coupons from this week's grocery circular?

"When I touched your skin, first in the parking lot when I reached to cover your wound, and then just now when I handed you the mug . . . " He hesitated. "My full angel fire was triggered. But not by me. By *you*."

"Angel . . . what? Is that why your eyes changed color?"

He nodded.

"My name is Titan. I am second in command of the sentinel angels. Your sister, it seems, was abducted by charmers—what you would call demons—six months ago on my watch. And for some reason, it seems the charmers are after you as well. And add to the fact that your touch brings on my full angel fire, a celestial power I have not had complete access to since before I fell to earth, and we've got ourselves a bit of a mystery."

Rose sat there with her jaw seemingly unhinged. Yet this man—Titan, he called himself—sat there as calmly as if he was about to start the Sunday crossword puzzle and referred to himself as a commander of . . . angels? No, this couldn't be right. None of it. But as she leaned forward to get up, exhaustion from the evening settled over her like a weighted blanket. Her reluctant butt plopped back down on the sofa.

"But there's another piece to this now."

"And what's that?" Her voice was so breathy from her panting, she hardly recognized it.

"You need to stay with me until we figure this all out. For whatever reason, the charmers have placed a target on your back." Titan rose to his feet. From her diminutive height seated on the couch, he looked like a giant, barely clearing the low cabin ceiling. But he was more than that. He was serious. Deadly serious.

He walked over to her and squatted down so he was as close to her eye level as could be. His eyes were still deep brown as they danced across her face. And for the first time, she got a glimpse of pain she hadn't noticed before. In the faint glow of the cabin's lighting, strained lines accented creases in his forehead, which she wouldn't associate with someone so young. He appeared no older than mid-thirties, though who knew how old he was. In fact, now that she was looking more closely, the worry lines were all over, from the corners of his eyes to the deep V between his brows. His eyelids even dropped more than they should, with each blink weighed down with invisible stress, she guessed.

Is this for real?

"Are you really an . . . angel?" She looked around his silhouette, scanning for a halo or evidence of . . . *wings.*

As if he was following her train of thought, he merely nodded again when she connected the dots in her mind. "All you need to know right now is that you're safe and you're staying with me. Tonight, you'll rest. Tomorrow, you can hit me with all your questions."

Well, that was good, she supposed. Because of all the questions her addled mind could focus on, only one seemed to be scrolling on a marquee through her brain.

Did he really say that my touch triggered his angelic power?

Titan left the woman on the couch sipping her tea while he went around back to fire up the generator. Habit would have had him using his own fire to make her tea, but like hell he'd risk it. Besides, if she was as inquisitive as he thought her to be, he was about to hit her with a boatload of abnormal. No sense in adding to it if he didn't need to. Additionally, his cabin was off the grid, which he preferred, but he wasn't a masochist. Mortals had invented many wonderful systems over the years, chief among them being well pumps, septic systems, and electric beard trimmers. He didn't come to this cabin often, however, especially in the winter, so what was stocked here was mostly canned goods and pantry items. Still, clean sheets and a hot shower went a long way toward improving one's mood.

He sure as hell hoped it would work for her.

When the low hum of the generator filled the night's silence, Titan went back inside and occupied himself with more domestic tasks. Action steps were his friend and went a long way in soothing his itchy proverbial trigger finger. Once the sheets in the bedroom were changed, he grabbed a short stack of clean towels and walked back into the living room.

"You're welcome to shower, if you'd like. The bathroom's right across the hall from the bedroom." He dropped the towels on the living room table and patted the top of them to get her attention.

But all she chose to acknowledge was the tips of her sneakers as her eyes remained downcast.

Titan sighed and headed back into the kitchen. He wasn't sure what he expected, exactly. He had just dumped a big-bang-sized bomb on her. Told her he was an angel, that demons were after her, that he had no clue she was a twin and had even less of a clue where her sister was.

And then there was the whole angel fire mess. How could he even begin to explain that when he barely understood it himself?

It was too much. And after all that, he just assumed she'd hop in the shower and hunker down for the night in a strange man's cabin, which he already told her couldn't be accessed by civilization?

Freaking genius boss move right there.

Pasta. He needed to make a big pot of carbs. Maybe she was hungry. Hadn't he heard something about low blood sugar affecting human behavior? No matter that it was nearly nine o'clock at night. He had no idea when she'd eaten last, but judging by her gaunt frame, any extra calories would be appreciated. Especially if he was there to make damn sure she was eating.

"Rose."

Titan barely missed the soft-spoken word that floated up from the living room. He was taking a stock pot down from the pot rack and wondered whether the clanging metal had him hearing things. He poked his head out of the kitchen entryway and looked at her.

And nearly dropped the pot on his foot.

She was staring at him, elbows on her knees and no-longer-hot tea still gripped in her hands. Her hair tie had been removed, allowing her mahogany hair to fall freely about her shoulders. Damn, it was long. If she stood up, he bet her hair would reach just above the curve of her hips. Titan choked back the inkling to sit beside her—as if she'd even let him—and touch it. Did it feel as soft as it looked? Were the waves cooperative when she pulled them into her bun? Or were they unruly and rebellious, preferring to sprawl and ensnare anyone and anything within reach? The thought was so foreign and struck him like a new flavor of ice cream he had never tried before, a delicious temptation that was no good for him.

"My name is Rose. Rose Meyer. And thank you. For . . . every-thing. For saving me from the attack, for bringing me here. For the tea." She held up her mug to him. And was it his imagination or did the slightest of ghosted smiles curl up one side of her mouth?

"And pasta. Let's not forget the pasta. That's up next." Titan quickly filled the pot, set it to boil on the stove, and joined Rose in the living room. "Now, this is an all-inclusive, mind you." He held out his arms to indicate the confines of the cabin beyond the living room. "We've got everything from your heat and hot water to your full-service shelf-stable pantry to your pillow-fluffing service and wood-burning fireplace."

That small smirk turned into a single laugh. It wasn't loud or large, but oh man, would he take it. Anything to lessen the burden he had heaped on her delicate shoulders.

"So, it's a wood-burning fireplace?"

Titan nodded and directed her gaze over to the neatly stacked logs in the corner.

"And what do you ignite the logs with?" Her mouth twisted, as if she was getting the feel of a new word before she said it. "Angel fire?"

Boom. There it was. Looked like they were going to do this after all.

"Yes," he said tentatively as he took a seat in the chair across from her and crooked his ankle over his opposite knee. "You ready to ask your questions?"

Rose nodded slowly. "I want to see it. I mean, I saw it. Back at the park. I saw the blue flame consume you, and I saw you shoot it out at those . . . demons. Is that what you do? Turn to fire?"

Oh boy. How would he explain all he was to a mortal who undoubtedly only knew of angels as fat cherubs or religious entities with cotton candy wings?

"How about I show you? Slowly," he said, raising his hands in front of her worried eyes. "I won't do anything without explaining things first. No surprises, I promise."

"Okay." A meager acquiescence.

Close enough for government work.

"But first—" Titan clapped his hands. "Pasta. I've got a jar of tomato basil marinara with your name on it, and something tells me we could both use some food."

"Can I help?"

The question was so casual, so innocent, yet it held all the weight of an aircraft carrier. Because offering to help implied a modicum of trust. Trust that he wouldn't hurt her and that his story was true.

It was a monumental gift, one he was determined to hold sacred.

And then he remembered Tung and the others. How they were going to meet him in Aurora. No doubt they would be concerned when he failed to report in.

"Absolutely. Come into the kitchen and keep an eye on the water. The utensils are in that drawer over there. I'll be right back."

CHAPTER 6

The red spruce's knotted bark grated against Titan's knuckles as he tapped out a beat and waited for Tung to pick up the phone. From outside, he could see Rose through the kitchen window as she stood stirring the pot of pasta. He couldn't help but keep an eye on her, even though she was more than safe. Titan mentally checked off the veritable arsenal of weapons he kept in the cellar and then chided himself on how one could possibly use them all at once. Or was he viewing it as more of a challenge? Bows and blades were his preference, but he also hadn't played with his Gatling gun in a while. Could be fun.

"It's about freaking time. Where the hell are you?"

Tung's terse greeting both soothed and rattled Titan out of his artillery daydream.

"I appreciate the love. I'm fine. Let's see, I went grocery shopping, watched some Netflix, killed a few charmers, and saved my missing woman's twin sister from getting her throat slit open by a bone blade. And you? You good?"

"Oh, cut the shit and explain. And that explanation better

include why you didn't call for backup. You of all people know the protocol."

Titan could commiserate, and yeah, he knew the rules all right. Hell, he and Tung had drafted them together. He hadn't intended to worry the team, hence the phone call. But hadn't anything he'd just said landed at all?

Through the thick layer of sarcasm you lacquered over your sentences? Really?

"You gave me a head start, Tung." The words reverberated so lowly in Titan's throat, they nearly came out as a growl.

"Yes I did. Because if I didn't give you action steps, you'd have punched out that streetlight and every other one in the parking lot. But I didn't give you permission to be foolish. You're my second for a reason. Now, explain. You found your girl's twin sister? Where are you?"

"Rose." Titan smiled despite himself as he spoke her name and looked back at the kitchen window. "Her name is Rose, and yeah, she's the twin sister to the woman I lost six months ago. Apparently, I haven't been the only one grieving."

"Holy shit. Where is she now?"

"With me. We're at my cabin. The charmers nicked her pretty good on the arm, but it's mostly healed already." Charmer bleedings were more about leaching out a soul than any bodily fluids, so physical healing time was usually quick . . . provided the charmer was stopped before its magic did the heavy damage.

Titan adjusted the phone, turned his back toward the cabin, and lowered his voice, even though Rose couldn't hear him. "The charmers were targeting her. I don't know why."

Tung's uncharacteristic silence greeted him. "You're sure?"

"Yeah. When I was scouting out the parking lot, I saw an elite charmer come through for her. Not a mystic. And once I took him down, I heard several more portals open up at the other end of the park." He let the seriousness of the words sink in before he continued. "Why would they send so many for a random soul?"

"They wouldn't. Unless . . ."

Titan held his breath as he waited for whatever dots Tung needed to connect to form the full picture. As much as he had a head for battle strategy and logistics, Tung was their prime for a reason. His foresight was uncanny in its scope. And frighteningly accurate.

"Unless she's somehow involved with the light. Or, at least, they suspect she might be. Otherwise they wouldn't have sent the artillery they did. And certainly not an elite."

"The charmer who first attacked her sister was an elite. And there were five charmers that I counted then."

Tung moaned as he processed the information. "There's a connection," he stated matter-of-factly.

"Well, of course there is. They're twin sisters. You can't get more connected than that."

"Easy," Tung warned.

Titan kicked his boot into the nearest spruce as he willed his body to calm. Deep breaths in and out and all that. Like that ever worked. Might as well tell a fired rocket to weasel its way back into the launcher, thank you very much.

"She knows about you, I take it."

Titan winced. "Yeah. Vaguely, at any rate. But she seems to be absorbing what she's seen and been told so far. But, yeah. We're going to be having some uncomfortable conversations. I can't avoid it. Plus, I need more information. She, too, has been looking for her sister all these months. And I don't know how yet, but she found herself a charmer cuff. Knew where to look for it, too. It was hidden deep in the bushes where her sister was last seen. And she knew exactly where to go searching. No way a random passerby would have spotted it. Either way you slice it, though, she's involved now."

"Damn. Were you tailed at all?"

"No. I made sure of it. I took a few detours."

"All right. Hang low for a couple of days. Make sure there aren't any surprises. Then come back to Aurora and we'll regroup."

"I'm not leaving her. She stays with me when we return. I won't risk it."

Tung's amused chuckle caught Titan off guard. "Of course. But you're to check in every twelve hours. I want you back here in two days. See you then."

Titan disconnected the call and threw his phone into his back pocket. As he jogged back into the house, a swirl of unease floated around in his stomach. In exchange for much-needed information, he was about to open himself up to a mortal. To share aspects of his existence he and his brothers had worked hard to keep secret for so long.

As he kicked the dust off his boots before opening the front door, he realized why those damn internal butterflies were so hell-bent on making him sick.

Because it wasn't just that he hadn't opened up to a mortal before. That was true. But more precisely, he'd never done it with a woman before.

And especially not a woman whose face had haunted him for the past six months.

Rose was three forkfuls deep into her second bowl of spaghetti. It wasn't anything special. Your standard enriched macaroni product smothered in a jarred tomato sauce that began its life cycle as more tomato paste than tomato, but she wouldn't complain. Couldn't. Her mouth was greedily taking in the cooked calories made by someone else's hands. And it was wonderful.

These past few months had been absolute hell without

Tammy. Oh, Rose was physically capable of feeding herself and did so as required. But when her every thought was consumed with her missing sister, personal health and nutrition went by the wayside. Carla, the doll that she was, always made extras for Sunday supper and gave Rose the goods each Monday morning. But outside of that, protein bars, bowls of cereal, and microwave meals had filled in the gaps.

"This is amazing," she mumbled around another mouthful.

"Wish I could take the credit on this one." Titan settled his empty fork in his bowl.

"You took the initiative on this one. That gives you the credit. Take it."

He softly chuckled. "Yes, ma'am."

Rose glanced up. Titan was sitting at the small table while she had taken up space on the couch. She hadn't asked him to sit away from her, and had even given him plenty of sofa room so he might join her.

But he didn't. He kept his distance. Perhaps to allow her the space he thought she needed? Whatever the reason, she didn't question it. In fact, she was grateful because it afforded her the opportunity to properly assess him.

An angel. Seriously? The concept was so strange. He looked like any other man she'd see on the street, albeit more muscled. His physique suggested he was more of a wide receiver than a celestial mall cop. A massively tall wide receiver who nearly had to duck to clear the doorways. And a well-groomed one at that. Titan's espresso-colored hair was cropped short but was still long enough for one to slide their fingers through. The tightly trimmed sides gave way to an even tighter full beard that framed an angular jawline. And those eyes. More of that deep brown, which was quickly becoming her new favorite shade.

What? Since when?

Rose shook the thought away and ducked her chin down a bit so she could continue her covert examination. His Henley shirt was open at the collar, with the first few buttons undone. But while artists and writers often lacked inspiration when looking at a blank canvas, she had a veritable geyser of feelings as she ogled the expanse of Titan's tanned skin. Every little twitch and dip called to her like a breadcrumbs trail, tempting her home.

Which was insane. He wasn't her home any more than Carla and Rob were. But he had been there when she needed help the most. Miraculously so, even, though she rolled her eyes at the celestial analogy.

And speaking of which . . .

"So, um . . . angel fire?" Rose inclined her head toward the fireplace.

Titan's easygoing expression dissolved slightly. His arms and shoulders tensed. Then he nodded and stood. "I would normally say we should start at the beginning, but who the hell knows where that even is?"

Rose appreciated his attempt at levity, though his stalling was only amping up her anxiety.

Titan raised his hand in front of her, all five fingers splayed out. Then, one by one, each finger began to glow. The light was a dull reddish at first, like the tail end of a sunset, but then ramped up from fiery oranges to golden yellows and finally to a brilliant bright blue.

"Holy shit!" Rose scooted back onto the sofa, even curling her legs up off the floor in a literal game of the Floor Is Lava. She had no idea what to expect because the man before her was literally holding freaking fire!

And was she seeing things or was that a smirk on his face? While he was on fire?

"He's on fire, and he's smiling," she panted to herself.

Titan walked over to the logs already settled in the fire-place, kneeled before them, and gripped one in his flaming hand. The wood caught, but slowly. No faster than it would if it were lit with regular kindling. The burn was appropriate and efficient.

Natural.

As soon as Titan was content with the flames, he stood, faced Rose, and the blue flames engulfing his hand extinguished. Well, not extinguished exactly. More like burned out or retreated into him, except without the smoke. Amazing!

"My brothers and I are sentinel angels, and angel fire is our last remaining celestial weapon."

"Brothers? There are more of you?"

Rose expected Titan to walk back to his seat at the table. But instead, he slowly walked over to the couch she was on.

He gestured beside her. "May I?"

She nodded, not exactly trusting her voice to deliver the message.

The leather cushions depressed as they gladly accepted Titan's weight. He rested an arm on the couch's back, allowing his hand to dangle freely at the wrist. The same hand that had just been on fire. Rose studied it closely before returning her attention to him.

No blistered skin. No discoloration. And all five fingernails are accounted for. Incredible.

"Angel fire is our last remaining celestial weapon."

"You said that already."

"Because it's important to the rest of what I'm about to tell you." Titan flicked his gaze to the fire before continuing. "Yes, I have brothers. There are seven of us, and we've been together since before humans were a thought. Our angel fire is our last connection to the Empyrean, the highest realm of heaven—our fire's source, and our home. The Empyrean is the birthplace of all high celestial beings. Our fire is a powerful celestial weapon, though we've mastered quite a few mortal weapons over the years as well." He smiled and turned back to her.

"We were—are—the Empyrean's champions. Protectors of

its celestial inhabitants and all the heavenly sources of light. Including human souls." He inclined his head toward her and smiled briefly. The fire had gathered some steam, and Rose marveled at the flames' reflection in Titan's eyes. "The charmers have a different view of things, however. They're demon magic users and the scourge of the Empyrean and all its celestial inhabitants. Everything that is light and life in the world, from sunlight to the spark of a person's soul, they condemn because they're relegated to exist in the dark. Light of any manner is their enemy. It kind of kills them. One hefty dose of the stuff snuffs them out like a three-year-old's sneeze on a birthday candle." He shrugged a shoulder and winked. Actually winked at her!

"They dwell in the dark, while all other celestial beings are able to not only roam free but thrive in the light. And like any shortsighted imp who wants what they can't have, they operate under the comic book supervillain mindset of 'if they can't have it, no one can.' So, they've made it their mission to abolish all sources of the Empyrean's light and shut the place down for good. No more souls allowed into heaven. No more souls ascending to the Empyrean. No more heaven period. With an eternal darkness over existence, they'd have free rein."

Rose barely had time to think about those implications before Titan continued.

"A long time ago, the charmers made a run on the Empyrean. It was a gruesome battle. We lost many." Titan's voice softened in quiet homage and remorse.

Rose wanted to ask more questions, but she and grief were besties. She sure as hell knew how to read a room, so she left him to his thoughts and waited for him to continue.

"But the celestial mages—the Empyrean's governing body and spiritual guides—made a last-ditch effort to protect the souls from being extinguished . . . and from blocking the charmers' advancing charge to take over the Empyrean. They empowered me and my brother sentinel angels with the ability to seal the gates."

"Gates? As in heaven's gates?" Whoa.

Titan nodded. "But the power was immense and new. The mages taxed themselves greatly to produce it and left themselves—and the Empyrean—extremely vulnerable. The spell all but drained the mages of their energy and power. It was the ultimate Hail Mary pass thrown to us, but we weren't prepared for the backlash we'd receive once we caught it. The mages had given us a final gift, without time to explain, before they were forced to be sealed inside the gates. Before me and my brother sentinels enacted the Sealing. Oh, we succeeded," he said with no small amount of pride, "but in doing so, we fell."

"Fell," Rose repeated. "So, you're fallen angels?"

Titan snorted. "I guess we technically fit that bill. But more importantly, when we landed in the mortal realm, we quickly learned that the Sealing not only prevented the charmers from gaining access to the Empyrean, but it sealed us out as well. And as a result, we no longer have access to our celestial powers. We lost all connection with the Empyrean. Our powers. Our weapons. Everything. Gone." Titan paused, fiddled distractedly with a loose thread on the couch, and set his gaze on her. "Except our angel fire."

"When was this . . . this fall?"

Titan plucked the thread free and absentmindedly fiddled with it. "About 65 million years ago, give or take a few millennia." He glanced up at her and shrugged a shoulder as if age was nothing but a number. "Mortals have always come to believe it was an asteroid that led to the extinction-level event that annihilated the dinosaurs. But, no. It was just us. Well, I don't mean to make it sound so casual. It hurt like a bitch. But regardless, the outcome was the same. All this is to say, we've been here for some time."

Rose sat silent, enraptured in his story as he inched closer to the burning question that sat impatiently on the tip of her tongue. *What does this have to do with me?*

"When we fell, well, let's just say we didn't come out of the oven the way we were put in. Our makeup had changed. Tung—Tungsten, our leader," he added for her benefit, "has more theories about the whys and wherefores. He suspects it had something to do with the mages and their frantically bestowed gift. But suffice it to say that we had been changed. Elementally. We could still access our angel fire, but only temporarily. With every use, we burn off the energy needed to rekindle it. Those energy stores, as best as we've discovered, need to be recharged each night while we sleep. The next morning . . . poof, back to full steam." Titan's fingers burst open for effect. "It's a great magic trick, but it makes killing charmers damn challenging. They can only be killed with our angel fire, so we've had to get creative over the years, infusing weapons and projectiles with the fire available to us so we can do more with what we've got. But it's taxing. And inefficient at times." Titan's shoulders sagged with the apparent frustration of the grind.

He looked back at the fire briefly before speaking again. "Until I touched you. More specifically, your skin."

"Is that what you were talking about before?"

He nodded. "When you and I connected in that way, my angel fire was called forth . . . and I sure as hell didn't do it. It was brief but vitally potent. And just enough for me to destroy the charmers in that parking lot in one fell swoop and get us away."

Rose's breath hitched when Titan's hand settled a hairbreadth away from her shoulder, as if the movement was both accidental and instinctual.

"I had it all, Rose. Every ounce of my full angel fire at my fingertips. I hadn't had access to that power fully since before I fell, before we sealed the gates."

Blood pounded in Rose's ears at the implications he was

creeping toward. Her heartbeat fluttered lightning fast at the base of her throat and sharp tingles bit into her skin as they bloomed up her arms and back.

"And it was all because of you. Whether you realize it or not, you are a key ingredient here. And most likely your sister is as well."

The bomb had been dropped and she was standing in the center of the blast zone.

"I have to go. I . . . I just need some air. Alone. Please." She scrambled off the sofa and bolted for the front door. Once she made it outside, she ran blindly into the darkness until her sides ached and her lungs trembled. But even as her sneakers slapped against the fallen leaves, her logical brain knew what her emotional one refused to acknowledge.

Titan was right. And she was so totally screwed.

CHAPTER 7

Panic fueled Rose's legs as she pumped them harder through the forest. Because this wasn't an area of the White Mountains tourists had access to, she struggled to get her footing as she raced along the inhospitable forest floor. Sharp, sap-coated branches and pointy pine needles swatted her in the face as she mad-dashed it away from that cabin and every unbelievable thing she had just heard.

She should have toughed it out, should have held her ground and wagged a big attitude-filled finger in his face and said, "You're crazy! Now tell me the truth." She should have risen up on her toes, grabbed that man by his invitingly open collar, and demanded he cut the bullshit and tell her where her sister was.

All of that sounded like perfectly logical reactions to the far-off news he'd just thrown her way. But instead, fear had gotten the better of her and it'd been all she could do not to leap out of that cabin and run away from the confusion. From the finely spun narrative of words and events that made no freaking sense.

Just like after Tammy's disappearance. When not a single thing in her life made sense anymore. Not the manner of her sister's vanishing, not the cold and shut-off reaction of her parents, not the missing leads and dead ends of the investigation. Nothing.

And after six months of head-spinning lost trails and sleepless nights, she found out that her sister was abducted all right, but presumably not by a person. No. But by a demon—a charmer, whatever. And the guy who saved her from the same fate happened to be an angel. And, oh hey, only she had some magic touch that recharged his D cells and gave him the full power he needed to take down the bad guys.

It'd be laughable. Comical. Except it wasn't, because it was real. Really freaking real.

But while she was lost in a thought cycle of disbelief and panic, running in the dark took its toll. She failed to notice the change in topography underfoot.

"Aaah!"

The toe of her sneaker snagged a tree root she hadn't seen, and Rose's ankle twisted sharply. Pain bloomed as she threw her palms out to catch herself. But the terrain was uneven, and while her left hand caught the ground, her right hand caught air. With the lack of light and her heightened panicked state, she had wandered too close to a steeply sloped embankment.

Her body was ping-ponged left and right as she barrel-rolled down the hill. Her shoulders and head took the hardest beating, despite her forethought to cocoon her head and neck behind the shield of her arms. When the rolling stopped, Rose landed on her back and skidded to a halt down the bottom portion of the embankment, finally landing on solid ground at the base of a large tree growing out of the root of the hill.

Everything hurt. From knees to nose, there wasn't anything on her body that wasn't throbbing in some manner. A whimpering groan rumbled out of her mouth as she slowly wiggled her extremities. There was the thrumming soreness of new bruises and the sharp stings of fresh scrapes, but nothing that told her she'd be a quadriplegic. Her ankle, though, was the blaring red flag in the assessment. That sucker had been twisted badly and obviously hadn't appreciated the Jack and Jill routine.

A shrill, whining bark off to her left broke through her body's alarm bells. At first, she mistook it for the ringing that had started up a tango in concert with the throbbing behind her eyes, but then the whining got louder and started to get more varied in pitch.

Rose opened her eyes and, unlike a moment ago when the lack of light caused her not to see where the hell she was going, this time she was blessedly grateful for the darkness. Her bruised and migraine-prone cranium thanked her.

Until hot, moist breaths puffed quickly against her ear.

Ignoring the pain, she frantically rolled over onto her hands and knees. The available moonglow was shit, but she didn't need a spotlight to detect the two black bear cubs standing in front of her.

She froze and then took in the tree in front of her. Especially the gaping hole at the base of its roots that was burrowed well into the embankment.

A bear's den.

Shit.

"Hey, there," she said shakily, the words a mix of fear and pain. "I'm not going to hurt you guys. I'm just going to back up and leave you to your little home."

Her knees were on fire as her wobbly legs relented to her brain's command to back the heck up right the heck now. It was October, and in New Hampshire, black bears typically started their hibernation in November but not always. And even though it was rare to see one out at night, it wasn't completely out of the realm of possibility, especially only a few hours after sundown. An inefficient glance around the den didn't immediately come away with signs of a mama bear, but she wouldn't be far away from her cubs. Rose needed to get the hell out of there and fast.

But the darn furballs didn't get the memo. With each backward hobble she took, eight lumbering paws and a set of curious black noses advanced on her.

"Oh, no you don't." She stopped and held her hand up in the universal sign of stop. "It's not playtime. It's bedtime. Go on back in your den, and I'll make good on my promise to leave you alone."

But the cubs' interpretation of her plea was for shit. Two warm, wet noses began tickling the tips of her fingers. Then one of the cubs pushed at her palm with the side of its muzzle, demanding attention. In that natural, inviting way people's hands tend to move around furry, cute animals, Rose's palm turned face up, despite her words and desire to flee. And dammit if that cub didn't lean in for a good face rub while the other one sidled up to her shoulder to sniff and rub as well.

"Please . . . please go back inside." The plea was made through pained tears. The situation had gone from bad to worse. She couldn't physically run away, not yet. And now she had her scent all over another animal's babies. In an area uninhabited by people. At night, when anything out of the ordinary for these cubs would automatically trigger a predatory response if the mama came back soon.

No, not if. When.

Rose pulled her hand away and struggled to get to her feet. The cubs circled her ankles and whimpered as they rubbed up against her, nearly knocking her off balance. The pain in her head and ankle was blinding, but she did her best to keep upright. Her ankle couldn't bear weight just yet, which she figured, but that didn't stop her from at least setting her toes down for balance. She'd hobble like a one-legged pirate if she needed to.

But where, Rose? Back to the cabin with the hunky angel spouting his "magic touch" nonsense?

The rustling of leaves behind her made her freeze. Crunching forest litter gave way to a much more ominous rumble. Rose slowly turned around, ridiculously put her hands in the air like she was under arrest, and cemented her heels to the ground while the rest of her stomach bottomed out.

A very large and very pissed-off mama black bear paced in front of her. Sharp, chuffing noises were directed at the cubs, she assumed, followed by a pulsing and threatening growl. Yup, that one was for her, all right.

Shit!

"Easy, girl. I'm not going to touch your babies, I swear."

Even though I already did technically, but that wasn't my fault!

Like reasoning with a predator protecting her cubs would help matters. If Rose wasn't so scared, she'd almost appreciate the mama's determination to stick by her children. But scared she was, so there was no empathy in the cards for the bear.

Rose kept her hands up and tried to back away, but where? The cubs had definitely seen their mama, but the darn nosy furballs weren't coming up with the good sense to get back in the freaking den. When she retreated one more step, her heel crunched down on one of the cub's paws. The poor thing yelped and then—natch—*that* was the moment he and his brother decided they should hightail it out of there and scurried into the den.

About freaking time.

But the damage had been done. As Rose tried to restore her misplaced balance, she took her eyes off the mama bear for a split second to secure more solid footing.

Right as lumbering paws charged toward her.

Rose heard the heavy strides of the bear before she saw them. She fell forward and scrambled for higher ground, up a boulder, behind a nearby tree, anywhere. But her ankle was lame, and her hope was even more so. She frantically scooched back and palmed the ground around her for something, anything to throw at the bear. When her knuckles bumped the rough bark of a branch, she gripped the thing and, with a groan, whirled it around . . .

And caught nothing but air.

Rose reared back with the branch again, desperately hoping she had time for another swing.

But she didn't. Mama was a few feet away from pouncing on Rose. The bear was so close that drops of the bear's spittle flew and landed on Rose's jeans. There was no time to swing the branch again. She merely held it in front of her, gripped it like a too-small safety bar on a roller coaster, and prayed it would catch the bear's open jaw when it came to that. Because she had no doubt it would come to that.

A streak of smoky silver dashed across her field of vision, tackling the bear to the ground. Long strands of her hair followed the whoosh of wind that came with the intrusion. Whelps mixed with growls and grunts as the bear fell onto its side and skidded across the forest floor.

No, not skidded. Was pushed.

Rose's heart beat frantically in her chest as she desperately tried to focus her woefully inadequate night vision on what the heck was happening. Flashes of what she thought was metal danced before her in the meager moonlight.

Then she saw the wings. Great expansive wings, which were as wide on each side as the bear on its hind legs was tall, rose in front of her. They were muted in the low light, but she could still make out every flare and angle to them. The feathered pattern she, oddly enough, expected to see was there, but the arrangement reminded her of roof shingles instead. Solidly strong and able to withstand any tenacious storm.

Awe quickly replaced fear as her gaze moved beyond the wings and landed on Titan's stoic profile, which was completely metallic, as was every inch of his body. Hair, beard, fists, boots. All of it was completely engulfed in the same metallic armor his wings seemed to be made from. Yet he moved freely and without restriction.

Titan's wide palms spread across the bear's belly as he pushed against what had to be three hundred pounds of pissed-off predator. Rose winced when the bear's long claws scraped against Titan's neck and chest. Viscous teeth and an unforgiving jaw clamped tightly around his wrist but didn't penetrate. It merely slid up and down his forearm in an attempt to seek solid purchase, but it never could.

"Easy, mama. We won't hurt your babies," Titan cooed to the animal. Once the beast was farther away, Titan stopped pushing and rested a gentle but seemingly firm hand on the scruff of the bear's neck. "You see that woman over there?" He gestured back at Rose. "She's very important to me, just like your curious cubs are to you. And it'd really bother me if you took a bite out of her." He leaned closer and whispered, "She's not that tasty. A bit tough."

Both the bear and Rose bristled at the remark.

"Your cubs are back safe and sound in your den. All I'm going to do is let you go, get my girl, and leave you to finish up your hibernation prep. All right?" The bear snorted and whined, but she didn't chomp her jaws or fight back.

No way that thing could really understand him. No freaking way.

And then, with a roll of his shoulders, Titan seemingly shook off his metallic skin like it was an annoying extra layer of clothing he no longer needed. Likewise, his wings, which had been a brilliant mix of menacing and miraculous a second ago, shimmered into translucent waves like summer heat off a blacktop and disappeared.

He was himself again. Or, rather, he looked like a normal man again.

But the transformation had done something to Rose as well. She swallowed down dry gulps of air and winced when her throat still burned with hoarseness. She squeezed her eyes shut as tightly as she could. Splashes of rainbow dotted her vision before she opened them again. All signs pointed to her still being alive and kicking.

So what she just saw had to have been real. The wings were real, which she could personally vouch for, but the metallic armor? How else could he have survived the bear's attack without a single maul mark or puncture wound? Heck, how did he even still have his hands?

Because he's not human, Rose. And he clearly has other means of defense.

Titan jogged into her field of vision. With his arms folded over his chest and a newly pinned scowl on his face, he had all the good nature of someone who just found out the neighborhood troublemaker had put urine in his gas tank.

He crouched down low and looked her over before softening his expression. "What's the damage report?"

"Ankle." She nodded toward her right foot, begrudgingly licking her figurative wounds.

Titan sighed as he put his arms under her knees and behind her back, being careful not to touch her skin.

She immediately swatted him away. "I can do it myself."

A low moan rose up behind Titan as the mama bear lumbered back into her den to be with her cubs.

"No, you can't."

"Yes, I can," she gritted out.

Titan dropped his hands from her and ran his fingers through his short hair a few times. Then he settled his forearms on his knees and caught her eyes. Exhaustion and frustration had added tension to his features where there hadn't been before. His fierce, angled cheeks and stern brow relaxed despite their determination. But it was more like the fight had gone out of them, instead of a natural softness and affection mellowing out his countenance. He was clearly just as tired as she was. Bone-deep tired.

And her little stunt hadn't done anyone any favors.

"Look, you're not that far from the cabin. There's a flatter path that goes around the embankment and heads back. It's a bit longer, but not by much. If you absolutely want to test that ankle and hoof it back, I won't stop you. But . . ." He held his finger up. "Let the record show that I'm strongly against it."

Rose nodded and did her best to keep the inclination to laugh out of her hidden smile as she pulled bits of crushed leaves from her hair. "Noted, counselor. And yes, I'd like that. Thank you," she said softly.

"Good." He nodded. "And while we're on the subject of likes, I'd also like it if you'd let me help you."

He wasn't touching her. Wasn't trying to manhandle or strong-arm his way into her decision. He just sat there with his arms on his haunches and tired patience in his waiting eyes.

He's letting you make a choice.

"Thanks. I'd still like to walk."

The disappointment and frustration were apparent in Titan's sigh, but he said nothing as he nodded and made to stand up.

"But I'd like you to help me, if that's okay."

He froze for a moment and then smiled. "Sounds like a fine plan." He tucked his arm underneath her shoulder, mindful of her exposed neck and hands, and helped her to her feet. "But once we get you home, it's a shower and sleep. For both of us."

Oh.

The walk back to Titan's cabin was agonizing, though not for its pace. Every now and then, while Rose was too intently focused on where to put her good foot, Titan would steal a glance at her. Her pert nose was often scrunched up in pain, and she did her best to bite back the winces, but nothing escaped him. Not the short pants of breath or the tighter her nails curled into the meat of his shoulder as she reluctantly placed more and more of her weight on him.

Her injuries stabbed him just as deeply. Because they were all his fault.

Talk about your oversharing. He should have known better than to unload everything on her so quickly like that. Had the circumstances been reversed, he no doubt would have been just as shocked. And pour on some long-standing grief and frustration and it was no wonder she'd bolted at the first opportunity.

He could only be grateful for being there in time. That would be his sole comfort in all this. But to protect himself from the bear's attack, he'd had no choice in the matter: he'd had to shift form.

He only hoped she wouldn't run again when she asked him to explain that little doozy.

Well, she can't exactly run right now, can she?

Titan mentally chastised himself for the internal remark and shifted her weight more evenly against him. The soft lights of the cabin poked through the dense spruce needles as they strode up to the front door.

"How's the ankle?" he asked as he guided her up the short steps.

"It's been better. I can tell it's not broken, which I'm grateful for. Most likely just a bad sprain."

"I have first aid supplies. After your shower, I'll bind it."

Once inside, she took back her arm from around his shoulder and sat on the arm of the couch. And paused. "Angels need first aid?"

He chuckled as he latched the door. "Sometimes. Though not often."

"Because of your metal skin?"

He bristled at the question, then he turned to her. "Shower first. Then you can pick my brain all you want while I wrap your ankle. Deal?"

She gave him the side-eye for a moment, but the coy upturn of her mouth took the bite out of the expression. "Deal. But I don't need help showering."

Titan held his hands up. "Oh, I know you don't. But even you have to admit your balance is a tad unreliable right now, and bandages and ice packs aren't going to do crap for cracked-skull syndrome."

They both knew his argument was sound. Why was she being so stubborn? He'd sooner saw his own leg off with a rusty steak knife than harm her. Whatever the reason, he hadn't a clue, but he'd continue to work his way up into her good graces and earn her trust, like he would do for any wounded animal.

Though he was beginning to suspect most of her wounds were far out of his healing reach.

Rose hobbled over to the bathroom, leaning on every door-jamb and chair back along the way. It was all he could do not to rush after her, sweep her off the floor, and put her in that damn shower stall. But he unwillingly reeled himself in. When she finally reached the door, she opened it before turning back to him. His breath caught in his lungs as he was assaulted by jade eyes of profound sadness.

"Tammy was my whole life." The words fell out of Rose with the weight of the great mountain outside their door. "She got me through our parents' divorce, got me through the end of a miserable high school experience and an even more trauma-tizing college one." The quiver in her voice gutted him, but he forced himself to stay silent and just listen. "Your parents are supposed to be there for you through all of your major life events, you know? Graduations, first apartment, first job. But ours weren't. Because they had chosen poorly and should never have been married, and Tammy and I got stuck in the in-between." Rose tucked her hand into the cuff of her sweatshirt sleeve and wiped at her eyes.

"When Tammy went missing, I didn't just lose a sister or a twin. I lost a piece of myself. The only person I could ever trust with anything. My parents were far too broken to step in and step up and preferred to silently turn a blind eye and grieve in their own way than care for their only remaining child." She dropped her chin and cast her eyes downward. He missed the eye contact, though he understood her need to look away. "So forgive me if I'm not yet ready to trust so openly. Yes, I have questions. Yes, I believe you won't hurt me. But I've been on my own for a long time now, so I don't know how to be anything other than who I am."

Titan just stood there as Rose's words settled over his skin. Strangely enough, his first thought was of his brothers. The seven of them had been together since they'd first been born from the eternal light in the Empyrean. They've fought together, fallen together, despaired and lost together. To have even one of them ripped away, let alone by a charmer, with no trail or information to follow, would cripple him. Utterly cripple and eat away at his warrior's soul.

And yet here Rose stood, battered and bruised and far too thin for his liking, but with a chin held high and an iron-willed resolve to keep going. To find her sister when no one else who loved her was willing to still do the same.

She was breathtaking. Such courage and determination. If he didn't know better, he would have sworn those two things alone would have been more than enough to call bright his angel fire. They were magnetic and inspired more profound feelings than any simple skin-to-skin touch ever could.

Titan walked over to Rose and didn't stop until her slim frame nearly brushed the planes of his chest. He longed to move closer, to take that final step and have her body pressed flush to his again, like it had been when they were flying. To soothe her with his fire's warmth and gently stroke away the tension of the past several hours. Instead, he merely stood there and gave her the space she so boldly requested.

"I wouldn't want you to be anything other than what you are. Ever." Titan's words were a tad raspy and almost desperate in their delivery. She looked up in slight confusion. "And you should know that you are not the only one who has been grieving. But there's time for that discussion later. For now, take your shower. Towels are on the rack and soap and shampoo are in the stall. I will be right outside this door the entire time."

Rose nodded as she turned the brass knob of the bathroom door.

"And sometimes," Titan added, stopping Rose before she entered the bathroom, "just knowing someone is there for you can make you that much stronger a fighter, whether you take the offered hand or not."

<hr>

Sure enough, the man held true to his promise and stayed outside the bathroom door the entire time. When she opened the vanity below the sink, looking for a washcloth, he told her through the door to look in the basket in the back. When she had a hard time figuring out how to get hot water to come on in the shower, he gently instructed her on where to settle each tap so the water ratios were right.

All through the door, without her ever saying an initial word.

Titan anticipated every single one of her needs well before she did. She wanted to chalk it all up to her being his guest in a however-many-years-old cabin in the woods, but her gut didn't honestly believe that. There was something more there. Something genuine and caring.

Something trustworthy.

When Rose finished up her shower, which was equal parts glorious and awkwardly painful what with her throbbing ankle and all, the only clothes she had to change back into were what she had been wearing. And no way was she going to try and mangle her injured leg into stiff denim. She might have been dumb, but she wasn't stupid.

She had her T-shirt and undergarments back on, while her sweatshirt and jeans rested in a pile in the corner. Her shirt had largely been protected by her outer layers, thankfully. But her bare legs were a no-no. Especially not in October.

And especially not in front of him.

Rose cracked open the door and looked out into the hallway. Titan's casual smile greeted her as he leaned against the wall, arms over his chest, with his booted ankles crossed.

"All good?" he asked.

"Almost. I, um . . . do you have a pair of—"

Before she could even get the words out, he dropped his arms and held out a pair of heather-gray sweatpants. "Figured you were done with the jeans for the night. And New England weather can be killer."

Okay, wow. He wins the award for most intuitive man on the planet.

"Thanks."

Rose shut the door and scooted her butt into the softest pair of sweatpants that had ever touched skin, she was sure of it. The lightest of butterfly kisses and smooth cotton strands caressed her thighs and calves as she settled the pants over her hips and rolled up the waistband a few times. She laughed to herself, thinking he must have a secret stash of fabric softener in a shed somewhere and that the man was a closet lover of luxury. But when she brought her hands to her nose, there wasn't even the slightest trace of artificial clean linen or bogus mountain breeze fragrance.

No. It was all Titan. Woodsy earth and deep balsam mixed with a mellow crispness. Her shoulders sagged as the scent did more to soothe her agitated nerves than any steaming, hot shower or scented candle ever could.

It was a fragrance she could get used to.

More than used to, in fact, and you know it.

Then she opened the door and slowly stepped out. Titan, of course, hadn't moved an inch from his post in the tight hallway. The man was like a darn K-9 in his dogged attention. But, despite his nearness, he was obviously respecting her boundaries. The action spoke volumes and made her realize that perhaps—and this was a *giant* scoop of perhaps on top of an uber-skeptical sundae—she might be able to trust him a bit. Either way, she was here, in his cabin—hell, in his pants—and the reason for all of that hung heavily in the air between them.

He'll help you find Tammy. And he wants to find her just as much as you do.

Rose exhaled, willing the tension and weariness to leave her body. No dice.

Titan's eyes assessed her, taking in the new addition on her legs. With a quick nod of approval, he gestured toward the bedroom.

The space was sparsely furnished but neat. A king-sized bed draped in an evergreen down comforter filled out the room, while a modest walnut dresser three drawers high sat directly across from it. The dresser had a smaller mate in a matching nightstand beside the bed. Nothing adorned the tops of the furniture save a single bedside lamp on the nightstand. There was not a knickknack or photo frame to be found on any surface. The only spacial intruder was a small basket containing a comb, nail clippers, and a few other small grooming items.

A crate with orderly arranged red cardboard boxes and white tubes of ointment sat at the foot of the bed, spotlit by the petal-shaped light fixtures from the ceiling fan above.

"C'mon. Lie down and let me look at that ankle. We can talk while I wrap it. After that, the room is yours. I'm locking the door behind me."

"Um . . . you don't have to do that."

Titan walked over to the bed and pulled back the comforter to reveal ivory flannel sheets.

Flannel. How irritatingly sensible. He probably never jaywalked and always carried ibuprofen on him, too.

Despite herself, she still smiled at the utilitarian makeup of his home. Everything about it was logical. No froufrou doilies or Egyptian thread count nonsense. Just basic, dependable commodities that he clearly kept clean and orderly, even though she figured this cabin wasn't his primary residence.

Everything about this man—no, *angel*—was logical, even in his obvious mysticism. Straightforward. Black and white.

Dependable.

Rose shook off her analysis and carefully crawled into bed, mindful of her ankle. As soon as her socked feet smoothed down the sheets and her back hit the upright pillow, her brain nearly went offline. "This feels soooo good right now."

A deep chuckle rose from where her feet lay. Titan had moved to the foot of the bed, taken a seat next to the basket of first aid supplies, and thrown back the comforter and sheets, giving him access to her ankle. And boy, did that thing not look happy to see him. Even though the pain was steadily subsiding and she kept her ankle covered in her thick sock, she was still swollen a plenty.

Warm hands gently lifted the angry appendage. Titan's touch was beyond careful. He was delicate, yet discerning as he tenderly poked and massaged each angry joint and muscle. Rose also took particular note of how he made sure not to touch her bare skin. When his fingers reached the swollen joint, she held her breath and waited for the flare of pain to come. But nothing ever did. In fact, it had been so long since she'd truly allowed anyone to take care of her, outside of Carla's Monday leftovers, that she wasn't sure she even knew how to receive the compassion. Her brain's receptors had long since lost the ability.

Turns out, they had a pretty darn good memory when the right stimulation was in front of them.

It was the first taste of bliss she'd had in six months. And it was over a freaking twisted ankle.

But just as her skin tensed against the frigid kiss of the gauze-wrapped ice pack Titan gently placed against her ankle, he said the most random thing. "Titanium."

The word came out of nowhere and was so absurd given the setting, she had to sit up a bit more to look at him just to confirm he had, in fact, said it.

"Come again?"

"My name. It's short for titanium."

Oookay.

"Parents can get creative sometimes." She shrugged as she offered her empathy.

"I named myself," he said, and Rose impatiently waited for him to finish wrapping her ankle. "How does that feel?"

She flexed her foot. "Better."

Titan nodded as he settled her ice-pack-wrapped appendage on a soft pillow. Once he picked up the bits of garbage from the packaging, he leaned back and looked at her.

Stern brows hovered dangerously low over piercing, studious eyes. She gasped quietly at the change in expression while her gaze dropped to generously full lips nestled deep within his beard. They had sealed shut like a castle drawbridge.

It was a test. Was she ready not to only hear his next words but listen? Truly listen? Even if what came out of that mouth meant there was no going back to the world she knew?

Her head dropped and rose so slightly, she doubted he even picked up on her hesitant nod.

Her concern was unfounded. He returned her curt nod in kind, silently informing her—again—that nothing would get past him.

"I named myself for the metal I command. The metal that adopted and transformed me when I fell from the Empyrean and landed here."

Rose leaned back and crashed her head onto the pillow. She supposed that was about as relaxed as she would get, because no way in hell was she going to sleep anytime soon.

Never in his entire earthly existence had Titan ever told any mortal about his true nature. Though he interacted with mortals regularly—a byproduct of the whole living-among-them thing—knowledge of the celestial wasn't exactly common, and it sure as hell wasn't his to share freely.

Looked like tonight was the first time for a lot of things.

"You called me a fallen angel earlier. You said it as more of a joke, but you weren't entirely off. I did fall. We all did."

Rose sat quietly and waited for him to elaborate.

"After my brothers and I enacted the Sealing, the reverberations of the mages' power were so intense, none of us were prepared for it. The onslaught of light and magic blasted through each of us and sent us careening down through every celestial barrier, every ward and veil separating heaven and the Empyrean from the mortal plane." Titan looked away from her intent eyes and focused instead on an exposed thread poking up from one of the comforter's seams. He fiddled with it as he took a breath to continue.

"The fall was excruciating and terrifying. I remember gasping and screaming as my celestial connection and source of power was snapped from me, like a fishing line severed by a ravenous shark or something. Whole parts of me, innate abilities, and celestial magic stores I had always known evaporated in a blink the farther I fell from the Empyrean and its eternal flame. My body was whipped left and right, and all my heavenly weapons had disintegrated from my grasp. Skin—skin that had never been affected by elements or earthly combatants before—had solidified around my form, only to flay open as I fell farther.

"For the first time in my existence, I screamed. I screamed in agony, I screamed for my brothers—who I knew were also falling, but I couldn't see or hear—I screamed for my loss." Titan shook his head as he willed that trauma to return to his deepest protected memories where it belonged.

"And then we landed in the mortal plane. The impact was tremendous and expansive. The gravitational force that pummeled me to the earth was like a fiery asteroid flying at Mach speed into my chest. It pushed us all down into the bedrock of your realm, into each layer of mineral and sediment, until the forward momentum finally slowed and we stopped moving."

Rose's mouth hung open as she shook her head. "How could anyone survive what you're describing?"

Titan quirked his lips and rolled his shoulders back a tad under her praise and astonishment. "I'm an angel, remember?"

And then she rolled her eyes at the joke. "How could I forget?" But the soft chuckle that escaped her told him she wasn't all that affronted. "So, you're immortal? Can't be killed?"

"Not exactly. When my brothers and I surfaced, we weren't the same. Something about our basic chemistry had been altered in some way. Most of our celestial powers had been lost to us, along with our heavenly weapons. But our bodies had somehow transformed to take on the traits of the metals embedded in the stone and elements around us. Not going to lie, those early days of exploration and experimentation had been terrifying but also profound. We learned that, yes, we can be injured and presumably killed one day. Though fat chance of that ever happening."

"Of course." She smiled.

Titan couldn't help himself in the slightest and wholeheartedly returned her smile. His cheeks damn near hurt with the foreign movement, but it was a good kind of hurt, like an atrophied muscle being nursed back to life.

"I was the first to be claimed by my metal. The titanium embedded within our rock cave had chosen me. The attraction was magnetic and all-consuming. The metal and its elements sliced through me and connected with my angel fire, which I thought was lost to me in the fall, as I had no longer felt its heat within me.

"The first transformation was agonizing. My skin knitted together in sharp excruciating pinches as metallic shards took its place and raced up my body. I thought I was about to die when my insides, one by one, turned to hard metal. I still remember the suffocation when my lungs refused to take in any more air and my tongue turned to solid titanium in my mouth, nearly blocking my airway."

Titan rose from the bed and took a few steps back from Rose. The bedroom wasn't that spacious, but it was large enough for what he had planned. He threw his shoulders back and let his metal take over his form.

What had been a terrifying experience all those years ago was a welcome metamorphosis now. Titan leaned into the change as the warm titanium quickly spread through his toes, tendons, and thighs before locking him tight around his waist and shooting up and over his torso and head. His body thrummed with power as his armor snapped into place.

And then, because he couldn't help peacocking just a bit, he released his wings.

"Oh, my gosh." Rose's stunned expression was nearly as prevalent as his wingspan.

Because this had been the first time she had been able to really get a good up-close-and-personal look at him in his transformed state.

He took a few steps closer to her. "Titanium is one of the strongest metals on earth, despite its light weight, and has an extremely high melting point. All these qualities are manifested in me in the flesh-born angel I have become. My size, my strength, my patience and level-headedness . . . all physical characteristics of my metal that now lives in concert with me. In this form, however, I exist as my metal and live fluidly with all its strengths and commanding properties."

Titan continued his forward movement and studied Rose's eyes carefully as they danced across every silver inch of him. Was she scared? Was she curious? Did she wish to run again? All questions that fluttered through his mind as he slowly approached her. But when his knees hit the edge of the bed, she hadn't retreated a single inch. Instead, her hand fidgeted closer toward him. The tip of her middle finger nearly brushed against his pants.

He had his answer.

Definitely curious. Thank the mages.

"But titanium aside, there is one core element to our makeup that stayed with us through the fall. That sat protected within while the rest of our celestial makeup was ripped away."

Rose's gaze climbed higher to meet his eyes. It was slow and studious and damn scorching. It didn't matter that he was standing in front of her, already tense and stoic as one of the hardest metals on the planet. Her assessment unraveled him and nearly threatened to dissolve his concentration and force him to shutter his armor.

"Your angel fire."

It wasn't a question. Though Rose's words were soft, the

connections she made were ironclad. Hell, Titan suspected there was very little that would ever get past this woman. And if this moment wasn't the first to prove it to him, he just had to look to the past six months of her refusing to take no for an answer when it came to the search for her sister.

He swallowed back the trickle of unease at the enormity of her insight and all its potential before continuing. "Yes. In the Empyrean, our angel fire was infinite. Once we landed on the mortal plane, however, we had been cut off from the eternal light. From our fire's supreme source." Titan drew his arms to the side and stretched his wings. "But we were not abandoned entirely." His body thrummed as heat flooded from his core and shot out through his closed fists and expanded wings. Electric blue flames danced in the reflection of Rose's eyes as he demonstrated his power, still maintaining intense care of his proximity to Rose and the furniture near him.

"Though we still had use of our fire, our connection was tenuous and its power limited. Each night, the metals and minerals found deep within the rocks and tunnels of the earth recharge us and fuel our fire. The earth's elemental energy, for some reason, calls to our new form and serves as a sort of celestial battery charger each night. And each morning, we wake rested and restored with our angel fire intact once more. A final gift from the mages, and all they could offer us before we sealed them tightly behind the protection of the gates . . . and fell."

Titan extinguished his flames. His wings relaxed on his back as he lowered them slowly. The tips of them hung limply, dusting the wood floor behind him. He wasn't yet ready to call them back into himself entirely. He wanted her to gaze at them a bit more, grow used to their presence and the aspects of his existence she'd have to face before they searched for her sister.

The demonstration, combined with the ordeals of the day, had drained him, however. Despite Rose's earlier touch, Titan bristled at the lack of remaining energy his angel fire had. Some

part of him had hoped her touch would have been more significant, more altering. And that had always been his problem, what
his brothers had always ribbed him about.

He often hoped for too much. Put too much faith in the
stuff.

Rose's shocked expression was difficult to read, and it
worried him. For the second time in as many hours, he had
hefted a canyon-sized ball of information on her shoulders and
was waiting quite impatiently to see how she would bear the
weight of it.

But he needed to be calm. Understanding. Really, really
freaking patient. Yet just as he was about to fill the silent space
between them with more celestial ramblings—of what? His
brothers? The Empyrean? The best ways to flay open charmers?
—his breath caught in his throat.

Because the edge of his wing had relaxed too close to the
edge of the bed . . . and Rose had laid her gentle hand flat along
his feathers.

Heat, blazing and unrelenting, flared hot against Rose's
fingertips after she smoothed them over the metallic feathers of
Titan's wings. While the rest of his body had turned back to
flesh, his wings remained giant sheets of feathered titanium.

They had been so close, *he* had been so close, she couldn't
help herself. Warmth radiated off that man like an engine room
furnace, and she was drawn to him like a cold-blooded reptile
to a sun-warmed rock.

She forgot what her direct contact produced. Foolishly
forgot how he'd told her what her touch did.

How it called forth his angel fire. Without his say in the
matter.

Electric blue flames blossomed under her touch and quickly

engulfed her entire hand. She screamed and jerked back, wildly shaking her hand and scrambling as high up the headboard as she could.

Titan grabbed her immediately, cupping her blazing hand against his chest, cradling it as best he could to recall his fire and snuff out the flames. But they wouldn't recede.

"Put it out! Put it out! Oh, God!" Rose's shrieks grew louder as the fire leaped out of Titan's fists and crept higher up her forearm.

"I can't! I have no control over it anymore!" Titan's eyes grew wide as the fire spread over her chest and down her other arm. Everywhere the flames appeared, his hands did their best to smother and pat them down. Rose cried as firm grips smoothed over her biceps, chest, and neck, but it offered little help to quell the maelstrom.

She thrashed her head frantically from side to side. Tears rose up and quickly evaporated. The heat . . . Oh, the heat! Her skin had surely flayed off her muscles by now. Her lips, nose, eyelashes, there would be nothing left in another moment or two as the maddening pain crept higher and higher up her neck.

Rose cracked her eyes open. Titan hovered over her, his face horrified as he screamed words she couldn't make out. His eyes, those deliciously dark brown eyes that had previously captivated her, flashed with a rippling rainbow before turning the muted silver of his metal.

And that was a damn shame, because she'd hardly gotten enough time to discover that side of him yet. A fierce, terrifyingly powerful side that would be her strongest ally imaginable in finding her sister.

But it was all over.

Blue flames consumed her vision as the heat pressed down on her body. She sank into it, stilling her arms and allowing her last breaths to escape.

Before firm, hard lips crushed against hers.

CHAPTER 10

Titan was trapped in a towering inferno of his own goddamn power. Logic fled him like rats scrambling for higher ground on the Titanic. None of this made sense. The other times he and Rose connected had never resulted in this. Had she previously called forth his fire? Yes. But had she ever taken it into her own body? No. And now that body was writhing around on flammable bedding and was mere inches away from lighting up the room.

The fire—*his* fire—had no effect on him as he roamed his hand over every inch of her emblazoned body, doing his level best to call the flames back into himself. But he no longer had control over it. Over anything.

Rose screamed and wailed beneath him. He had never been more helpless in his life. By appearance, she looked unharmed. Her clothes, skin, and hair were not scorched or singed. But that didn't mean she wasn't suffering. Wasn't feeling every ounce of unimaginable heat and ferocity as the fire licked over her body. Angel fire was a byproduct of the Empyrean's eternal light, the source for all light and life in existence. His fire burned, yes, but never produced smoke. It was created from too perfect a source to not combust purely. Rose's lungs would be clear to breathe freely.

If only she would open her eyes and realize she still possessed the capability. That this was no normal fire. And she was no normal victim.

Titan glanced up at the blue flames as they rose higher within the room. The walls of his cabin were stone by design, as the metals and minerals in the rock were needed for him to recharge at night. But the roof was good old-fashioned log cabin construction and would ignite like tissue paper if he couldn't get Rose to call his fire back soon.

Dammit!

He needed to snap her out of her pain. Make her realize that the flames weren't consuming her the way she no doubt believed they were. If he couldn't control them, perhaps she could. But how to split her focus?

No sooner had the idea come to him did his resolve enact it.

Titan crawled over Rose's thrashing body, pinning her to the bed with his legs lest she errantly kick out and spread the fire. Once she was braced to his satisfaction, he settled on his elbows and cupped her head in his hands. Without another thought, he lowered his mouth to hers.

The fire responded all right, but again, not in the way he anticipated. Instead of the flames jumping from one source of combustion to the next, they retreated inward and proceeded to engulf him and Rose entirely.

A rush of energy pulsed through him as his angel fire connected with him once more. But not solely. Not as completely as it had before. But it was enough. He would take the modicum of control and rein it in with all he had.

Titan wrapped his arms around the woman beneath him and lifted, rolling them to the floor and away from the flammable bedding. Yet, as he settled his charge beneath him, cradling her within the flaming cage of his arms and wings, he tensed.

Because Rose's lips moved against his. The soft petal pushes were slow at first and unsure, as if sampling a new delicacy. But they quickly picked up the tempo, seemingly satisfied with what they found.

And Titan couldn't have agreed more. This hadn't been the plan. Hadn't even been a loose nugget of an idea when he brought Rose here. But now that she was here, beneath him, and somehow stealing his angel fire from him? Unmanning him, as it were?

He wasn't about to complain. Especially not when the flames began to recede, reabsorbing back into his form. And not when Rose's screams from a moment ago had suddenly turned to hungry whimpers against his mouth.

Bless the mages, she tasted divine! Like sweet cider and honeyed spices. Plush lips plied against his as her flavor worked its way deep into his senses. Her hands, which had previously been limp at her sides, crept up along the insides of his wings. He shivered as her touch fluttered against the grain of his feathers. The movement would normally irritate him, much in the way a feline preferred to be pet in one direction only. But under her touch, he was more than content to be pet in whatever direction she wanted.

The flames had all but subsided, with only a few wisps of flaming tendrils snaking over their upper arms. But within the cocoon of his protective wings, the air was very much on fire. Titan's kisses increased in their boldness as he lavished extra attention on her plump upper lip. To his delight, she immediately returned the favor, alternating her lips against his. When the slightest kiss of her hot tongue painted his lower lip, he groaned into her mouth.

"Rose . . ." His angel fire was long gone, but the temptation of her kisses grew to be too hot to ignore. Soft, encouraging moans left her mouth as their tongues danced back and forth. Her mouth fit his perfectly and sealed her to him like an airlock securing a lifeline for space flight passengers. The sensation was perfection and left him breathless.

His newfound treasure shifted beneath him. When the slender fingertips brushing his wings froze, his body stilled as well. Dammit! All good sense had escaped his head, and his cock apparently saw fit to take over command. This was not right. None of it was right, despite the feel of her against him and the simmering heat of her that had been reduced from scorching flames to a magnetic ember. His mouth broke the kiss and pulled back from its target despite Titan's growing desire. He removed his hands from her neck, lingering at the soft valleys under her ears, and braced his palms on the floor at her sides. Titan pushed his upper body away from her, allowing Rose's rapidly blinking eyes to adjust to the scene.

"What—" The words died on her tongue as she coughed and swallowed a few times. "What the hell was that? What just happened?"

"You stole my fire. Not maliciously, I mean. I know you didn't do it intentionally. But you definitely took it into yourself when your hand brushed my wing."

Rose's eyebrows shot up at the revelation, and then she took in the cage of silver feathers cocooning them to the hardwood floor. "I'm all right? How? I was on fire." She glanced down at her arms, which were pinned to her sides underneath Titan's body. "Or, at least, I thought I was."

"You were." Titan rose from the floor and sat back in front of her. "But you weren't hurt. Angel fire doesn't harm the one who summons it. It's a part of them. Or traditionally, it always has been. For some reason, my fire didn't physically harm you. But you felt it. You felt the pain of fire all over your body, right?"

She nodded furiously as she sat up, drew her knees into herself, and held them close to her chest. Like a cornered, frightened animal. *Shit.*

His head sagged in his hands as he covered his face. None of this made any sense. She shouldn't have any affinity over his fire. He was born of it! And she was mortal. The phrase "out of his element" came to mind. He would laugh if it wasn't so disgustingly accurate. And it was all made worse by the fact that doubt and fear were etched on every inch of her face. Unacceptable. He was here to keep her safe, to protect her from the charmers hunting her. But how could he protect her from himself?

"And after?"

Rose's quiet words penetrated his worries. His head shot up. "After?"

She shrugged a timid shoulder. "After the flames." Her gaze moved from the crests of his wings above his back to his face and, more specifically, his mouth. "You kissed me."

Angel up, buttercup. She deserves an explanation.

"It was all I could do to distract your mind from the pain you were obviously in. Since I couldn't control the fire, I needed you to try and do it. I suspected you could, that you had to, but not when you were lost in your turmoil."

She nodded, though with a heavy dose of uncertainty. "So . . . you thought kissing me would help me focus?"

The line of thought sounded like crap even to his own ears. But if he had to do it all over again, he would. And he would hardly call it a hardship. It definitely fell into win-win territory. That was a sacred space he hadn't found himself in for a very long time.

Before he could respond with a boatload of he didn't know what yet, she spoke. "Well, I guess it worked."

He blinked. That didn't sound like a complaint at all. Was she not angry at him, then?

"Yeah, it worked." He tested the words out on his tongue, still uncertain whether her responses were genuine. The slight curl of her lip and bashfully averted gaze was all the answer she would provide.

And he would freaking take it. All day. And twice on Sundays.

"So, what do we do now?" she asked.

Excellent fucking question. Titan looked over at the bed. Smoldered patches and scorched linens lay jumbled on top. And parts of the mattress had been burned clean through, exposing its inner stuffing and springs.

"I have some sleeping bags. We'll camp out in the living room. Tomorrow morning, I'm going to take you to my brothers. I was going to hang low here for another day, but they might have more answers than I do about what happened. And the more information we have, the better."

"And my sister?"

Damn, she was like a dog with a bone.

"One thing at a time. If the charmers were hunting you before, this newfound ability of yours would entice them all the more. Until we can get answers, you've got one hell of a target on your back."

Titan had his work cut out for him.

Rose clenched her teeth together as the fire coursing through her invaded her dreams. The heat had been so intense, so engulfing, she was sure death was a second away from incinerating her out of existence. The flames were around her legs now, snaking around and wrapping her in a blanket of molten fury. She kicked and thrashed, rose up and slammed back down. She did all she could to escape the burning as it coated her body in roaring agony.

Muted cries wormed into her consciousness. They were soft at first, barely audible whispers of her name, but spoken urgently. Desperately. Her jaw ached with tension, but something about the voice poking through her veil of pain gave her hope. Perhaps it was a distraction born from trauma. Her brain's last-ditch effort to trigger her mental gate control theory of pain, where a new and stronger stimulus would divert her attention away from the old.

Her name, now spoken with loud harried energy, punched through the pain. The frantic voice was edgy and raw, desperate and determined. And familiar. Oh so familiar.

Harsh tugs pulled her down, as if her legs were caught in a binding. But the only thing trapping her was the pain and the flames that were incinerating her from the inside out. Another sharp tug and cool, crisp air rushed through the wide legs of the sweatpants she wore.

Titan's sweatpants. Which still lay softly against her skin.

"Rose, wake up!"

Her eyes flew open and took in a face full of heaving, sweaty angel who looked as though he had just wrestled an alligator and nearly lost an arm in the process. But he stared solely at her, with no regard for anything else in the room that might be on fire or close to it.

I'm not on fire.

She looked down at her legs and saw long lines of totally intact and not at all singed gray sweatpants. In the corner next to the couch, however, lay the balled-up sleeping bag she had been wrapped in.

Oh.

"It was a nightmare," she whispered, still in awe of the dream's brutal strength and stark vividness. It was so lifelike!

"Yeah, I got that." The remark came out with a slight snort. "The next time your mind decides to relive past trauma, remind me to get out of the range of fire. Holy crap, woman. Has anyone ever told you that you kick like a mule?"

Rose would have laughed if the image wasn't rooted in so much confusion. But then she glanced up at Titan, who sat with one hand on his knee and the other pressed tightly to his ribs.

The wince on his face screwed his features up sharply, and she got the impression he wasn't used to outward displays of pain.

She didn't remember kicking him. The pain, however, she remembered crystal clear.

"I would say sorry, except I'm not in the habit of apologizing for things I don't remember doing."

Titan's shoulders bobbed in a silent laugh. "Note taken."

Rose ran her fingers through her hair and rested her palms on her scalp. She was so done with all of it. "What the *fuck* is going on? Seriously, I sailed past overwhelmed hours ago. I'm now firmly in freak-out mode, and I have well and truly reached my breaking point. Last night, I left work to hunt down a lead I had on Tammy. The first real lead I'd been able to get my hands on in months. And when I finally track the thing down, I find myself stepping in steaming piles of celestial shit everywhere I go."

She brought her hands down and began ticking off her fingers. "I've been stabbed with a bone knife. And who the hell uses one of those, by the way? I've been flown like freaking airline cargo across the state, manifested some magical angel woo-woo, almost broke my ankle, nearly got mauled to death by a bear, got set on fire but technically didn't, kissed a pseudo-tin man metallic angel, and can't go to sleep without reliving the whole bonfire routine. Oh, and I'm absolutely zero steps closer to finding Tammy. Did I miss anything?"

Her chest heaved with the rant, but oh, did it feel good. To say everything and be completely unencumbered by any sort of thought process. She should have cared how it was all perceived. How her tirade made Titan feel. After all, none of this was his fault. Well, nothing intentional, at any rate. But there was only so much a strong woman could carry before the weight of her burden came crashing down on top of her.

"Coffee."

Rose blinked. "Excuse me?"

Titan gestured toward the kitchen. "You forgot the part where the pseudo-tin man metallic angel makes you coffee in a travel mug because he *really* wants to hit the sky and get you the hell back to his brothers where we can all search for answers together. *Safely.* And find Tammy."

Well, shit. Did he have to do such a good job of cutting off her lady balls and making her sound like a tantruming toddler?

This time, Titan most certainly deserved her apology.

"I'm sorry." The words, heavy with exhaustion, fell out of her. And the tense lines in the corners of Titan's eyes, along with his drooping eyelids, made her realize she wasn't the only one running on fumes. And that was when she noticed her sleeping bag was the only one in the living room. "Did you sleep at all?"

A quick shake of his head was all the answer he volunteered as he got up and walked to the kitchen.

"But I thought you had to recharge your angel fire each night? Don't you have to sleep to do that? And what if those charmers find us when we head out?"

"They won't." His gruff reply unsettled her as he fiddled with the lid of the travel mug. It was such a human action. Securing one's coffee before heading out of the house. She briefly wondered what other human tendencies her angel had. "Charmers and sunlight don't mix, remember?"

"But sleep and angels definitely do." She crossed her arms and stomped into the kitchen just as he turned to hand her the steaming mug. And darn it if she didn't nearly curl herself around the thing, pop the lid off, and dunk her mouth in it, burns be damned.

"Look. I don't like surprises. Or you not being protected. I wasn't going to take a chance, especially not one that can go wrong when we're both asleep and vulnerable." He stepped toward her and laid his palm on her shoulder, careful not to touch her skin. "Our den is about thirty minutes away. That's where me and my brothers live. Once we get there, you'll be safe." His other hand smoothed over her ribs and squeezed slightly. The gesture had a weight to it she wasn't sure how to interpret. "Once I get you properly fed and watered, and I know you're in good hands, I'll rest a bit. I promise."

It was a small acquiescence. A macho line he was throwing her way to calm her down. But as much as she hated to admit it, again, his reasoning made good sense. And she also didn't suspect he made promises lightly, especially not ones he wasn't sure he could keep. But they couldn't stay here forever. And she needed answers more than she needed to be right.

Damn pragmatic angel. She was beginning to see why he was second in command.

Rose relented with a sigh and a swat to his abdomen. She smiled when he tensed at the unexpected blow.

"All right, tin man. Take me to Oz."

CHAPTER 11

If Rose could ball herself up any more tightly, she would have. But that was kind of difficult to manage when the only thing you had available to help with maneuverability and leverage were the hard planes of a warm male chest against your cheek. Not to mention the iron-bar forearms holding you securely against said chest.

Still, it didn't take away the fear of contact. The fear that, if her sleeve cuff inched up just a tad and brushed against the sliver of bare skin that peeked out above his waistband from time to time, their little angel express would turn into great balls of fire.

No offense, Jerry Lee Lewis, but I'm not in the singing mood at the moment.

"We're here."

Rose leaned her head back from Titan's chest and looked behind her. The view was utterly unspectacular. But then again, she wasn't sure exactly what she was looking for. A great expanse of evergreens carpeted the hilly landscape, while voluminous reds, oranges, and yellows provided interspersed sunbursts of autumn's bounty. The annual leaf peepers would no doubt shoot their loads at the site, which was astonishingly breathtaking and could only be achieved through air travel. Or angel travel, as it were.

But she didn't see any sign of a house or other dwelling. As she turned her head in all directions, nothing other than vibrant fall foliage and rolling stone structures stood out. But her ears did pick up on one familiar sound. She craned her neck. Off in the distance, the mellow whirrings of high-speed engines growing low, then loud, then low again clued her into a nearby highway of some kind.

Titan's heels touched down on slabs of stone. The landing was smooth as butter, without even the hint of a jerk or abrupt halt. A perfect deceleration and stop. She could definitely get used to angel flight, that was for sure. And she was even able to take her coffee to go!

Once Rose's feet were firmly on the ground, Titan retracted his wings. This time, she made a special note of the fade, as she was coming to call it. The way his hard, smooth metallic wings settled tightly against the column of his back and shimmered into transparency, until nothing remained of them and he looked like any other man.

Well, not *any* other man. But mortal, at least.

Gosh, was she really using that word as casually as one might say blonde or redhead?

She waited for him to release her. If she were being honest with herself, however, she wasn't all that impatient to separate just yet. Because while they were flying, it had been just the two of them. In the daylight, there was no threat of charmers. No bears or fire or anything other than solid warmth tucked into her front and crisp wind tickling her back. For a few precious minutes, she was untouchable. And safe.

Titan's chest rose and fell with a deep inhale. Was he having similar thoughts? Did he find himself with a curious urge to linger a tad longer? As the thought entered her mind, she decided to take one last inhale as well. The scents of balsam and earth crept in and wrapped around her, anchoring her to this place and time.

Or was it this man?

His arms around her back gave one final pulse, barely a squeeze, before falling free. He took a step back from her and walked over to a low slab of granite tucked in and lying flat on its side at the base of an embankment. The front of the stone was jagged and uneven, with bits of crushed leaves stuck in dried ivy branches on its surface. The granite slab couldn't be any taller than three feet.

Titan squatted down in front of the rock and skimmed his fingertips along the edges. Rose sucked in a breath. The dark gray hues of the stone's center were wholly unsurprising. What *was* surprising, however, was the shiny metallic border about an inch in thickness that snaked along the granite's perimeter. It wasn't a clean line, but one made to serve more function than form, one that was thinner in the center and higher on the edges, as if it was holding together two unlike surfaces.

A seal.

Could this be an entrance?

The tips of Titan's fingers glowed blue as tiny flames licked over his hands. Before he went to touch anything, he paused and looked back at her. Eyes of shimmering silver held her attention.

"This should go without saying, but there's no going back from this. You can't speak a word of what you're about to see to anyone. I've pledged to keep you safe, and—"

"Safety is a two-way street with me. I get it. And I won't say anything to anyone. I'm kind of invested at this point, remember?" She held up the coffee mug and shrugged. "I mean, you gave me French press coffee. I have to assume the food on the other side of that slab of granite is top-notch as well."

He dropped his head and shook it. Likewise, the smile on his lips didn't go unnoticed. The crisp burr of his tenor-toned laugh was infectious. She vowed to herself to find more opportunities to hear the sweet melody.

"Oh, we definitely take our food seriously, too. C'mon, let me show you."

Rose was content to follow him, but there wasn't anything around that screamed enter-this-way. But then Titan turned back to the stone and carefully slid the tips of his glowing fingers against the metal seal. Blue flame followed his movement as his hands settled into the crease and skimmed over the entire edge of the border. In his hands' wake, molten metal shimmered and dripped down the craggy slide of granite, scorching tangles of ivy as it flowed. Titan's fingers continued their path until they had completed the loop at the top where they began, connecting the river of metallic liquid.

With the seal loosened, Titan extinguished his fire and settled his palms on the flat of the stone, mindful of the ivy. The barest of grunts left him and his arrows hardly jostled along his back as he pushed the stone free of its holding. The great heavy thing settled back inside the newly created entrance as if it were used to the maneuver. Titan extended his forearm all the way into the opening, pushing the stone back farther. When he retreated, a wide empty hole was left in the stone's wake. Rose suspected the slab now hung inside on a hinge of some sort.

So freaking cool. Fraggle Rock ain't got nothing on this.

Titan took a seat, let his legs dangle into the hole like he was getting ready to careen down a water slide, and looked back at Rose.

"Hop on." He swatted the tops of his wide thighs. Even his baggy cargo pants did little to subdue the powerful nature of his legs. "It's a good drop down." He extended his arms wide, offering the protection of his embrace. An embrace that Rose's body still remembered all too well.

"All right."

She made to climb onto his lap, at first sitting with her back to his front so they were facing the same direction. But he quickly corrected her.

"Face me. It's safer to hang on that way."

Well, okay then.

She turned and adjusted her position as best she could to keep the friction low, but she couldn't help it when her bottom rubbed against his groin. She was still wearing his sweatpants, and the soft barrier did very little to hide his endowment. Her breath hitched at the contact.

He cleared his throat and moved her a tad to his left. Again, he was always mindful not to touch her skin. And something else, apparently.

"Tight fit." He grunted.

She squinted at his joke. Because she wasn't entirely sure it was a joke. But that was all the thought she gave to the matter as Titan snaked his arms around her and slid them both down the hole. Rose leaned forward on his chest as her stomach flew up into her throat. The sensation of falling was exhilarating and terrifying, like how she'd imagine bungee jumping or skydiving would feel. Her stomach and surrounding organs seemed to fly northward, while her skin tingled in a rush of tightly knitted goose bumps.

Rose's arms clenched more tightly around Titan's neck and even reached so far as to grip the arrows and bow at his back. In her panic, she clung to any and all parts of Titan available to anchor her. His snug embrace increased its pressure at her back, though not out of fear. No, it was more of a reassurance. A silent gesture in the dark to confirm that he'd done this a million times or more and that the manner of descent was no more threatening than riding a city bus. As Rose's apprehension slowly fled her body, Titan's boots landed them on firm ground.

This time, there was no lingering in each other's embrace. Titan stepped back from her, turned, and did the universal not-so-subtle hop that all men did when an adjustment of masculine proportions must be made.

Guess that answers the angel anatomy question regarding compatible parts.

Rose turned to give the man some privacy. Not that it did any good. Pitch black greeted her. But though her vision wasn't up for getting first billing, quite a few of her other senses fired online right quick.

Titan whispered a few words she hadn't paid close attention to, but she gathered he was going to replace the stone door. While she waited, deep earthy scents assaulted her. The air was surprisingly cool for being underground, as she presumed, and heavy with a subtle, almost salty moisture. They were surrounded by rock, but the rock was so alive it nearly hummed with energy. Though she couldn't yet see it, the trickling of water and slight patter of tiny critter feet were familiar. It almost reminded her of those old quartz mines she'd visited on field trips when she was in high school.

Then a bright blue hue rose behind her.

"Door's up ahead." Titan gestured as he held his hand high, now lit with the blue flame she was growing used to. And sure enough, down at the end of the carved-out tunnel was a massive door. Made up of, yup, more metal.

Rose turned to Titan with a single questioning eyebrow raised. The glow of the blue flame against his angled jaw and beard stood out in stark contrast to the simmering silver glow of his eyes. Gosh, would she ever get used to that?

"Metal entrances. Metal angels. And a built-in blowtorch," he said, wagging his fingers. "Best security barricade out there."

"I can see that."

He settled his non-flaming hand against the small of her back and guided her forward. She melted into his touch as she walked. She had never had a man's hands on her back, let alone on her body period, this much in her life. Yet the more contact she had with Titan, the more unsettled she was when he wasn't near. Almost as if her body was forming some sort of symbiotic connection to the angel, with touch recognizing touch and heat recognizing heat. Embarrassment and wonder bloomed on her face, warming her cheeks. She had never been more grateful for the darkness.

Titan's hand fell away from her back, and like before, he used his fire to liquify and loosen the seams of the massive door in front of them. But also, like before, there were no handles. No grips to grab onto and shut the door. It was literally a floor-to-ceiling slab of metal.

"How do you close the door behind you? There are no door knobs or handles."

"Magnetism." He leaned his shoulder against the door, settled his weight low, and pushed. With a low groan, the door slowly gave way.

"Ah." She nodded assuredly, as if she should have known that already.

Bright light and boisterous chatter filled the room behind him, but he was blocking her view. "All of the entrances to the den contain traces of our different metals. But they're predominantly made up of iron, which is magnetic. The bits of other metals, such as titanium for me, allow us to access and control the doors through the iron's magnetism. Think of it like a specialized key for each of us. It works on the surface seals the same way."

"Surface seals?"

"The seal around the granite slab at the surface's entrance. It's made up of iron but mixed with our other metals. That's how we can all melt it down and reseal it. By manipulating our metals that are floating around within the iron."

"Fascinating," Rose said softly as her fingers brushed up along the rough slab of iron. With the light from the room illuminating the door, she was able to look more closely. Tiny bits of sparkling metals dusted the surface of the black iron. Silvers, pewters, and deep shimmering charcoals were abundant. And then there were the more tawny tones of brass and bronze mixed into the foray. Every little twinkling speck was a calling card to a different angel and gave them access to their home where no one else could enter.

He wasn't kidding when he said this place was secure. Holy smokes!

Heavy footfalls drew Rose's attention away from the door. A man of immense size and stature filled the entryway to what she could only describe as a great living room turned underground bunker from her brief glimpse of it behind the man's back. So many things assaulted her senses, but none more so than the towering figure who stood in front of her and Titan. This man was just as tall as the angel at her side, but where Titan's physique was tightly toned and athletic, with strength more evenly dispersed through every limb and muscle, this man had power in spades. And it all emanated from his hulking, brawny torso. Intimidating, but not carelessly so. As if his size and strength were as much a tool and reflection of his station as any other person whose body answered to the demands of their profession. Tawny tinted hair fell in waves to his shoulders. Under the muted lights, flecks of amber, gold, and caramel glinted throughout his mane, and Rose could only be reminded of a lion. A leader of predators and fierce protector of family.

Rose instantly knew the prime sentinel angel stood before her.

"You're Tungsten." She bowed her head slightly, unsure how to properly address a celestial leader.

The angel with golden hair smiled before her, seemingly pleased at her assertion. "Yes. I am Tungsten. Tung, if you wish. We are an informal lot here." He moved to stand aside a bit and clasped Titan's hand, allowing her to see more of the space.

And what a space it was.

The great room was a carved-out cavern large enough to rival the lobbies of opera houses, which made her question just how far below the ground they actually were. The walls of the room were not walls at all, but grand expanses of raw slabs of rock that circled up and over to complete the ceiling. Except there were no stalactites or weeping trickles of activity like there had been in the other tunnel. Oh no. Here, the ceiling was shaved smooth, with elaborate and oddly powerful light fixtures hammered into the stone at even intervals.

The room itself reminded Rose of a studio apartment times infinity. Large sandstone-colored sectional sofas were dotted throughout a central living space, complete with deep walnut coffee tables. Solid support columns of smooth granite were pillared around the room and served as dividers for the different purposes and functions of the space. To Rose's right, behind one pillar, were rows of targets. Some were circular and obvious in their bull's-eye shape, while others were no more than black outlines of a human body with white delineating markers. Next to the targets was a massive breakfront housing various weapons from a litany of blades and swords to firearms Rose had precisely zero knowledge of.

Her gaze fluttered to the great hall's left. Beyond another pillar lay a covered pool table surrounded by floor-to-ceiling stacks of books encased in glass, no doubt for protection from the damp environment. A large wooden lectern stood tall and proud in the forefront of the tomes next to the pool table.

Behind another pillar, sectioned off toward the rear of the cavern, was kitchen equipment. Flashes of stainless steel stove handles and—was that an espresso machine?—stared back at her, while, on the other side of the pillar, a dining room table seemingly as long as the space was tall filled out the central living area. Decorations and ornamentation were scarce, but amenities and utilities were abundant. It was all Rose could do not to gape and gawk at the underground den's immaculate luxury and amazing existence.

"It is good to see you back and in one piece. Though, if I may say so, you look a little worse for wear." Tung's eyes softened at the corners with a sad understanding of the events his brother had been through the past twelve hours.

"What he's trying to say is you look like shit. Even calling you death warmed up is too generous. I wouldn't want to insult anyone's good memory, you know?"

Rose nearly swallowed her tongue as she looked at the other man standing behind the leader. Tung crossed his hulking arms over his chest and pinched the bridge of his nose while Titan dropped his head and cursed.

"Good to see you too, Chrome." Titan strained to keep his words genteel, more for her benefit, she suspected, as he rolled his eyes and turned to grip Rose's shoulders. "Time to meet the gang. You ready?"

"Ready as I'll ever be." She shrugged.

Titan nodded. "Good. But first, let me get you that top-notch food I promised you."

His hands gently squeezed her shoulders in a silent show of encouragement and was that appreciation as well? She wasn't sure, but one thing she did know after being a woman working years in a male-dominated industry . . .

She was more than well-versed in giving as good as she got.

CHAPTER 12

As Titan watched Rose push her finished plate away and lean back in her chair, the vice around his chest eased for the first time since yesterday. The meal was simple fare. Nothing more than a generous heel of that morning's sourdough bread Iron had baked, yogurt topped with cinnamon-spiced sauteed apples, and the fluffiest damn scrambled eggs his forearm had ever whisked. The plate had been full. But the soft moans and choice licks of Rose's petal-pink tongue as she devoured her food were far from satisfying. It only tortured him more.

Because the idea of her in his home, with his brothers, under his astute care tempted him in painful ways. Inexplicably, his urges toward Rose had taken roots and grown into boisterous desires. The obvious malnutrition Rose had suffered since her sister's disappearance ate at his own malcontent. Had she been in his care all along, he would have seen to her health. Seen to it that the sheen of her brown hair never would have faded, that the vitality never would have left her buoyant spirit.

But it did, and it was all because I didn't save her sister.

"Chrome, huh? Please don't tell me you have a garage of motorcycles camped out under here somewhere."

Rose's voice jarred him out of his morose thoughts, only to be replaced with gouging pinpricks of exhaustion. God, he was damn tired. He needed to rest and recharge his fire, but not until Rose was completely sated. It was the least he could do for her. He peered up and saw her take several gulps of freshly squeezed orange juice. He glimpsed her slender neck and the gentle swallows of her throat as she took in more of the meal he'd prepared for her.

He could watch that vision for eternity and never tire of it. Even though he had no right to. The cold sweat of his glass' condensation slickened his palm in spite of the tension he squeezed against it. His fingers flexed so tightly around the vessel it threatened to shatter all over his lap. When Rose finished her drink and set it down, he then numbly shook his head.

Exhaustion is getting the better of you.

Chrome leaned back in his chair and folded his arms behind his head. The hind legs groaned under the strain as the chair's front legs lifted off the ground. He waggled his eyebrows at Rose and smiled widely, letting every single tooth in on the party.

"You want to see my hot rods?" More waggling. More smiling.

Titan kicked his foot out and hooked the toe of his boot behind one of Chrome's supporting chair legs. The chair toppled and the big man stumbled backward with all the grace of a felled tree. His ass hit the hardwood, followed by the loud stomp of his bootheels.

"I'm pretty sure hot rods are cars, not bikes," Rose said with all the gentleness of a mother but with none of the scolding bite. "And I'd love to see more of your home, if *that's* what you meant." Her eyes squinted in admonishment as she peered over the table at the prone angel on the floor. "It's a lovely offer, especially when made to an outsider."

She rose from her chair and walked around to Chrome, who still lay splayed out on the floor, and squatted before him. Her smile was cordial yet teasing, and Titan got the impression she'd often dealt with men who needed the benefit of getting knocked down a peg or two from time to time. He couldn't help but smile at his girl.

No, she's not my girl.

Then Rose extended her hand to Chrome in assistance. Titan pushed out of his chair and snatched Rose's arm away a moment before Chrome touched her bare palm.

"Ow! What the—"

Titan wheeled Rose around and hurried her to the other side of the table. The great hall of the den was massive and served a multipurpose function, encompassing eating spaces, gathering grounds, and even some small-range targets for weapons practice. But at that moment, the expanse of his home was nowhere near large enough for his liking. His own touch he could monitor, ensuring nothing was accidental. But the others? How could he protect them all, including Rose, from uncontrolled angel fire? And would another angel's touch trigger it within her in the same manner as his?

The thought was pure vinegar on his tongue.

Titan's breaths sawed in and out of his chest as he tucked Rose firmly behind his back. Tung was at Chrome's side, helping the angel to his feet. Neither of the men looked pleased, Tung especially. The golden-haired angel squinted his dismay at his second.

Shit.

Titan stepped forward, still well aware of Rose's presence behind him, and cupped the back of his neck. He looked at Chrome and softened his expression. It was as much of an apology as he could muster given the freaking road flares in his temple and the unanswered questions surrounding the woman at his back.

Then he remembered why he'd brought Rose here in the first place.

To keep her safe from the charmers, to help find her sister, and to get answers. With his brothers' help.

Titan sighed as he dropped his arm and settled it on his hip. Best to let the grenade drop. The pin had already been pulled. "Rose can command my angel fire."

The statement killed any potential words on either of the angels' tongues. They both stood there in silence, Chrome slack-jawed and wide-eyed and Tung tight-lipped with his brow furrowed in confusion.

Then Titan told them everything. About how the woman he'd lost six months ago was Rose's sister, about the charmers hunting Rose, the transference of angel fire, everything. It all poured out of his bone-weary mouth so fast he wasn't even sure the words were coherent. But they had been, judging by Tung's pacing and Chrome's constant gaze on Rose.

"Bless the mages," Tung muttered into his hand as he rounded the back of a sofa. "How is this possible?"

"Wait. Just wait." Chrome threw his hand up and shook his head in disbelief. "When you say you felt your full fire again, what do you mean, exactly? Like, full as in . . ." Chrome was gesturing with his hands for Titan to continue.

"Full as in the way I used to command my fire. Full, without limitations or the constant trickle of depletion. Like it was before . . ." Titan choked off the words and looked at the floor. "Before we fell."

Soft gasps drew his gaze up. Chrome and Tung were staring at each other, disbelief and awe flooding each of their stern features.

"Um, excuse me."

Titan and the other angels turned to look at Rose, who had

stepped out from behind Titan's shielded back but still hovered close to his side. "Is there somewhere I can take him to get some rest? He explained to me about the need to recharge, and he's been up a full day without sleep. I'm new to all of this, but even I can read a room and tell when a person is running on fumes."

Her delicate plea's soft desperation flooded the great hall. And for the first time since Titan had returned to the den, Tung's gaze assessed his weakened state. Titan's leader cursed softly and walked over to them, though careful to keep his distance from Rose.

"Of course. How inhospitable of me. Please forgive me. We are not used to entertaining guests." Tung glanced over at Titan and sighed with a look of stern compassion. "It seems our priorities are in need of a realignment." Tung stepped back and pointed his arm toward a tunnel leading out of the great hall. "His living quarters are at the end of the tunnel, the last door on the left."

"Thank you," Rose said softly. She nodded and tucked Titan's arm into the crook of her elbow.

She was truly leading him around by his tail, but even in his exhausted state, he was still humble enough to realize he didn't mind it all that much.

Rose nearly sagged with relief once they were inside Titan's quarters and the door was solidly shut behind them. Unlike the outside entrances, this door thankfully had a handle. And as simple as the task of opening a door was, she had never been more thrilled to throw herself into usefulness and heft the door open.

Once inside, Titan left her standing by the door and nearly stumbled over to the king-sized bed in the center. Much like his cabin in the mountains, his suite followed the same orderliness.

Neatly made bed: check. Cleared-off dresser top except for a small wooden box of grooming essentials: check. But where his cabin had windows and drapes, this suite of rooms had none. In fact, none of the spaces she'd seen in the den had windows.

Well, der. Hello, underground bunker.

And though she should have been more concerned with getting Titan into bed, she couldn't escape a nagging question of practicality. "How do you have electricity down here?"

Titan toed off his boots and lifted his weapons from his back before tossing them on the floor with a groan. "Geothermal energy. A few miles down, there are hot water reservoirs. We use the steam to rotate our underground turbines, which activate our generators."

Titan paused in his explanation, allowing Rose to detect the faintest hum of a distant engine, accompanied by the barest of vibrations. They were almost soothing, the way a rocking chair and white noise machine might be for an infant.

"We have all sorts of utility rooms at the far end of the den. Massive caverns we built long ago to accommodate turbines, floor-to-ceiling generators, and anything else we need to live comfortably and independently as the times change. Ventilation systems have been tunneled into the surrounding rock and granite, venting out to interspersed locations along the nearby highway, so all the fumes and byproducts don't build up in the cavern. Our air is cleaner than anything up above, I promise you."

"I don't doubt it. And I thought I heard motor noise earlier. So, we're near a highway?"

He nodded. "Yup. We're in Aurora. Or, technically, under it."

Amazing. All this time, angels had lived right under Rose and she'd never even known it.

An exhausted male groan snapped back Rose's attention to Titan and his overall sorry state of affairs. And then it snapped to something else entirely.

Titan's biceps bunched as he raised his arms and grasped the fabric of his shirt behind his neck. On an effortless tug, the thin Henley slid over his head before getting snagged on his ear. Another pull and the fabric popped over his short brown hair and fell away from his arms and chest, baring his torso.

Rose couldn't remember the last time she'd been with a man, let alone one as mouthwateringly captivating as Titan. It was probably about a few years shy of never. And she suddenly realized why.

Because none had ever held her rapt attention the way this angel did, even weary and drained as he was.

Titan lifted his head and locked eyes with hers. And that was a mistake, because even if there was a blazing inferno behind her about to sear her hair off, she couldn't look away. Not for a single second.

His shoulders and forearms were long and chiseled, as if also carved from the very granite the angels lived within. Every sharp dip and vivid curve of his muscles drew her eyes down to his center, where a light dusting of dark hair kissed the wide planes of his broad chest. His full lower lip dropped open as he sucked in deeper breaths, each one taking his sinful torso fuller in breadth than Rose thought possible. And it was also no surprise that the smattering of dark hair coating his pectorals was neat and trimmed. A delectable, teasing taste of rugged maleness, rather than being overgrown and wild.

The sight pleased her greatly, though she didn't stop to examine the why of it.

Rose's breath intensified and her core simmered and fluttered to life where long-frigid coals had always been. Titan's chest angled down into perfectly narrow hips. Her gaze danced over rigid abdominals and that delicious indentation on each hip that started at the sides and descended below the waistband of his cargo pants. Rose's tongue jutted out and lightly moistened her lower lip before she sucked it inward. She hadn't even been aware she'd done it.

Oh, but he had.

Titan's eyes snapped to her mouth. Knuckles paled with tension as his fingers tightened a death grip on the edge of the bed.

She had no idea what was happening. She should be helping him rest. Urging him to recharge after all he'd done for her. She most certainly shouldn't be standing here, in his room, eye-fucking him when he was in such a vulnerable state. This should be the last thing on her mind. And it always had been. Between her horrible home life, and Tammy's wildly bubbly and happy presence to counterbalance it, she simply hadn't had the occasion to focus on her own pleasure. Guys brought drama she simply didn't have room for. And since there was no shortage of batteries at the drugstore, what was the point?

And then Tammy had disappeared and Rose's life had gone to shit. Even deeper shit, if that was at all possible.

"Come here."

Rose felt more than heard Titan's almost primal command. She hesitantly walked toward him and shook her head. "You need to rest."

Sure, her head was solidly behind the statement, but the throbbing tightness between her legs told a whole different story. Still, she didn't stop until her toes were an inch in front of his and he was eye level with her chest. A metallic rainbow flashed through his irises before the molten orbs settled into the stark silver she had grown used to.

"I want to . . . touch you." His words came out in a whispered, painful exclamation. Because, damn, she wanted it, too. She wanted to feel his hot mouth on hers again, relish the slick heat of his tongue as it danced across her own. She wanted to skim her trimmed nails along every ridge and bend of his defined muscles, feel the warmth of banked heat on his lips as he dragged them across her hypersensitive skin.

Heat. Fire. No.

Rose shook her head in painful protest again. "Your fire. I don't want to steal it. I don't want—"

"I know. I won't. *We* won't." Sweat kissed the crisp edge of his hairline. His body nearly shook with his powerful restraint. "But damn if I'm not thinking about it."

The declaration was a confusing and jagged blow to both of them. Because Rose remembered all too well the agony that resulted when they touched each other without barriers. Engulfing flames of fire that neither of them could control. She stared down at his face. The dark slats of his eyebrows were slanted in frustration and helplessness, but the firm set of his jaw was holding the front lines of his determination to keep her safe . . . from himself.

Rose ached to touch him, to pull him closer to her body to both give and seek comfort. But she couldn't. His bare skin taunted her everywhere she looked, to the point that even if he did put his shirt back on, her traitorous fingers would no doubt seek out his bare body regardless. Everything about this man, from his body to his soul-deep goodness, was fiercely magnetic, and she worried she'd never be able to pull away.

But then another memory floated back to her. An image of Titan kissing her, embracing her. Of him plundering her mouth with needy urgency as he rolled her off the bed of his cabin and smothered every inch of her with his hard body. She closed her eyes and recalled the burning, the mind-splitting terror of the flames coating her skin. But then her subconscious presented a different image. Another memory. One of the flames receding under Titan's touch. Where the feeling of blistered, boiling skin melted away and was replaced with a mellow simmering heat that blossomed between the two of them. A welcoming, arousing heat that some basal part of her knew was no more harmful to her than the trembling warning her stomach gave when she descended a hill too quickly.

"Rose . . ."

Titan's strained whisper drew her attention to his fingers, which hovered tentatively above her temple. He didn't touch her, merely went as close as he could to brushing his hand around the curve of her cheek. When his thumb stopped a hair-breadth away from her trembling lip, still never making contact, she let her lower lip fall. Nervousness mixed with thunderous temptation as she let out a breath and allowed herself to commit to the action she was about to take.

Her uncovered hands reached up and cupped the sides of his face. They tingled as the coarse fibers of his beard tickled the soft spaces between her fingers.

And then she brought her mouth to his and let go.

Titan was on fire. Someone had turned on the nuclear option, and every spare inch of his body ignited in an uncontrollable roiling inferno.

But the flames were all heat without pain. Tumultuous energy without havoc and anarchy.

All traces of exhaustion were promptly shown the door. His gut recoiled as his angel fire ripped out of him and was called into action under the relentless torture of Rose's incendiary kiss. The tips of her short fingernails bit into the sides of his scalp as her lips moved harder and hotter against his. With each sucking pull of her mouth, his fire rose up to greet her needy command.

His cock responded in kind. Every press of her bare skin against him tugged his arousal closer to her deft little touch, willing it to rise to her beck and call. As far as he was concerned, it *was* hers. She owned and commanded every single inch of his being, and he bent to her will like a cobra beguiled by a snake charmer. His angel fire rose higher, bloomed brighter in his body, nearly shaking the flesh of his mortal cage in unrelenting power. Tight pinpricks assaulted his eyes, even beneath the fall of his lids. Titan's fire was so immense, so all-consuming, his eyes fought back tears as he touched the fullness of his celestial flame again.

And then he remembered what his fire, his power, did to Rose the last time they had connected in this manner.

His eyes shot open. The bridge of Rose's delicate nose and the sweeping fan of her long lashes caressing the tops of her cheeks filled his vision. And that was all. Well, not all. He took in the graceful line of her jawbone as she opened her mouth wider against his. Marveled at the barely visible flutter of her pulse hammering against the curve of her wrist as her sweatshirt sleeve shimmied down. He was attuned to every part of her. His celestial senses were heightened over each pump of her heart, each inhale of her needy breaths. It was a scorching overload of sensation, and his cock jerked in a powerful strain at the assault.

But blue flames were not among the swirling furors between them. Oh, the heat was there, most definitely. But it remained churning within him at full bore, nestled safely behind the cage of his self-control, instead of launching as an outward threat to those he wished to keep safe. As it always had been for him when he dwelled in the Empyrean.

Titan pulled back from Rose's mouth. The tight smack of their lips' release was a mournful noise, one Rose attempted to chase as she leaned forward to claim his mouth again. But he stopped her. By the mages, he actually stopped her! When his cock was nearly weeping with need and his balls were drawn up so tightly they rivaled the granite around them. Still, he managed to stop. But when her chasing lips frowned into a petal-perfect pout, she opened her eyes.

Finally!

"Rose, how do you feel? Are you . . . in pain? Burning?" If her pinky toe even sported as much as a sunburn, he'd heave himself across the room. Hell, he'd even ask Chrome to shear a chunk of his wing off in retribution. But she said nothing. Just sat there as her eyes fluttered in confusion, as if she were coming out of a trance, before her gaze darted over her body. His lips dried with rapid inhales as he anxiously followed her line of sight. He looked on with rapt attention as she inspected her chest, legs, and farther down the length of one arm and then the other.

Silence.

He gripped her sweatshirt-clad shoulders and gave her the barest of insistent shakes. "You need to say something here, petal. I need to know what you feel. What's hurting you? Right the fuck now."

That halted Rose's investigation. She looked at Titan and quirked her head to the side. A single raised eyebrow was all the notice he received that she wasn't being burned alive by his power but, instead, had chosen to mock him.

"Petal?"

He blinked. "Of all the things I was frantically spitting out to get your attention, to see whether you were hurt or worse, *that's* what you latched on to?"

And then the little minx flashed him a perfect row of white teeth. Right before they imprinted on her plump lower lip and sucked it into the moist haven of that mouth he craved more of.

"You're teasing me. Right now. You're freaking teasing me?" His body was practically housing a supernova and this woman wanted to play cute?

Oh, it's on, sweetheart.

"I'm not teasing you. I'm just marveling at everything. Because, yeah . . . I feel fine. No burns or heat or anything. I can't believe it." Her slight chuckle of exasperation added a tempting blush to her cheeks and did jack shit to douse his arousal.

"No dice. I need more confirmation than that."

"What? Uf—"

Titan gripped Rose by the waist and hauled her onto the bed, pinning her under his chest. He took advantage of her surprise by sliding his palms up under her sweatshirt and T-shirt until the whole of her stomach was exposed for his inspection. And pleasure.

"If I touch you here," he said, circling the rim of her navel with the lightest of caresses, "does it hurt?"

"Titan . . ." His breathy name on her lips was all the confirmation his logical brain needed that his fire wasn't hurting her. Oh, she had most definitely called it forth again, along with his nearly painful erection that was so hard he could use it to hammer out another suite of rooms in the bedrock, but that was where her influence ended. At least on his fire. For the first time in agonizingly long eons, his connection to the eternal flame swam and swirled within him. His muscles effortlessly recalled how to cage and temper it, as if no more than a single day had gone by without it.

His soft sweet petal beneath him gave him a miracle, and he would see to it she received proper recompense.

Rose's hips squirmed under his hold as he flattened his rough palm against the smooth heated skin of her belly. He regretted the coarseness of his hands, wished his touch was less abrasive and more gentle. But then she placed her hands on top of his and slowly slid them around her skin, leaving a searing trail of heat even he could feel in its wake, before inching them higher up her torso. Until the tip of his middle finger bumped the edge of her bra.

Her breath hitched.

Titan shifted his gaze to Rose's eyes. And swirls of shimmering rainbow rippled through irises he had known to be pure pools of muted sage a moment before.

"Your eyes . . ." He let the words fall out of his mouth before he had a chance to think better of it.

Incandescent hues of his heated metal flickered on a final

wave before turning the solid patinated silver of titanium. Her dark lashes blinked while brunette brows dipped in confusion. And then, as fast as it appeared, the color of his manifested angel fire retreated, revealing the true green of Rose's eyes once more.

"What? What is it?" Panic and worry coated her words as she tried to sit up and look down at her body.

But he settled her more solidly against the comforter and cradled her delicate face between his hands. "Nothing. Just . . . feeling really damn lucky at the moment."

She shook her head in the telltale sign of not buying his bullshit, but her tenuous smile said otherwise. "I feel something, too."

Titan froze. Could she feel his angel fire? Was he harming her with his presence after all?

She pursed her lips as if struggling to find the right word. "Warmth, but greater. Heat, but without the incendiary crackling nature. Kind of like the warmth of a heated blanket, but with a weight to it, with rippling tingles going up my body. As if you turned up the dial suddenly."

He debated whether he should tell her about her eyes, about his suspicions, but the doubt only lasted a second. He would never keep anything from her, when she was the very thing that was restoring him.

But all that could come later. He was on overload. His connection to this woman, to his fire, to all the elements around him, was becoming too much. His hands itched to run up her skin, to feel bare every tingling, scorching curve that had been tucked up against him the past day. Tantalizing and teasing every part of him to stand at attention and await her command.

Titan gripped the edge of her sweatshirt with one hand, while his other stayed poised to deploy. He just needed one final confirmation.

"I'm going to ask you again, petal. One last time. If you're in pain or you're just not trusting yourself. Or, hell, if you want me gone because my mug is a hair too ugly up close or, fuck, you're just not feeling it, I need to know. Now. Because since you've been in my arms from that first moment in the park, every part of my body has been itching to memorize every curve of yours. Do. You. Want. This."

Rose didn't answer at first. At least not verbally. But she didn't waste a minute in gripping the hem of her sweatshirt and top and ripping them over her head. Once she was free of them, an expanse of flushed, heated skin lay open before him. Rose's breasts strained against her gray sports bra with each harried rise of her chest. Titan's tongue nearly darted out to claim the rigid peaks of her nipples protruding against the thin fabric.

"Yes. I want this."

He. Fucking. *Moved.*

Titan hooked his thumbs under the elastic band of her bra and peeled it off her. The rounded mounds of her breasts sprang free and her dusty rose-colored nipples stood erect and wanting, as if greeting the man they mocked while hidden.

He leaned down and attacked her right breast. Laved and licked at the taunting rigid tip that had been pressed up against his body for too damn long. During every wind-whipped second he'd held Rose in his arms as he flew, he'd had to hold back a groan. Pretend that the twin peaks and soft lushness molded against his chest weren't there, constantly driving him to painful distraction. But now they were here, and Rose was bare before him from the waist up, and she was allowing him to feast.

He didn't deserve even a fraction of her considered praise, but he was too weak-willed to help her see the light.

Soft pants escaped Rose's parted lips. Titan spread his wide palm over her other breast and kneaded the delicate pillow. Though life and grief had ravaged her body, producing ribs too prominent and hip bones too assertive, her breasts remained full and vital. His fingers caged her protectively, borderline aggressively, as he swept his thumb slowly over the teasing peak before turning his mouth to its supple offering. He groaned against the lushness of her body.

"Oh, petal . . . do you have any idea how hard you make me? How painful it is to have all this sweetness tucked up against me while I'm supposed to be focused on shielding you, protecting you?" Titan rolled his hips against her inner thigh, impressing upon her the hardness of his cock. Rose sucked in a breath as she pressed firm fingers down the length of his back. They stopped short when those toying hands reached the waistband of his cargo pants and slowly burrowed under.

He claimed her mouth as her explorations went farther. Rose's palms stretched as they clutched his ass, tightly spreading him wide in her grip. So hard the bite of her short nails shot painful pleasure directly to his dick. He hissed as the damn thing nearly wept for release.

Right before Rose broke away from the kiss.

"I appreciate the protection," she breathed out as she leaned up slightly. One of her hands left his ass to crawl around to the front of his pants. "But I'm not some delicate flower. Despite your cutesy nickname."

She smiled and winked at him. The brat. And then her not-so-delicate hand, as she rightly pointed out, made a torturous fist around his dick and squeezed. He practically roared as he dropped his head and bit into her shoulder. Hell, she'd be the death of him. He was going to explode in every way possible under this woman's commanding touch. But it would be bliss. Pure fucking bliss.

"I can take care of myself." Her words were firm and assertive in his ear as she worked his cock in powerful, firm strokes. He nodded breathlessly.

"I know, petal. Fuck, I know . . ." He couldn't think, couldn't breathe. Hell, he was supposed to be giving *her* pleasure. Seeing to *her* comfort. How the hell had she turned the tables so quickly?

"But . . . just because I *can*, doesn't mean I have to. Or even want to."

Titan shot up and looked at her, making sure he damn well heard that right. The quirk in her smile and the flush of her kiss-swollen lips spoke volumes. As did the glaze of her eyes and the too-hollow indentations of her cheeks. He was reminded how tenacious her spirit had been over the past several months and still was. Despite her despair and loneliness, her perseverance always took center stage. But it was damn near killing her. So no, she didn't need him. Of course not. At least not for this. But she *wanted* him. And she was making sure he understood the difference.

Ten. Fucking. Four.

"Understood. Loud and clear. Now lean back." He cupped the back of her head and gently guided her down to the bed, its softness accepting her weight. Once she was settled, he tenderly removed her hands from his body and pinned them above her head. He stared at her for a second, at how open and alive her half-naked body looked beneath him. How her breasts made his mouth go dry with need and how her skin radiated his fire's warmth back to him. It pained him to lose the close connection, but the anticipation of caring for her the way she deserved filled that void until it overflowed with want and desire for this woman. "I've got you. Let me take care of you."

Rose's chest heaved as she nodded slightly but quickly.

Titan smiled and leaned over her hips. His tongue traced the rim of his sweatpants on her body as he slowly peeled them off her. Gray cotton underwear met his mouth as he placed light kisses on the fabric. High at first, directly over her pubic bone. Then lower. His tongue slid a slick trail of temptation along the soft cotton until it nestled against her sweet opening. With a final flick, he pressed the underwear lightly against her crease, the cotton depressing temptingly into her greedy core, before he shucked it off her body entirely. A quick gasp from Rose was all the reaction he got, as if she was holding back for some reason.

Nope. That wouldn't do. He needed more.

His thumb found the delicate nub of her clitoris in an instant. He toyed with it at first, oh so delicately and gently, rising higher with her as he chased each throaty breath and soft whimper. Those sounds were ecstasy and torture. He gritted his teeth together as his dick grew impossibly harder, straining for friction against the too-soft padding of the mattress. But he would take the pain, drink it down wholeheartedly, and order another glass before he failed to bring Rose the pleasure she deserved. His precious petal.

Titan's fire intensified within his chest as Rose arched off the bed with each touch, her breasts reaching ever higher toward the ceiling. His hands itched to roam over the beautiful arch of her back and the long column of her neck. But neither temptation called to him more than the plump nub he relished playing like a priceless Stradivarius. Without further thought save utter fucking delight, he brought his mouth to it. Rose gasped and clutched his hair in her fingers. The sting against his scalp spurred him on as he suckled and nursed his woman to her most pleasurable peak.

Warm, wet heat coated his mouth as his hands pushed her thighs wider and his tongue dipped low into her channel. It was the most perfect nectar he had ever tasted . . . at an altar so divine it was only right he was on his knees.

Rose's mewls of pleasure climbed higher as he worshiped her. Every cry, gasp, and squeal he coaxed out of her was a song his heart sang. A chorus of hope and passion and fiery praise for the woman in his arms. As her hips jerked forward and a guttural moan left her lips, he rose and captured her mouth. He kissed her through her orgasm as he held his hands protectively around Rose, until the last tremor settled over her skin and her body was replete with pleasure.

"That . . . was . . ." Rose panted against the cage of Titan's shoulder as he floated kisses across her sweat-slicked forehead.

"It was exactly what you wanted, petal. And it was everything we both needed—"

Loud shouts and heavy footsteps rose up from the hallway. Titan's arms tensed around Rose as he looked to the door.

"Titan! We need you!" Hammering fists pounded against the metal entrance like a battering ram.

"Leave me! I'm fucking busy!" Titan growled out the words as his fire burned hotter within. It was all he could do not to shift into his metal skin at the intrusion.

More banging. "Steel's hurt."

The words about his brother calmed his composure enough that he was able to recognize Chrome's voice on the other side. "The charmers fucked him up last night. Bad. Iron just got him home, but . . ." The smart-mouthed angel trailed off, and Titan began to understand the gravity of the situation. Chrome was never meek in his tone. Ever.

Shit.

He threw the comforter over Rose's body and hauled himself to his feet, frantically tossing her clothes her way. "I'll be right there," he called to Chrome as quick feet stamped down the hall in retreat.

As he watched Rose punch her arms through her sweatshirt, tension roiled in his gut. She looked at him and shooed him out of the room. "I'll be right behind you. Go."

He nodded reluctantly. A millisecond after she put on the last of her clothes, he wrenched open the door and bolted. Worry and unease assaulted him as his boots flew over the ground. Because he had foolishly allowed himself to forget about the threat they all faced. And the irresistible temptation he couldn't afford to lose.

CHAPTER 14

Rose slid her hands over her face as she hesitantly rounded the corner into the great room. Her body thrummed with a jumble of nerves and emotions. And, yeah, some pretty stellar aftershocks if she was being completely honest. Titan's mouth, his hands, even the coarseness of his beard as it caressed her skin lit up every single neural pathway in her body like an airport runway.

Because she had never been worshiped before. That was the closest word she could think to describe the attention and care that angel lavished her with. As if he'd fired up a spotlight and showered down long-starved affection on even the most sheltered of her hidden places. It was all-consuming and immense. There was nowhere to hide from any of it. And it struck her as both exhilarating and overwhelming that she didn't want to hide from it at all.

But when Chrome's interruption invaded their sacred cocoon, the reality of her world had come crashing down again. Guilt pricked her insides at how she had given herself over to her needs—wants, not needs, she corrected herself—and allowed her thoughts to carelessly drift from finding her sister.

That was the whole reason she was even still hanging around him, right?

Screeching metal scraped over stone, and heavy footfalls kicked away chair legs. Rose looked up and saw three massive men carrying a motionless body into the great hall. Titan and Chrome worked to clear the dining table and bring lamps over while Tung shuffled backward, supporting a sagging head of shaggy hair so blonde it was nearly white.

"What happened?" Tung barked the question as the angels laid the still body on top of the table. Two of the ones carrying the man let go of him gently and worked to strip him of his weapons. Blades of every size and shape flashed in the lamplight as the angels, both sporting red hair, though one had it more closely cropped than the other, carefully laid the weapons on the couch.

"A pack of mystics used hydrochloric acid bombs. Blew Steel out of the sky right before they portaled away as the sun rose." The clipped words came from one of the men who had been carrying the unconscious man. Another angel, Rose assumed. She huddled behind a stone pillar, not wishing to distract them as the angels all furiously worked to aid their fallen brother. But as bodies moved and furniture was cleared, her eyes kept drifting to the brawny bulk of the veritable giant who had just spoken. The third angel who had brought in the unconscious one.

Thick wrists cuffed with brown leather slammed the edge of the table. The flannel of his button-down stretched taut over bulging strength. A full russet-colored beard, much longer than Titan's, framed a stern face with a large brow. All manner of gray grime and rust-toned streaks painted the angel, as did the other two who had come in with him.

Titan stood next to the big angel, shears in hand, and was clipping away fragments of the unconscious angel's clothing. His hands peeled away layer after layer of flaking, rusted fabric.

Some he was able to cut through, but others he used the tip of the shears to chisel off.

What the hell had happened to him? Was that . . . rust on his body?

Rose watched on, her body taut with tension as Titan effortlessly slid into his role as second in command.

"Fuck, he's completely corroded. Was he in metal form, Iron, when the bombs hit?"

The bearded man next to him nodded. "Yeah. The bombs were altered somehow. Enchanted with dark magic. He was airborne. And when the acid hit him, it didn't just splash his body. The shit coated and clung to his frame like a goo eating him alive. He drew his wings back in and fell instantly. But when I reached him, I couldn't fucking touch him!" The giant shook with simmering rage as his eyes darted over the still body of his brother.

"Hey." Titan dropped the shears and put a calming hand on the wall of Iron's chest. "This is not your fault." His voice fell to a whisper Rose could barely make out, so she strained her head farther around the pillar to hear. "This is not the same as before, and you know it. That stubborn, logical part of you knows it. But right now, I need you to get the chamber ready. Chrome will need all our help on this one. *Steel* needs your help."

Iron nodded silently, his lower lip shaking, and moved away in a hurry. His lumbering strides were so large, so fast, that Rose didn't have time to get her foot out of the way quickly enough. The toe of his boot hammered into it, and she cried out when the sting hit. She hobbled away from her pillar and hopped on one foot, trying to nurse her throbbing toe through her soft sneakers.

Hard hands gripped her shoulders, halting her movements.

"Who the hell are you?" The thunderous roar that erupted out of Iron nearly blew her hair back as she stood frozen under his touch. Her heart hammered out a fearful rhythm before Titan's booming words commanded the room.

"Remove your hands, Iron. She's with me."

Rose turned to see threatening titanium eyes staring daggers at the man holding her. Though Titan's hands continued their work of aiding the man on the table, his fierce eyes and stern expression had a different agenda. When the giant angel didn't move immediately, Titan's fingers tightened around his shears. He dropped them and was about to move when Tung intervened and quickly advanced to the big angel's side.

"Iron." The angel's name spoken in their prime's voice was calmer, yet still commanding. Tung's voice got through where Titan's threat didn't. "This is Rose. She is Titan's guest and is not to be harmed."

Iron's tense hands flexed on the caps of Rose's shoulders before they fell away completely. She released a shaky breath.

Tung walked up next to Rose to place her at his back, stood in front of the confused angel who had yet to step away from her, and gripped his bicep. "Titan and I will reveal everything. But right now, Steel needs us. Chrome is nearly ready. He just needs you to get the oxygen chamber."

Iron looked at Rose a moment longer before he nodded and ran off, presumably to get what was asked of him.

When he was gone, Tung turned to Rose. "Please forgive him. Trust does not come easy for any of us, but especially not for Iron." Tung winced at the poor excuse of an explanation and quickly changed the topic. "Are you all right?"

Rose had to give the man credit for doing his best to give her his full attention, but the angel's side glances and turned shoulders to the commotion on the table gave away his true concerns in the moment.

"Yes, I'm fine. Just a stubbed toe. But what happened to him?" Rose jutted her chin toward the still angel. "Will he be okay?"

Titan and the others had stripped the unconscious angel of his clothing, and his skin looked no better than the blackened, peeled-off fabric that now littered the floor. Expanses of scaly dark char appeared where healthy skin should be. Crumbling flakes of pitted metal, jagged and decomposing at the edges, coated the angel over his torso, upper arms, and upper thighs. His face and hair were unmarred by the corrosion, but they were still dusted in charcoal-colored grime and streaks of rust.

Behind Tung, Iron carried a massive inflatable cylinder over his head. The thing must have been at least seven or eight feet long and three feet in diameter and looked like a giant navy-blue oval vitamin with gauges on the side and a see-through plastic window on top. The angel plunked it down on the floor next to the dining table. Rose watched on as the rest of the men descended on the task of slowly, carefully loading up their fallen brother into the chamber, while Chrome fiddled on the side with hookups and connections.

"I hope so." Tung's tense words were laced with uncertainty as he watched the scene with her. It made her wonder . . .

"Can angels die?"

He paused a minute, and she recognized the action as a trademark of his leadership style. Measuring his words before delivering them, as if he only had so many to use in his lifetime so choosing the right ones was imperative.

"I suppose we can. In this life on earth, we are immortal but not indestructible. We have lived long and will continue to do so, should the mages see fit. Aging and disease do not harm us. In our metal forms, there is not much that can debilitate us . . . outside of the natural flaws and objections to our metals." The last words were said softly, and Rose regretted that he felt compelled to say them at all, given his fallen comrade.

"Acid, prolonged water exposure, extreme heat, or fickle brittleness . . . all things nature has put in place to balance out the metal elements." He cleared his throat as steady beeping, along with the first hisses of an open oxygen tank, filled the room. "But despite our elemental properties, our flesh and bone bodies can still be injured. Steel is . . . well, I confess, this is the worst we've seen."

"He's ready. Chrome." Titan stood and nodded to his brother. The others took several steps back from the chamber.

Chrome rolled his wide shoulders and pumped his fists as gleaming flashes of bright silver metal fluttered over his large frame. The angel was a solid wall of glistening chrome, and Rose briefly marveled at how the sight of such transitions had become less jarring for her, almost normal. Routine.

His metal knee scraped against the stone floor as he laid his palms on the surface of the chamber, which Rose now realized was no more than an inflatable hyperbaric chamber she'd heard of professional athletes using. A soft wheezing sound emanated from a white box with a yellow oxygen tank strapped to it. A long coil of clear plastic tubing connected the chamber to the box. Rose turned back to Chrome as he dropped his head low, clenched his eyes, and furrowed his brow in concentration.

"What's he doing?" Rose whispered.

"He's forming a protective layer over Steel."

Rose startled at Titan's tenor-toned words behind her. How the hell had she not even noticed when he'd moved closer to her? His hand fell to the small of her back and rested reassuringly in the low dip just above her backside. The touch wasn't animalistic or possessive, merely necessary for both of them. She leaned back into the connection and stood closer to him.

"Hydrochloric acid rapidly corrodes steel and many other metals. The charmers have been weaponizing anything and everything they can against our metal forms. This latest bomb hit Steel and quickly ate away at him. They also cursed the acid so it couldn't be easily removed."

Rose sucked in a breath, horrified. Titan's palm moved to her hip and gripped her tightly to him.

"Chrome can manipulate chromium, specifically chromium oxide, which protects metal from corrosion. But he needs oxygen to do it, hence the hyperbaric chamber. With Steel in the chamber, Chrome can create a protective passive layer of chromium oxide over Steel. It'll help him resist the corrosion. Technically, Steel's metal is an alloy . . . made up of many metals and elements. He has always taken to the chamber and Chrome's manipulations far better than the rest of us."

"So, he'll be okay? God, he must be in so much pain." Worry choked her words, and she barely got them out.

"He's unconscious, so he most likely doesn't feel much." That was all the consolation Titan would offer Rose.

She nodded and hugged herself before realizing Titan hadn't exactly answered her first question.

"We don't know." His words answered her before she had a chance to repeat herself. But they were clipped, and the strained, stoic expression on Titan's face spoke of his uncertainty.

Tung's deep timbre filled the silence. "Chrome's protective layer is just that. Protection. He's never tried it out on existing corrosion. We've all used the chamber for various minor injuries, but never anything on this scale. And even those smaller ailments can take an hour or so in the chamber for Chrome to heal. This is . . ."

Rose's stomach nearly turned at the implications of the angel's words. She had just gotten here, just discovered about the vile monsters who had abducted her sister and who were, apparently, after her as well.

I just met Titan. I can't see him lose a brother and go through the agony I've experienced.

She had no idea what prompted her to move forward. But her legs carried her out of Titan's embrace and away from the two towering angels at her side. Murmurs and whispers of her name faintly rose at her back, but she ignored them. All her focus was on the giant blue capsule-like chamber on the floor and the gleaming angel who had his head down in concentration.

The other angels hovered around the chamber and stared at her in confusion. The two red-haired ones she hadn't yet met exchanged questioning glances between themselves and then looked to Titan and Tung behind her. Iron, the largest angel in the room, stood at the head of the chamber, opposite Chrome's position at Steel's feet, and eyed her warily, but he didn't move. Thick, russet brows settled straight over commanding bi-colored eyes, one hazel and one brown. The distinction surprised her, and she was tempted to gaze a bit longer at the anomaly, but her inexplicable intentions kept pulling her toward the angel in the chamber.

Rose kneeled at Steel's head and peered through the clear plastic barrier that doubled as a pitiful excuse for a window. She squirmed at the large chunks of charred, pitted flesh that hung off him like weathered roof shingles.

"Who the hell is that? What is she doing?" The uncertain whispers came from the redheaded angel nearest her right, the shaggier of the two redheads whose hair nearly kissed his shoulders in unruly waves and who sported a trim goatee. His brother, the one with the closely cropped hair, said nothing but merely shook his head and gripped the other angel's arm, halting him as he made to advance toward her.

Rose placed her trembling palms on the flexible plastic of the chamber and sucked in a breath as her fingers hummed with the vibrations of Chrome's power.

As if summoned, Chrome lifted his head, and bright silver eyes met Rose's. His metallic mouth opened as if to speak, but the words died on his tongue. Bright, warm light of the purest white imaginable flooded out of Rose's fingertips. She sucked in a breath as the gentlest soothing heat coursed through her body. The reaction was intense and profound. So much focused, exuberant energy swirled within her chest that she had no choice but to exhale and let go. Release what was happening to her into the vessel underneath her palms.

Pristine light blossomed within the chamber. All the angels standing around it reared back and braced their forearms over their faces against the blinding onslaught of energy. Boots rushed behind her before Titan, too, halted his advance, sliding to his knees at her side.

As fast as the onslaught of light and power came on, it dimmed. The aching tightness all throughout Rose's body receded, leaving only the vibrations underneath her hands—the thrums of Chrome's power—just as steady as they had been when she'd first kneeled.

"Holy shit. Look!"

The gruff shout of the shaggy red-haired angel called attention to Steel's nude and battered form within the chamber. Rose sucked in a breath. Black, pitted skin previously tinted with angry rust and vile corrosion glowed vibrantly as a net of immaculate light stitched bright strands across the injured site. The cords weaved and knitted themselves together over every blemish, forming a mesh net of tightly packed light. Once every strand was connected and tethered tightly, the net glowed brightly with a single pure pulse before it dimmed and faded. In its wake was newly healed skin.

Eyes of every color watched on as Steel's skin was reassembled like a magical patchwork quilt. Chrome had returned to his flesh state, but other than that, no one moved a muscle.

It wasn't until a solid thud at Rose's back drew everyone's attention away from the miracle in the chamber.

Tung crashed to his knees on the stone ground and held his head in his hands. Golden locks shimmied through his splayed fingers as he shook his head in disbelief. Then he raised his head, sat back on his haunches, and looked at Rose. His expression was one of awe as a slow smile grew on his face. "I never thought I'd see it again, yet here it is before me."

Titan turned to face his prime sentinel. "What are you talking about?"

"The Empyrean's eternal flame—"

"Is still in the Empyrean," Titan said firmly.

"But its guiding light is here, in the mortal realm. It's what the charmers have been after and what we've been tasked to find and protect."

Rose shook her head in confusion as her heart rate struggled to settle from her little magic show. "Can someone explain to me what he's talking about? And what the hell just happened to me over there?" She threw her finger back toward the chamber, where Chrome was bent down at the white box, monitoring oxygen levels.

"Rose . . ." Tung hurried to his feet and grabbed her hands. Before Titan or Rose could stop him, he gripped them tightly. Rose braced herself for a potential fireball, but nothing happened. "You carry the Empyrean's guiding light inside you. *You* are what we have been searching for all these long eons."

Her cheeks itched and pricked with rising heat and unease as she shook her head. Titan stood back from her and could only gaze at her slack-jawed as the connections began to form.

And then Tung dropped the other proverbial shoe.

"But if you have a twin sister, I'm willing to bet she has some of the light within her as well. And if that's true, if the Empyrean's light on earth has been fragmented and strewn about the mortal realm, there could be others who serve as its vessels."

"So, Tammy . . ." Rose's throat tightened at the prospect of all she was hearing. And then she looked into Tung's softened, slightly sad steel-gray eyes, though his jaw was set firm with determination.

"If the charmers have Tammy, then they have found a portion of the Empyrean's flame . . . its guiding light on earth."

"And their goal is to destroy the light so heaven and the Empyrean will be shuttled into eternal darkness and those monsters will have free rein over everything." The words left Rose with no small amount of despair. Her hands flew to her forehead. "Oh, God! Tammy!"

Titan scooped her against his chest before a single one of her tears even had a chance to fall. "Not going to happen, petal," he whispered for her ears only. "We'll find her. By the mages, we'll find her and bring her home."

A raspy breath rattled out of Rose as she leaned back and nodded at Titan before turning her attention to Tung.

"Now. We start looking right now. It's time to find my sister."

CHAPTER 15

Heat seeped into Rose's fingers as they curled more tightly around the mug of tea Titan had given her. Peppermint tea, the same kind he'd offered her when she was at his cabin after that charmer attack. God, was it only last night that it happened? Her mind and body seemed to have aged a million lifetimes since then. But she did her best to let the tea's spicy herbal aroma seep into every part of her. It was a comfort she desperately needed. That and Titan's solid warm hand as he constantly rubbed her thigh beneath the table. The gesture grounded her and was a steady reminder that she was not in this alone. Whatever the hell *this* was. Because last she checked, humans didn't magically spew forth celestial light and heal dying angels.

Tea. She definitely needed more tea.

Rose cautiously sipped the steaming drink and eyed the others at the dining table. Around her sat the contingent of angels and, holy crap, did she feel small. Tung commanded the head of the table, with Titan to his right, as appropriate. The wood of the chairs strained as all around her, wide, solid frames of muscle shifted in their seats. Chrome sat to her right, though

134

every so often he'd rise from his seat to go check on Steel, who was still in the chamber.

Titan had already made the introductions for the other three angels she hadn't officially met yet. Across from her were the two red-haired men, Bronze and Brass. Though, now that she was able to meet and view them up close, stark differences stood out beyond their hair length. Bronze sported the unruly hair and trimmed goatee Rose had first noticed, but his stature was similar to Titan's athletic frame. Iron and Chrome had bulk in spades, but Bronze had a more agile and lean physique, though still powerful. His height, like that of all the angels, was commanding but not nearly as intimidating as the others. He had been the first to shake her hand once she and Titan realized it seemed to be safe to do so. Bronze's charming, boyish wink and flashing smile instantly warmed her to him. The angel exuded golden retriever energy.

Brass, on the other hand, had not taken to Rose so quickly. Oh, sure, he was polite and respectful but more reserved. He retreated into himself when not actively engaged in conversation, which Rose didn't mind. He was much like her in that regard. At least, her of the past six months. With Brass's shortly cropped hair, more auburn than a true vibrant red, and his incredibly calm demeanor, the quiet warrior was an easy person to be around, despite his tranquil nature. There was no strained need to fill the silence. It was refreshing.

And then there was Iron. The angel was so large and hulking that she was concerned about the even weight distribution at the table and silently questioned his choice of an end seat. He had been cordial and respectful when Titan properly introduced them, but it had seemed forced. Strained. The quick drop of her hand after he shook it didn't escape her notice. Nor did the bi-tonal eyes that she caught glancing at her every so often. Oh, they'd dart away as soon as she spied him, and he'd return to focusing on the grain of the wood as his thick fingers absently stroked the table. But it wasn't lost on her. Still, if Titan and Tung trusted him, she could, too. Though she wondered what Tung had hinted at earlier and what exactly had happened to that angel in the past to warrant their leader's soft words of explanation.

"I still can't believe it. All these years and we've finally found it. I mean her. No, that's not right. But the light is her, so technically, maybe?" Bronze's hair swept across the tops of his wide shoulders as he animatedly worked out his thoughts for all to hear.

"Well, it's nice to meet you, too." Rose quirked her lips at the angel. "But I'm going to need more information on this whole light thing. Not going to lie, that sort of scared the crap out of me back there."

"Well, I've been sliced up seven ways from Sunday." Bronze shook his loose fingers up and down his body and twisted his face up in disgust. "Had all manner of muck pouring out of me through holes that definitely weren't included on the original model, and I've never seen anything like that."

"Oh, fucking hell." Chrome groaned. "Do we have to hear about your holes again? I'm the sorry ass who had to patch you up. So don't remind me." He shuddered, and the tingling aroma of sharp, icy peppermint from his gum mixed with the scented steam from her tea.

"We need more information." Titan's words refocused everyone's attention on the larger matter at hand.

"And I need a primer on this whole light thing." Rose crossed her arms over her chest and shook her head. "I feel like I'm being thrown into a triathlon with pool floaties and flippers while everyone else has wetsuits and the endurance of a . . . a . . ."

"Triathlete?"

Rose looked up at Bronze, whose toned arms were spread as

widely as his grin as he leaned back on the rear legs of his chair. "What? I was just trying to help you out."

Brass snickered lightly while Chrome hid his smile behind his fist. Chrome lifted a brow and glanced at Rose coyly. "The joke landed, okay? They don't always. You gotta give him credit when they do."

Rose couldn't help herself. Seeing the big angel laugh into his hands and do his best to hold back a cackle was all the permission she needed to let her own laughter free. And damn, did it feel good. She couldn't remember the last time she'd laughed. Her sides hurt from the deep chuckle and it was a refreshing type of innocent torture.

Until she remembered Tammy. Her exuberant boisterous laugh that could fill a room and entice everyone in it to join her.

Shit.

Her laughter died on her lips. But Titan's hand cupped her shoulder and drew her near to his solid chest before the weight of the memory had a chance to bury her.

How does he always know what I need?

She looked up at his profile. Titan's full lips were pressed together, nestled within the soft confines of his beard. Lips that had seared blazing trails of heat over every inch of her body. Lips that had delicately caressed her forehead and whispered quiet assurances when scary things got scarier. All silent promises and intense ferocity. The enormity of it all, of *him*, both took her breath away and steeled her resolve.

"The eternal flame in the Empyrean was lit by the prime mages at the time of this realm's creation." Tung's words drew the attention of everyone at the table.

Rose struggled to look away from Titan's strong profile, but his slight shoulder nudge when he caught her failure to give Tung her full attention convinced her.

"From this light, all celestial beings were created, including the celestial mages and the sentinel angels. The flame resides in the Empyrean, the highest realm of heaven, and it is our eternal task to protect the flame and the Empyrean at all costs. It is the source of the Empyrean's power and a beacon for all pure light."

"Light that attracts souls," Titan chimed in, then turned to Rose. "When a mortal dies, their soul is called home to the flame, and they reside for eternity within the sanctuary of heaven's gates. When a soul is returned, the eternal flame brightens and strengthens and gifts mortals with new births and souls. It's a pristine cycle that has never been broken. Until the charmers were discovered. Since then, we suspect all new births contain a soul made up of the essence of another who has already come before them, but who is not able to ascend through the sealed gates. I believe mortals refer to it as reincarnation." Rose's head swam with the idea of it all, of her soul somehow existing for lives upon lives before it got dealt the short straw and wound up in her. But it was Titan's mention of the enemy that made her shift uncomfortably. She'd be damned, though, if she'd let her unease cause her to shy away from what she needed to hear.

"Discovered?" she asked.

Tung nodded and picked up where Titan left off. "When the prime mages created the eternal flame, it was not without an unintentional counterbalance. After all, light cannot exist without shadow. So, in the wake of the eternal flame's creation, a realm of darkness also formed. The celestial mages had always asserted that the darkness was barren and, therefore, harmless. Until one day when they noticed that souls called forth from the mortal realm never appeared in heaven. And no light ever returned to the eternal flame."

"When you say 'never appeared,' you mean what exactly? The people died but their souls were stuck in the in-between or something?"

Tung settled uneasy eyes on her in the same manner one would deliver bad news to a child. "I'm afraid not. No, the souls were intercepted."

"What? How?"

"Charmers. It was then that we learned of their existence. The mages deduced that unintended byproducts were created when the eternal flame first sputtered to life in the great void." Tung leaned closer to Rose and rested his elbows on the table. "Those byproducts were, at the time, undetectable traces of magic, which had been littered through the darkness in the flame's great wake."

Rose shook her head. "I don't understand. What does that have to do with the light?"

Tung thinned his lips and gestured his hand toward Rose, curling his fingers outward as if searching for words. "Think of the way an earthly flame behaves. It gives off carbon particles if there is not enough oxygen during the initial reaction."

Rose nodded, doing her level best to keep her chemistry-flunking head in the game. But then a thrilling chill coursed through her as Titan's knuckles calmly stroked along the curve of her spine in support. She smiled, though never taking her attention from Tung, and hooked her ankle over Titan's in a silent show of thanks.

The gravity in Tung's tone deepened. "Well, instead of carbon particles, the eternal flame gave off magical byproducts. And it was from those byproducts that the first charmer, Cyro, emerged."

"Fucking shit under my shoe," Chrome muttered.

"And somehow, Cyro had the ability to manifest more of his kind. *That* was how we discovered their existence. Because those souls who departed their mortal bodies and began their ascent to heaven? They were intercepted by the charmers and their lights were snuffed out. Over the ages, the charmers have gotten smarter, craftier. Under Cyro's command, they have been able to seek out light and extinguish it at rates even we struggle to combat. And their ranks have changed and grown into three classes. Mystics, elite, and apex. Mystic conjurers wear a gold band around their necks and arms. They are spell-casters who manifest magic from a distance, like the ones who threw the bomb at Steel. Elite are the warrior class who prize hand-to-hand combat above all else. They are fierce and formidable and wear two gold bands on their bodies."

"Fierce and formidable my left nut!" Bronze barked out before leaning over to get Rose's attention. "Rose, remind me to show you my trophy room. I've got more elite gold rings than Sonic the Hedgehog."

"Right. I'll have to see that sometime," Rose said with an uneasy laugh.

Tung rolled his eyes at his brother before continuing. "Apex conjurers are the third class and make up the high order of charmers. They are both expert warriors and lethal spellcasters and are signified with three gold bands on their bodies." Tung's tone deepened as he held Rose's gaze in earnest. "And they hold a personal fondness for unspeakable evil. If one should ever cross your path—"

"Run." The short word rumbled out of Iron, who had remained silent through Tung's explanations. The angel didn't look at Rose and just sipped his beer casually, as if they were talking about draft strategies for fantasy football. Occasionally, his eyes wandered over to the chamber where Steel still lay but always returned to his beer.

The gentle lilt of Brass's voice softened the tension slightly. "The apex are the crafty ones Tung mentioned. They're responsible for the enchanted hydrochloric acid bombs and for the bone knives. When they learned we can manipulate metal, they had to get creative with their weapons." He shrugged, gave her a grim smile, and went back to picking at his fingernail.

"If the Empyrean's light is lessened by the souls not returning to heaven, then . . ." Rose's words trailed off as her understanding of the dire circumstances increased.

Tung leaned back in his chair. His charcoal eyes pinned her

to the spot before he answered. "If the sun were to be extinguished tomorrow, how long do you think it would be before every creature in the mortal realm perished?"

A rattled breath rushed out of Rose at the enormity of it all.

"Hush . . . hush." Titan's soothing words settled over her in blanketed comfort as he flexed firm fingers around the back of her neck. But even as Rose melted into his touch, the unnerving glances from the other angels added to her rising discomfort. Bronze and Brass zeroed in on Titan's hands on her, and the soft murmurings he whispered for her benefit were clearly picked up by the others in the room.

Was she breaking a rule? Were outsiders forbidden from touching angels? If that was the case, then what happened between them in his room earlier definitely would have raised some pissed-off eyebrows.

"But I wonder whether the eternal flame did not have some other unintended magical byproducts as well," Tung mused.

Titan's head shot up. "What do you mean?"

"What I mean is . . . what if sparks of the eternal flame landed in the mortal realm after all, but those sparks were actually the guiding light we've been tasked to seek out all these years? After all, the mages were never able to elaborate on their frantic directives while we were enacting the Sealing. There was no time for clarification, if you recall."

"You mean it's some sort of failsafe?" Titan quirked his head to the side.

"Yes. What if sparks of the flame somehow exist in souls on earth and have managed to latch on and move dormant through human souls over the ages? As long as those sparks are here in this realm and hidden, the flame can dim but never truly go out. If creation is at the flame's core, and that spark somehow lives in Rose but is dormant no longer, it would explain how she was able to save Steel's life. And why she was even drawn to his fallen state in the first place."

"I, um. This is . . . just . . . a lot." Rose rested her head in her hands and did her best to blot out every outside stimulus. It was too much. It was all too much.

But her concerns fell on deaf ears as animated voices swelled around her. Excited theories and hopeful shouts swirled throughout the room in a dizzying hurricane even Titan was unaware she cowered under. Until his reassuring and commanding voice broke through the din of the excitement.

And solidly placed the storm directly over her head.

"When I first touched her, my full angel fire was triggered. Every touch since has strengthened my connection to my full power. My lethargy is gone, and that debilitating need to recharge my fire each night is lessening the stronger our bond grows." Titan's words rushed out of him as his palm flew to his forehead. He leaned back in his seat. "By the mages . . . What if my touch triggered a spark of the Empyrean's eternal flame that had been hidden, lying dormant, in Rose this whole time?" He turned to her quickly and leaned his head close to her in hushed confidence. "When we were together earlier, your eyes changed color. They took on the hues of my metal briefly, before fading back to their natural green. I didn't know what to make of it at the time, but now I wonder whether the cause is celestial in nature after all. But from within *you*, not me. From the eternal flame."

Silence swept over the room, and Rose's heartbeat pounded like a drum line in her ears. She shook her head as they chattered about this light inside her, as if she were a host for some celestial parasite. Her skin crawled and her stomach twisted at the hopeful rise in each of their voices. Of the awed smiles and pats on the back at this miraculous win they'd somehow discovered while her life had been, and still was, in utter shambles. She was in no position to be anyone's beacon of hope. If anyone shone brightly under adoration, it was Tammy. *She* should be here, serving as the bright and shining hope to a room full of angel warriors, not Rose. All Rose wanted was her sister back, and her exhausted soul couldn't handle anything beyond that.

Rose squeezed her eyes shut and jerked as hot tears dampened the sweatpants covering the tops of her thighs. This was all too fucking much. She needed to get away from this, from them. She just needed to *breathe.*

Rose shot up from the table. Titan dropped his hands in surprise and looked at her. He was about to speak, but she just held up her hand to silence him.

"I need some time to myself. This is overwhelming. I need . . . just . . . I need to be alone for a bit."

"Rose!" Her name on Titan's lips nearly pulled her back, but it wasn't strong enough to quell the rising panic in her chest.

She scooted around the table and ran back to the hall, easily retracing her steps to find Titan's room. Thankfully, it was unlocked and she had no trouble slipping in.

Exhaustion had her flopping down on the bed, face-first. She was so overloaded and bone weary that she didn't even pick up on the shouts behind her or the loud crashes of equipment that toppled over. As if a captive animal was breaking free of its cage.

CHAPTER 16

Paralyzing confusion and indecision froze Titan in his seat. He was torn between wanting—no, *needing*—to chase after Rose and aiding his brothers as they rushed to Steel's chamber. The angel within thrashed and writhed as he frantically punched and kicked at the flexible walls of his confines. Sharp hissing and the metallic thunk of a fallen oxygen tank pierced his ears. Chrome caught the tank before it could roll anywhere and quickly shut off the valve while Brass and Bronze worked frantically to unzip the chamber. Rounded joints and blunt fists pummeled the inside of the polyurethane chamber's casing while a great rumbling roar rose from within.

Titan's feet itched to run, however, to upend the ten-foot-long farmhouse table and shoulder his way through whatever doubt and worry Rose carried inside her. Communication and understanding would ease her consternation. Any time things got tense with his brothers, whenever heads got hot and training fell by the wayside, he would sit their asses down and insist they hash it out. All his leadership skills were for shit if he couldn't understand the genesis of fracturing. Known enemies were not nearly as powerful as unknown enemies.

But she'd requested solitude. And even through the excitement of their revelations, the logical and strategic side of him held him fast to his chair. He fisted his hands and slammed them down on the table. Again, he'd allowed his world to pile up so high on Rose's delicate shoulders when he should have been bearing that weight for her. It was no wonder she'd fled, that she needed space alone.

Away from me.

The rejection stung harsher than any acid.

Metal clanging against stone steeled his resolve to help his brothers. He was of no benefit to Rose at the moment and even less of a benefit as a chair warmer. Even alone in his room, she was safe. With Steel punching through his restlessness after waking from a healing coma, his brothers were less so.

With a painful grunt, Titan tore himself away from staring at the hallway to his suite and ran into the muscled foray.

"Hold him steady. For fuck's sake, grab his leg!" Chrome barked orders as one by one, each angel had a hold of Steel and lifted him so Iron could shuck away the deflated chamber from underneath. Steel's powerful body thrashed and kicked against the hands that restrained him. The angel's skin was dotted with perspiration, and his muscles tightened with each twist of his traumatized frame.

Titan grabbed a nearby blanket from a couch and put it down on the stone floor. "Settle him here. Gently."

Once Steel was on the blanket and wrapped loosely, Titan patted the sides of his face. "Easy, Steel, easy. You're home and safe."

But the trauma of Steel's ordeal was etched starkly on his wan face. The angel's bleach-blond hair was soaked in sweat and clung to his face and neck in slick tendrils. The tense wrinkle between his brows and the slight shiver of his bottom lip sent mixed messages. Yes, he was alive, but he was lightyears away from being well.

"Why is he so hot? Was it Rose's light . . . fire . . . whatever she did?" Bronze was the first to ask the questions as the angel kept a firm grip on Steel's ankles.

Titan shook his head. "I don't know."

"Well, I'll say this: his head may need to catch up with the program, but his body's totally healed. All the acid burns and corrosion are completely gone." Chrome was on his knees, examining Steel's flank, when he sat up and scratched the back of his head. "His skin's completely mended. Hell, all his old scars are gone, too. It's like he's been buffed to a high shine with an extra coarse macro grit sanding belt. Shit..." He shook his head in disbelief.

"I suspect Rose's light did exactly what it was meant to do." Tung kneeled at the side of Steel's head and placed a wet kitchen towel on the angel's sweaty brow. The instant the connection was made, Steel's seesaw breaths slowed. His chest rose with a great inhale and slowly settled down as a satisfied moan escaped his dry lips. Then his hand, no longer held down, reached up and clasped the wrist of their prime.

Ice-blue eyes poked through heavy and weary lids as Steel looked up and met the angel who held the cool towel to his brow. Then the side of his mouth rose in a lazy half-smile.

"Hey." The word was raspy and garbled against his straining vocal cords, but it held all the nonchalance of a bike messenger who casually gets taken down by a city taxi from time to time only to dust himself off and chalk the experience up to an occupational hazard.

Cheers and hollers erupted around the room as the angels all released a collective sigh of relief.

Tung patted Steel's cheek and helped the angel sit up. "By the mages . . . welcome back."

"How do you feel?" Titan asked.

Steel shook his head and dropped it in his hands for a moment before addressing the question. "Great. Well, not great.

But way better than I was. Sore, kind of tight, like my skin crisped up, scabbed all over, then peeled off in chunks." He lifted his arms to inspect the damage. His left hand quickly flew to his right bicep where Titan knew there had been a bone knife scar from a charmer skirmish years ago.

At least there had been previously. Nothing but pink, new flesh remained.

"Wow," Steel marveled as he stroked his unblemished skin. "I don't know what you did this time, Chrome, but you better keep up with the Wheaties. They are doing wonders for my complexion."

"Ass," Chrome mumbled through a held-back smile. "Glad you're back."

"Same." Brass leaned over and dropped a set of clean clothes into Steel's lap. The blond angel was just about to pick up his shirt when he sucked in a breath and slapped his forehead.

"The charmers! I almost forgot."

The angels all slowed their movements at the mention of their enemy.

"Forgot what?" Titan asked.

Steel bolted upright, clothes in hand, and quickly dropped his meaty legs into his athletic pants. His restless hands haphazardly threw his T-shirt over his head and then quickly spun it around his neck when he realized it was backward.

"Fuckers have a holding facility," he breathed out as his arms punched through his sleeves. "For mortals. It's an abandoned mill along the Ellis River. Shit, what was the name of it?"

"A holding facility? For what? Their mystics create portals freely so they can travel back and forth between the dark realm and here. What could they possibly need a holding facility for?" Tung's rapid-fire questions were roaring Ping-Pong balls off the cavernous walls, with each one failing to land on an answer.

To say Titan's frustrations and tensions were high was the motherfucking understatement of all understatements. His head was there with his brothers, doing its level best to analyze the information.

But his heart was back in that bedroom with Rose. *His* room, where he could make her feel at home and gently peel back every single burden he'd placed at her feet. Where he could finally—*finally*—talk to her about Tammy. Explain to Rose his involvement in her sister's disappearance. How, for the past six months, only raw dogged determination at finding her, the only woman he'd ever failed to protect, had kept him going. How Rose had never been alone in her grief, even though she hadn't met him yet. He would scoop her up against his chest, lean them both against the headboard of the bed, and take on every ounce of her fatigue and stress as they recounted their shared memories of Tammy's abduction until . . .

Abduction. Tammy was abducted, not slashed on site to have her soul bleed out.

"Holy shit . . ." Titan's realization and barely there curse was enough to draw six pairs of hell-bent eyes on him. He cleared his throat as the unease of what he was piecing together twisted his stomach. But if it was true . . . "I think I know what they're holding in that mill."

"What?" Steel asked.

Titan met everyone's eyes and, one by one, asked the questions he needed them to answer for themselves. "When a charmer goes after a mortal, how do they bleed the soul?"

Bronze snorted at the softball question. "You kidding me with this? All right, I'll take the preschool bait. They pick their kills based on the mortal's life and the aura they give off, whether they were upstanding citizens, did a lot of volunteer work, never fucking jaywalked. Whatever shit fits the charmers' metrics of having a pure and bright soul. Then they stalk 'em, slit their throats with their magic-laced knives, and sit back with a bag of fucking popcorn as the light of the poor mortal's soul bleeds out into the smog of the city. With heaven and the Empyrean sealed up tight, the soul has nowhere to go. So they snuff it out of existence."

"And it ain't quick," Chrome added hesitantly as if wondering why they needed to recap the history lesson for Charmer Killing 101, but he trustingly played along. "Oh, don't get me wrong, the charmers have used their magic to speed up the process of getting the soul out of the body, but the death of a soul is not something that happens on their schedule. It could take hours. And since mortals can't travel to the dark realm with the charmers, everyone's stuck there in the middle of fucking Main Street or the kiddie playground until the deed's done. With the exception of your girl six months ago, it's an on-site job. No abductions. Um . . . generally speaking, that is." Chrome lifted his shoulder and looked down as the words settled.

"But what if their process didn't work?" Titan faced the hallway to his suite, still addressing the angels. "What if a vessel for the eternal flame's spark, like Rose, didn't behave the same way as others? What if, to extinguish the spark, the process was entirely different? And the charmers needed more time to figure out how to get the job done?"

"Wait, you mean— Actually, I don't know what you mean." Chrome swallowed his words.

Tung just stood there in silence, arms crossed over the bulk of his chest, with his inquisitive gaze resting on Titan. And then their prime pieced together the puzzle. "He means that, if Rose's sister carries the spark within her soul—and we're working off a monumental *if* over here—the charmers haven't figured out yet how to remove it. And since mortals can't travel to the dark realm, a holding facility in an abandoned mill would satisfy many objectives."

Hushed curses traveled around the room as Tung's words sank in.

Because with that realization, a new type of threat also reared up. One of abduction and torture, instead of quiet loss.

The realization for Titan, however, was far more unsettling. Because it meant Tammy could still be alive . . . but had been held captive by the charmers all this time.

150

CHAPTER 17

The coarseness of the bathroom floor's grout shaved smooth a jagged edge of Rose's fingernail as she absently ran her hand up and down the grit between two white marble tiles. Swirls of gray skimmed in and out of each two-inch hexagon slab as her fingers followed the grout lines. They were the smallest rough patches she could find in a suite of rooms full of abrasive surfaces and daunting expectations. Hell, even the cool marble under her butt expanded out wider than her entire living room, kitchen, and bathroom combined.

A glass shower stall so large it boasted a matching tiled bench seat stood across from her. To its right sat a jetted tub worthy of its owner's size and stature . . . a size and stature she tried very hard not to dwell on at the moment. Sparkling porcelain and shimmering glass twinkled every which way she looked. And all Rose could do was press her tailbone farther down into the marble as she gripped her knees, hoping the pain would somehow wake her the fuck up.

Her forehead hit the tops of her knees as she exhaled. But when the warm air that left her lungs merely stagnated in front of her, having nowhere to easily escape, she sat back up again and leaned her head against the vanity. She tried to wrap her mind around just when, exactly, the world had gotten so freaking big.

Prior to her stroll in the park, her life had been about finding her sister. Every breath she took into her lungs had been focused on sustaining her body long enough so she could find Tammy. And now? Those breaths had to do more, go further. They had to fuel this unimaginable light inside her that somehow elevated her status on the importance scale to literal holier-than-thou proportions.

Rose held out her hands in front of her and wiggled her fingers. Whatever was inside her didn't affect her motor skills. She was able to walk and move like normal, able to eat and breathe like normal. And when she turned her attention inward, scanning her body for anything that felt off, nothing threw up any red flags. Although, there had been changes, that was for sure, but none she suspected were due to any angelic light inside her.

For starters, the sharp pangs in her stomach had lessened. Where eating had been a bodily necessity before, here, with Titan, he seemed to view it as an act of service. Before she could even think about shutting down her hunger, Titan had been there with a hot cup of tea or a freshly prepared meal. It didn't matter whether it was an appropriate mealtime or a common eating hour. Her unspoken needs always seemed to blossom brightly and boldly in his thoughts in a way that hit differently from Carla's Sunday leftover casseroles.

But another tension had lessened as well. Her tiring need to go it alone. Faith. Support. Encouragement and teamwork. All these things had jumped ship along with her loved ones once she refused to give up searching for Tammy. The abandonment had stung, but not nearly as bad as when all those other things had left as well.

Here, however, with Titan and his brothers, purpose and

motivation refired her cylinders. Here, she could be a team. She could work with others, have a network of support, intel, camaraderie. She could have . . .

Titan.

"Rose, it's me."

Her name in Titan's smooth tenor tones drifted through the door. Of course. As if the angel knew she was thinking about him, his voice magically appeared on the other side of the bathroom door.

No, not magic. You're in his living quarters. Stop being childish.

"Hey." The word was weak on so many levels. But it was the best she could offer given the circumstances.

"Can I come in?" Muffled worry punctuated the short question.

Closer now. His voice was closer, as if his forehead were kissing the cold metal of the door and his lips were close enough to fog it up with his breath.

"Yeah. I just—"

"You don't need to explain a damn thing, petal."

The bold crispness of his voice had her looking up. Titan had already opened the door. His intent eyes immediately sought hers out and hardened the moment he took in her curled-up form on the floor.

She knew what was coming. Knew it before the worn fabric of his pants protested as he began to drop his large frame to her level. Knew it before his boots shifted position, toes out, to better accommodate his balance in his anticipated crouch.

But before he could come any closer to her, she held up her hand and stopped him.

He froze and cocked his head to the side. But he didn't move. He just squatted there and waited for her to take the lead.

In the pause of the moment, she took advantage. Her eyes glanced up at him and drank in every solid inch of the man who not only renewed her own hope but gave her some of his.

And for the first time, Rose understood just how much power he regularly held in check around her. How much power he was allowing her to control with just the slightest flip of her fingers. It was staggering.

He was staggering.

Every one of his actions made her feel cherished. Without any questions or expected reciprocity. Even once he knew about the eternal-flame-spark-thing inside her, he'd never once told her how she was to perform. What she would need to do in her newfound role as a celestial candlestick. The only thing he ever insisted was that she stay close, under the cocoon of his protection, until they could figure out the next steps to find her sister.

And now, here he was, inviting her into his circle of trust, all while practically asking for her drink order and how she liked her eggs cooked.

Rose extended her arm to Titan. Her palm lay face up, and her fingers were curled in invitation. He didn't hesitate to accept her offer. Rough skin scraped along her hand as his solid weight settled into her. She held his eyes for a moment. His stern brows sank heavily over wary pools of espresso-colored irises as he no doubt struggled to get a read on her actions. The hard set of his chin and the grim line of his full mouth beneath his beard were steely, yet reserved.

He was waiting for more information, waiting for her, and was poised to react any way she needed him to.

Rose's other hand cupped the side of his face. The warmth of his cheek peeking above his beard increased as a glowing flush bloomed under her hand.

"Leonardo." She spoke the word with solid assurance and nodded. "You are definitely Leonardo."

Rose bit back a laugh at the angel's stalled-out expression.

"Um, come again?"

A soft chuckle finally escaped her mouth as she dropped the hand she held and cradled the other side of his face with it.

"Leonardo. The leader of the Teenage Mutant Ninja Turtles? The brother who was responsible for corralling his other brothers to fight Shredder and the Krang?" Rose couldn't keep the excitement out of her voice as Titan's look of confusion grew.

"It was a television show. Then an arcade game. Then it morphed into a whole slew of movies, some bad and some so bad they were good. And each ninja turtle had their own weapon, their own quirks, and their father was a giant rat named Splinter."

The corner of Titan's lips rose in an amused smile.

"I gotta tell ya, I'm wondering who you think the rat would be in this comparison."

She smiled and let him take both of her hands. His warm lips pressed chaste kisses against the inside of her palms. She shivered at the light scratch of his beard as the fine hairs of his mustache brushed against her delicate skin.

"The easy answer would be to say Tung, but I don't get the tough-love vibe from him. I doubt he forced you to run training drills without your weapons or practice fighting hand-to-hand blindfolded."

Titan's shoulders bobbed with a laugh.

"But this," Rose spread her arms out and gestured around them, "definitely solidifies the metaphor. The ninja turtles lived in a sewer under the city. You guys live in a cavern nestled under a valley near the White Mountains. All that's missing is the pizza."

"You should see Chrome's pizza oven, then. He takes it very seriously. The man's got two types of baking stones, a baking steel, at least three different pizza peels, and has these bread proofing box things to make sure the dough rises at the right temperature."

Rose's eyes widened with delight. "Really?"

Titan nodded and smiled. "But where are you going with all this, petal? I doubt your mind was on mutant turtles back there." His eyes fell a bit, and his hands holding hers tensed.

"I just meant that you're a really great leader. Second. Whatever. Everyone trusts you . . . and I need to trust you, too." God, why were those words so hard to say? It was like the truth was buried six feet under cold, wet sand and she had to use a bulldozer to drag it out, only to dust it off and present it for a vulnerable inspection. "I was scared. Freaking terrified, actually. But there hasn't been a single time since I've met you where you've given me a reason to not trust and believe in you. So," Rose drew in a ragged breath and silently wondered whether the supposed magical light inside her could offer up a hefty dose of courage right then, "all this is to say that I'm on board. Whatever light lives within me, whatever this connection is between us, I'm willing to throw my all into it if it'll help us find my sister."

At the mention of Tammy, something changed in Titan's features. He grabbed a seat next to her on the cold marble tile. He didn't say a word at first. Just picked up her hand and traced his fingers over every knuckle and raised vein. His ministrations were oddly soothing and did far more to ease her mind than any of the deep-breathing-into-her-knees hooey she'd tried when she first shut herself in the bathroom. She couldn't help but envision his touch like that of a loving mapmaker who painstakingly charted every swelling curve of a river and angular jut of a mountain.

Her wrist shifted as he carefully turned her hand up and continued tracing her palm, this time following the creases that slashed horizontally across the expanse of her hand. Every now and then, his blunt fingernail would dip into each valley, causing her breath to hitch and a thrill to tingle throughout her body. The sensations went beyond calm and were almost trance-like. Under Titan's deft fingers, which were rough and calloused on the outside but intentioned and magical against her, all the long-held stress seeped out of every pore in her body. Pores that had been clamped shut under fatigue and duress for too damn long.

And for him to be able to take it all away with a simple, stroking touch?

The sigh that fluttered out of Rose held six months' worth of tension. And boy, did it feel good to let it go.

Rose lolled her head to rest against Titan's shoulder, not even caring about how forward the act was or how intimate holding his hand was. Hell, they had gone way past intimate less than an hour ago.

But any doubt about the action quickly skittered away when Titan's head rested against hers.

"Your trust is the most sacred gift to me." The statement was so final and held so much weight to it, Rose nearly shivered as the vibrations of his words against her skin, and the intensity with which he said them, cascaded over her.

And when he pulled away to look at her, she nearly whimpered at the loss. But when his eyes flashed the sharp gleam of titanium, she tamped down her inner mewling over the angel before her and put her senses on high alert.

"What is it?"

"I think I know what happened to Tammy."

If Rose's ass hadn't already been on the floor, her tailbone would have fractured something fierce at the velocity it would have hit the marble.

She shook her head in confusion. "You do?"

He nodded grimly. "I was there when she was taken. I was out on a routine patrol when it happened. I had my hands full and was playing fucking defense to four charmers. My brothers had their own assaults to deal with. We were in the thick of it with really shitty odds. And then I saw you. Or your sister. She was in front of her car's trunk when another charmer, an elite I hadn't seen originally, grabbed her.

"I dove at the fucker and pierced him straight through the neck with an arrow. But when I turned, a mystic had your sister around her middle. Before I could even get up, the mystic whispered a spell. A portal appeared behind them and the mystic escaped. With her."

Even though it hurt like hell to have the scenario recounted, Rose nodded her understanding. But she still shrugged her nose up and shook her head. "I know all this. You've already told me." And, boy, had that not been an easy pill to swallow. But, while the old Rose would have lashed out and found fault with Titan's role in Tammy's disappearance, the new Rose saw the bigger picture. Blame truly was just a game, one which never resulted in winners.

His searing gaze silenced her interjection. And the low rumbling growl that vibrated within Titan's Adam's apple warned her of another danger entirely. "Charmers don't abduct people, Rose. But with your sister, they did."

"What . . . ? Why?" Disbelief warred with confusion as she struggled to get the words out.

"Because we think she's harboring a spark from the flame, like you. And they haven't figured out how to get it out of her yet."

Yet.

That word dripped like poison as it floated into Rose's comprehension.

"When you say . . . *yet* . . ."

Titan didn't nod this time. Didn't move his head or look anywhere other than directly at her. And for the first time, Rose understood what it must be like for the prey he targeted.

"There's an abandoned mill along the Ellis River. We think it's being used as a holding facility. We think . . . Tammy might be there. And we're going in to get her."

CHAPTER 18

Rose had never seen so many muscled-up behemoths in one place before. True, she was probably the furthest thing from a gym rat and definitely didn't hang with the CrossFit gang, but even still, the massive bulk of bodies that took up space in the den's great room was intimidating.

Or, at least, they would be to anyone who hadn't spent the last hour observing how very much like the ninja turtles they could be.

Bronze had all the makings of a Michelangelo. His affable, lighthearted manner was always ready with a foul-mouthed joke or lewd gesture. He reminded Rose of an older brother, perhaps one who was always in trouble with the law. And, likewise, one who always managed to escape said trouble.

Wide expanses of rough leather strappings crisscrossed his chest and back as he strapped in bronze throwing daggers. The glint of the blades, however, spoke of power more than just the qualities of the metal. At his back sat a bronze halberd. The length of the shaft, however, was shortened to accommodate flight and one-handed fighting. But the precise curve of the half-moon blade at its zenith was like a deadly sickle. Any momentum Bronze propelled into the handle would ricochet through the gleaming metal with destructive force. The thing was nasty and not something Rose wanted to find herself on the business end of. Like, ever.

Chrome's weapons vest was a stark contrast to Bronze's bladed glory. Oh, sure, Rose spied a few short blades being tucked into the massive angel's thigh holsters. But for the most part, the man was a walking wall of pure, calculating gunmetal, with an emphasis on the guns. And that was in his flesh form.

Firearms of every shape and size imaginable blanketed his chest, back, and sides. The bulk of the gear alone was enough to weigh Rose down to the ground. But it wasn't bulk for the sake of it. No, Chrome was smart. Much smarter than he let on. Once she got past the foul mouth and cigar smoke, she marveled at his comprehension of biology, medicine, and weapons manufacture. She'd learned that every single gun in the den was modified and reinforced by Chrome for improved accuracy, trajectory, and speed. The ammo as well.

A true Donatello.

The clicks of magazines being loaded and blades being sheathed drew her attention behind her. Brass, Tung, and Titan were huddled together over weapons of every shape and sort splayed out across the dining table. While she knew Titan, her Leonardo, favored his bow and arrows, he still kept knives on him as part of his close-quarters tactics. Brass and Tung, however, seemed to be in Chrome's camp with a preference for heavy-metal artillery.

Titan grabbed a Ka-Bar from the table and sheathed it at his hip, but not before glancing up at her and giving her a small smile. And was it her imagination or did he flex his arms a bit as he twisted them around to secure his bow in the sling at his back?

Her heart fluttered. She couldn't help the smile that slowly spread across her face, so she bit her lip and turned to hide her impending rise in color.

Only to face Iron.

Of all the angels, he was the one who still unsettled her. Perhaps it was the weighty beard and thick shoulder-length dark red hair hiding most of his facial features, but she had never quite managed to get a full read on him. All the others had been above and beyond friendly, almost to the point of annoying in that brotherly sort of way. Steel, for example, who stood next to Iron as he strapped on every manner of bladed weapon imaginable, had taken a liking to her almost instantly.

And why not? She was freaking likable, goddammit! Or, at least, she used to be . . . before her sister got abducted. Before the world had abandoned her and turned its other cheek on a twinless twin who obsessed over a perceived lost cause.

But Iron had never warmed to her. Never said much beyond what was required. Although, it also seemed he never spoke much to anyone. So, perhaps she shouldn't take it so personally?

Iron clutched a wide iron double-bladed ax with a shortened handle before fastening it to the hip holster on his side. His shoulders bunched as he turned without moving his hips and adjusted the iron mace at his other side. The weapon was as long as the ax, but instead of twin blades on top, three metal points jutted out from a blunted and bulbous hunk of rounded iron.

That angel was blunt force trauma personified. And had Raphael-caliber attitude oozing from his stubborn celestial pores.

"Now, do you remember what we talked about?" Titan walked up behind Rose and softly laid his hands on her shoulders.

She turned to face him. "Yup. When we get to the mill, I'll stay out of sight with Steel."

Titan nodded. Then the corners of his eyes crinkled. "You

know, I was expecting you to fight me on this. I figured you'd want to try and go in with us, that'd I'd have to lay out all the reasons why you should stay behind."

Rose scoffed. "I'm not an idiot. I don't have the muscle you guys do. And no way am I about to put myself into a potential damsel-in-distress situation because of some misplaced pride. My goal is, and always has been, to get my sister back. And the best chance for that is for me to not get in your way."

"You know, I could really get used to you bossing me around."

"I'm not bossing you around. I'm agreeing with you."

"But your hands are on your hips. So, you know, bossy."

Damn, did she want to kiss him. The sly smirk of his full lips just called to her, even through his witty banter with her or the stern orders he gave to his brothers. She was quickly melting under the bright light of his presence, and the stupid giddiness of the thought was doing its best to plaster a permanent smile on her face.

She had forgotten how good it felt to smile so often, or smile period.

"Hey, Rose! Got something for ya."

Titan cursed softly and rolled his eyes at the intrusion.

Bronze came jogging up to her with a knowing smile on his face and all the energy of an untrained puppy. But despite his exuberance, she admired how every single one of his weapons refused to jostle an inch out of place. It was a testament to his warrior nature and that, floppy hair and goofy grin aside, he was just as lethal as any other angel in the room.

"Here, a little pre-battle present."

He handed Rose a knife. No, knife was being generous. The thing's hilt was practically the same length as the blade itself, which barely reached past the tip of her middle finger anyway. The object in her hand was one solid piece of metal, except for a thin cutout in the middle spanning the length of the blade and a hole the size of a coaxial cable at the juncture of the blade and hilt. Rose took the offering and rolled it around in her hand. The bare knife was as no-frills as it got. The thing didn't even have a proper handle! But a quick poke of her finger at the double-beveled tip told her all she needed to know about the pointy end. This little thing could very much still do some damage.

"And what is this, exactly?" Rose asked.

Bronze shrugged. "Didn't want you to feel left out."

"So, you got me a baby knife? Without a real handle?"

"Hey, don't worry! There are five more where that came from."

"Ah. So the baby knife wouldn't feel left out as well?"

The bastard winked at her before trotting back over to the table.

"I asked him to get them for you." Titan took the knife from her and placed it into a holster where its five siblings were already settled. And then he dropped to his knees before her.

"What are you—"

Titan grabbed Rose's knee and crooked it over his shoulder. She was so stunned by the act, she nearly tore a chunk out of his arm as she grabbed it to steady herself. The position went way beyond intimate, even bordering on inappropriate. Hell, they were in a room with his brothers! If he thought this was the time to get frisky, the man had more rocks in his head than this damn underground cavern.

But before she could tell him off with the meager amount of bite she could muster, he grabbed the knife holster and brought it up to her thigh. All too late, she realized where he intended it to be fastened.

The holster hugged her thigh like a lover. Its sharp tightness and taut straps tugged at other parts of her, and oh, how she wished they had more time. More time to resume what they had started, more time to learn about each other. But as quickly as the thought entered her mind, an image of her sister potentially held captive in some abandoned textile mill replaced it.

She couldn't think of herself. Not until Tammy was home and safe.

Even if Titan's fingers lingered a little longer than strictly necessary once all the buckles were secure.

Loud, raucous whistles chorused behind Titan, but neither of them gave a fig about the intended distraction. Because their heated gazes were locked on each other like tractor beams. Bright, metallic, celestial tractor beams.

Titan slowly lowered her leg to the ground, but he never removed his hand from the outside of her thigh. Likewise, her hand never left his shoulder, even though her balance had returned.

"They're throwing knives. You shouldn't have to use them at all. But if you do, they're good for a fifty-yard target."

"You're . . . you're trusting me with these? What if I drop them or lose one?"

"I'd trust you with a whole lot more."

Rose stood there, speechless, as Titan gave one final squeeze of her thigh before he stood from the floor.

"All right, petal. Let's move out!"

"Did . . . did you just quote Optimus Prime to me?"

Her snarky angel winked at her. "I may never have thought of myself in ninja turtle terms before, but *everyone* knows about the Transformers. And Optimus was an amazing leader. Autobots? Decepticons? Pssh . . . c'mon. They're classics."

Rose stood there, mouth agape, as Titan turned and walked toward the door.

Yup. I could really get used to a man like this.

As far as abandoned textile and cotton mills went, Titan figured this one was pretty standard. The thing sported the expected four-story brick rowhouse-style structure, abutting the Ellis River. The bones of the building still had the original window frames, but the paned glass had been blown out long ago. To the far side of the building, settled on the north bank of the river, was a decrepit mill wheel. And decrepit was the nicest term Titan could come up with for the condition of the thing.

The mill had originally been built in the mid-1800s to manufacture cotton and wool. And, much in the way of all things human, the bright and shiny glitz of cheaper overseas manufacturing had caused ye olde mill to go bye-bye.

But that was something mortals seemed to forget about quite often. That just because the business changed, and advances to the process were made, they somehow thought they were absolved of all ties to the original infrastructure. One by one, abandoned buildings, which were once houses of immense power and opportunity, were left to clutter the earth like plastic in the ocean. Their only remaining value, more often than not, was the land on which they were built. And even then, location was king. If it wasn't center stage in a retail district or large enough for a new development, mortals would just let 'em go and walk away like they were a pair of out-of-style jeans that were too tight in the crotch and sat too low on the ass.

They never once considered what other manner of pest would take up residence in their abandoned garbage emporium.

Nor had Titan, for that matter. A problem he and his brothers were there to correct.

Titan and Rose, along with Bronze, Steel, and Chrome, sat huddled along the perimeter of the property, shaded amid a thicket of spruce trees. Thank the mages for evergreens, as leaf cover was their much-needed friend right then. Dusk was creeping in close. As soon as the sun went down, they'd lose the protection of daylight and the charmers would be out in full force.

"It doesn't look like much of anything. Do you really think she's in there?" Rose asked.

"We went through all the options. This is the only abandoned mill in this part of the state. And the charmers wouldn't be popping up in this territory unless they had a reason to be here." Titan gripped the back of her neck and massaged away the tension she always seemed to carry there. The act had become as natural as flying and something his hand did at the slightest hint of her unease.

Steel scoffed. "Oh, they're there, all right. I wouldn't risk scorching my hide over bad intel."

The strands of Rose's long hair fluttered against the inside of Titan's forearm as an abrupt strong breeze blew behind them. He and the others turned around.

Tung, Brass, and Iron lowered their bodies to the ground. The setting sunlight at their backs glinted off their fully metallic, winged forms. Rose cupped her hand over her brow like a visor and squinted at the angels. This was the first time she had seen the rest of his brothers in their metallic silhouettes, and she hadn't cowered in the slightest. That was no small feat, especially when it came to the sheer size of Iron and Chrome. All of them together, however, were a powerful force.

And he was made that much more powerful with Rose by his side. Was bringing her here a tad on the stupid side? Absolutely. But he'd never claimed to be strictly smart. Merely savvy and logical. Most of the time, at least. And he would make damn sure she stayed out of sight until the rescue mission was complete.

He'd incinerate the entire forest if it meant clearing a path to Rose's sister. To finally bring her home.

Tung's deep voice resonated through the small copse of trees they were sheltered under. "We've got another half hour or so until the sun goes down fully. Now's our opportunity. Steel was right. By all appearances, this mill looks completely discarded. But Chrome and I counted eighteen rooftop security cameras. All active."

Bronze folded his arms over his chest and scoffed. "Cameras? Really? That's what they're using?"

"I can't say I blame them. Why waste the energy on magic when mortal tech can get the job done, at least as a rudimentary first defense?" Chrome shrugged.

Bronze sneered at his brother, while Titan gave them a look to shut down the argument. Once they quieted down, Titan voiced the obvious immediate concern. "Can we disable them?"

Iron turned to Titan, and it wasn't lost on him that the brawny angel refused to make eye contact with Rose. "No need. Our way in isn't through any area in the cameras' ranges. It's through the water wheel."

"Wait, what?" Rose asked.

Iron tensed at the unexpected shrillness in her voice, clearly unused to explaining himself. "The wheel is in the river. There's no door there."

Even though Rose was staying behind, Titan appreciated her keen observation. Even without being on the reconnaissance flight, she knew why Iron's original suggestion sounded off. Pride swelled in his chest, and he tamped down his urge to hug her close and kiss her.

Iron cleared his throat before clarifying. "All the doors are under surveillance, as Chrome pointed out. But the mill isn't the only thing that's time-worn and damaged. Right behind it, where the iron gears feed into the side of the building, is a gaping hole in the brick. It's covered by the wheel and the size of the wheel's slats itself. Unless you know it's there, you ain't finding it. We have to go in single file, though, as the hole isn't that large." Iron's gaze bounced from each of the angels, even though he addressed Rose's question directly. Finally, his eyes landed on her. The brief nod of Iron's bearded chin was all the acknowledgment he gave her for the insightful question.

"Then let's go. Time's a-wastin'." Titan stepped away from Rose just enough to allow his full wing span to unfurl as his skin quickly shimmered from a heated rainbow into the bright sheen of his titanium. But just before his metal skin inched over his face, he leaned down and snatched a quick kiss from Rose. The little breath she sucked in joined the chorus of clanking and slicing metal around him as the rest of his brothers also changed form. Once everyone was settled, he smiled at Rose's awed expression.

Because as soon as he brought her sister back safe and sound, he couldn't wait to put that look on her face again.

The wall of acrid heat hit Brass and Titan first as they crawled through the dilapidated brick, closely followed by Bronze and the others. Of all the angels, their physiques were the leanest of the bunch, even though by mortal standards they resembled well-toned tight ends who still had to lean down to fit through most entryways. There was no movement or signs of life at all as they stepped quietly onto the worn stone floor. The smell, however, was pungent and raw, like the smell of a rotting corpse baking in the desert sun. Thankfully, their metal forms protected them from the elements, but they did jack squat against the stink.

"Oh man, that's awful," Brass remarked as he stepped through the hole with his metallic forearm braced against his nose.

Titan merely nodded as he stepped aside to let the rest of his brothers through. He reached around and grabbed his bow, an angel-fire-infused arrow at the ready as he scanned the abandoned space. Behind him, coughs and groans grew in intensity as, one by one, each of them was hit with the blazing stench.

"By the mages, that's fucking foul," Bronze coughed out. "How many dead rats do they have in here? And are they building a flaming shrine to the suckers? Because holy hell, it's hot!"

"Appearances would say this place is abandoned, but that's where appearances end. We're only on the lowest level. There are three more floors above," Tung said, looking around for an access point to the upper levels.

The floor was an expansive barren warehouse filled with old abandoned worktables, sewing stations, and looms. The great iron gears and shafts that had led them in there from the water wheel connected to giant vertical poles nearest the edge of the room. When the wheel turned, those poles would engage and turn as well, powering all manner of weaving and looming machinery connected to it. But this space hadn't seen any such action in a very long time, judging by the wetness weeping through moldy stones down the walls. Great big cakes of decaying rust coated everything, except the wooden chairs and table tops, which had become rotten and withered with an elemental decay of their own.

"Shit."

They all turned around and looked at Brass, who hardly ever cursed. He was frozen stock still.

"Ammonia." His glinting golden chest expanded as he sucked in a deep breath. The air came out of him on a rush as he looked around. "They're cooking up ammonia here. Heated magically somehow."

"I can smell the acid as well," Chrome added. "Also magically modified, the way those bombs that hit Steel were. I'm willing to bet the heat is coming from whatever they're brewing, along with the stench."

Now that Titan breathed in the air more completely, the enchanted chemical weaponry was as clear as day. And fuck it all that he hadn't figured it out sooner. Ammonia, while not corrosive to steel or iron when mixed with water, was highly corrosive to brass. On its own, however, it was bad news for all of them to varying degrees.

Titan cursed. The charmers were hatching up heavy artillery that the angels were very fucking vulnerable against. The risks had just skyrocketed in an unfavorable way.

They should turn back. Weapons of this magnitude were new and something they were not entirely prepared for. Not yet. Hell, if it hadn't been for Rose, he could have lost a brother.

Rose.

Just the thought of her, huddled at the edge of the property with freaking knives strapped to her thighs, on an endless hunt for a sister he should have never allowed to be abducted in the first place . . . it was all too much. Her pain was his. Her anguish was caused by his failure to the sacred mission the mages had entrusted to him.

And none of this circuitous thought process was helped by the unrelenting strength of the metal that coursed through him.

That strength manifested as stubbornness, arrogance at times, but always fueled his path to good.

A path that now led to the upper levels, where his feet began to take him.

"We go together. Weapons out. Be prepared for anything. Remember, we find Rose's sister, we get her, and we get out. This is a rescue mission, not a takedown. There will be time enough for that, I promise you." As Titan growled the words, eyebrows shot up around him, but no one voiced any concerns. The only sounds he heard were the slices of sharpened metal leaving their sheaths, the clicks of safeties disengaging, and the creaking tension of cocked triggers under steady and eager fingers.

The head of Titan's gleaming arrow shimmered with his fire as he aimed it in front of him. Soft clicks from his boots, metallic from the change, kissed the stone steps as he slowly advanced higher and higher. His titanium skin was a blessing, as the heat from the enhanced noxious fumes rippled over his metal form the farther he climbed. By the mages, it reeked. Had he been in his flesh state, his vision would have been clogged with relentless tears from burning. With each step higher he took, sounds grew louder. Clanking of bowls and glass. Whooshing whirls and sharp claps of dark magic. Titan's gaze slowly followed the tip of his arrow as he pointed it around the stone wall of the staircase, grateful as ever that the lighting inside the mill was so poor.

And what he saw nearly made his stomach bottom out.

He quickly threw up a hand behind him, signaling for his brothers to halt. Because about twenty feet from them stood a cluster of at least six charmers. Pale heads practically devoid of all pigment and snaked with shimmering tattoos of teal and gold were bowed over a table. The single gold bands around their throats, the only bands visible given their bulky outerwear, signified them as mystics. Magic users.

Beyond that single table were dozens more tables just like it, each with varying numbers of charmers at each station. Most were in their natural form, but a few walked around with mortal flesh-colored visages, magical disguises some used when interacting with the mortals. Through their perverse enchantments, the ghostly pallor of their skin—so translucent as to see nearly every vein—would turn to any human skin tone they wished. Their tattoos would disappear as well. The only features remaining that would still tie them to their true selves, for those who knew to look for them, were their lack of hair, unnaturally golden eyes, and the irremovable gold bands around their necks and arms.

Pops and cracks of blue lightning flared sporadically about the room as mystics opened portals freely for transport. The swirling circular lights of magic flared brightly as more and more elite charmers stepped through to join the mystics, accepting coats and jackets from the others once they were settled into the warehouse. There must have been at least a hundred of them, with more coming through the portal every few minutes.

"Oh, shit." The barest of whispered curses was all Titan could spare as he afforded a glance through the nearest sad excuse for a window. They had ten, maybe fifteen minutes tops before the sun fully set and these beasts would be able to move freely among the mortals. He tried to tamp down his rage, did his best to keep the fingers on his bowstring steady as he was slammed with the implications of all he was seeing. But by the mages, they couldn't let this infestation loose on the mortals. Now that they knew where the charmers' earthly nest was.

Titan's arm shook with the tension of his indecision. Until a larger cluster of charmers caught his eye.

In the center of the floor, where the greatest mass of them gathered, lay a large pod on a wooden table. The pod almost resembled the hyperbaric chamber Chrome used back at the den, except there was nothing inflatable about it. The tube had a metallic base, with the upper half consisting of a solid clear casing from end to end.

And it was fucking glowing.

He dropped his arrow and focused harder on the sight in front of him. But as he squinted and jockeyed his head from side to side, trying to improve his vision as the charmers kept walking through it, the movement of bodies around the chamber suddenly stopped.

The surrounding charmers, elite and mystics alike, parted as another figure, whose stature exceeded the others in the room by at least a foot, walked over to the chamber. The new charmer had the telltale look of all the rest of them, but he wore dark sweeping robes that hid everything else. The fabric was so eerie it practically moved on its own as it swept behind the charmer's wide gait like an inky trail of poisonous velvet.

Ominous pale hands poked free of the robe. The room fell silent as he spread his massive palms wide, lifted them high into the air, and laid them across the clear barrier of the chamber. Before the charmer's hands touched the chamber, however, the billowing sleeves of his robes fell loosely down the rigid stance of his arms, puddling at his shoulders. Arms bulged with strength and fought against the confines of his gold bands.

Three gold bands. The mark of an apex charmer. A warrior of the demon class that was the most lethal combination of combat and highly skilled magic.

The glowing muted gold light that had flared around the chamber rippled and writhed as the charmer's palms connected with it. His expression hadn't registered so much as a wince or even an intake of breath. Nothing. Just the rise of his broad chest as he slowly inhaled. The light mimicked the maneuver and receded away from the chamber's walls, gathering and seeping back into the palms that called it. The chamber remained, now only lit from the inside, much in the same way jewelry cases are constructed to illuminate the gems within. The internal glow was a muted brightness compared to the show Titan had just seen, but it was more than enough to see the chamber's contents.

Titan lowered his weapon and settled his forehead against the cool stone of the stairwell as he ducked his head down. Despite his honed strength and practiced tension, his muscles were moments from collapsing.

Because even though Titan had a limited viewing angle, he easily recognized the soft fall of chestnut hair and the gentle upturn of the inhabitant's pert nose.

He silently cursed a blue streak. Because Rose's sister lay imprisoned in that damn chamber.

A chamber that was currently being fondled over by the most lethal viper in the largest poisonous nest.

CHAPTER 20

Cold stone scraped against the metal at Titan's back as he retreated his post and slid down the stairwell to face his brothers. Deeply set brows and tightly thinned lips were plastered along all of their faces. But he had no time to address their impatience at that moment. Two of his fingers cut through the air as he waved them back in the direction they came. Understanding dawned on each of their expressions as they silently backtracked. Only when Titan's boots landed on the stone of the lower level did he relax the grip on his weapon. His fingers tingled at the release of the tension.

"The floor is flooded with charmers of all classes. At least a hundred. With half a dozen open portals shuttling more as we speak." Titan bit out the words. Eyes of every shade of metal shimmered at the news. Angel fire was high in everyone, which was great when they were gunning for a huge release of power. Not so great when they were up against a whole boatload of baddies yielding weapons both known and unknown.

"Wait. You said *all* classes?" Chrome whispered insistently. "As in—"

"Apex. At least one."

Bronze and Chrome both muttered curses as they rested their hands on their hips and shifted their weight on their feet. Hushed murmurs had settled over the barren floor. Brass walked up to Iron and clasped the giant on the shoulder before whispering something in his ear. The newly hardened and stern set to the giant angel's bearded chin was the only indication Titan had that Iron didn't like the newsflash. But as soon as the slightest inkling of hesitation appeared, it ghosted away and russet-brown angel fire flashed in his eyes before settling into the silver gray of his metal.

Titan sighed as he prepared to deliver the rest of the bad news. Time to put their other nut in a vice.

"I also saw Rose's sister, Tammy. It looks like she's being held in some chamber pod protected by magic. Magic that's controlled by the apex." Again, Titan looked toward the decrepit hole they had crawled through, where the water wheel was connected to the mill. The day's light was barely there now. Only muted cracks of pale glowing orange crested above the rim of the broken stone. They had precious few minutes before the sun would go down completely and the charmers could leave the confines of the mill.

They could leave. Any moment, the charmers could freaking leave! Leave and find Rose huddled in the forest. The sheer number of them alone would be too much for Steel to protect her from, even at his best.

The fierce hardness of his metal gnawed at him as if he were a stubborn bull in a matador's ring. A stubbornness that often-times clouded his better judgment and impacted his ability to lead his brothers. He knew what he wanted to do, what his metallic body thrummed with the need to do. But an all-out attack on a room of surprised and unknown enemies was fine for a suicide mission. Less fine when you had others to consider.

The firm weight of Tung's strong hand settled on Titan's

shoulder. Their prime's charcoal-gray eyes bore into Titan. And despite Titan's willful determination to wallow in his obstinance, he couldn't. Not when Tung reeked of righteousness and support. The prime angel's expression was all manner of encouragement, unwavering trust, and gentle guidance. There was no questioning tone, no shutting down of options because Titan had just led his brothers into the shittiest of shit shows. Just solemn and compassionate understanding that the cards were stacked against them, but even more so against Titan. And they would just have to manage that as best they could. Together.

"If it was one of us in that chamber instead of Tammy, do you think any of us would weigh the risks differently?" The nurturing tone of Tung's wisdom seeped into Titan's addled mind.

"No." The answer was firm and quick. "But Rose is not one of us, and neither is her sister. I can't insist—"

"Are you sure about that?" Tung's knowing glance and raised eyebrow were infuriatingly insightful. It was all Titan could do not to swallow his tongue in surprise.

"C'mon, Titan. Let's square-peg-round-hole this shit. I didn't get all dressed up in my Sunday finest just to have no one see me. Look, I even strapped on my favorite dirk." Bronze gestured toward his waist and patted the sheath of his weapon.

Brass looked at him wryly, though he couldn't entirely hide his smile. "It's Thursday, not Sunday."

Bronze shrugged. "Same difference."

"No. It's either the same or it's different."

"Enough," Tung barked as loudly as he dared and leered at the bickering angels before turning back to Titan. "Well? What's the plan?"

Titan opened his mouth to speak. But before the words could get out, a whooshing gust of air flew past his ear. The grunt at his back had him and his brothers whirling around toward the stairs.

A charmer stood at the bottom step, mouth agape like a fish. The familiar handle of Iron's mace dangled from the demon's neck. The blunt end sat firmly in the charmer's forehead, not so neatly embedded in his skull. Black blood seeped out of the depression and oozed around the bumps and ridges of the mace's bulbous end. Rivers of liquid kohl mingled with the gold and teal tattoos as the mystic's body crumpled to the stone floor.

Titan and the others whipped their gazes around to Iron, who was still standing there with his arm extended in front of him and his powerful legs braced apart. His stance resembled that of an Olympic shot-putter. His chest barely rose, however, as if the exertion required to throw his mace and hit his intended target was no more strenuous than putting one's socks on.

"Time's up." Iron walked toward the charmer, gripped the handle of his mace, and rocked it back and forth in the skull until it sprang free.

Time was definitely up. And Titan had all the votes of confidence he needed.

"Iron, you're with me. We make a straight shot down the center of the floor to the chamber. I have no idea what kind of magic that thing's tripped with, so we've got to fly it and Tammy out of there in one piece for now. Tung, give us cover. The rest of you three, have a fucking field day. Consider it open season. But the goal is to get in and out with Tammy. Understood?"

Knowing smirks and flashes of angel fire coated the room in crackling energy.

Titan turned, palmed his weapon, and stepped over the charmer as he funneled his brothers up the stairs, no longer caring about their silence or stealth.

All he cared about was getting Rose's sister out of there. And maybe taking down an apex in the process.

***

Titan burst through the stairwell with the speed of a search-and-destroy missile. The moment he cleared the confines of the stairs, his wings whipped out behind them. Great sheets of aerodynamic titanium took him above the reach of every charmer in the room. The slack-jawed stances and frantic scrambling of his enemies were so delicious, he sorely regretted that he couldn't stay and play longer.

But then the bullet brigade behind him swung into action. Shouts and screeches rang out all through the mill as Chrome, Steel, and Brass rained hell down on the scattered ants around the room. Glass and tables clattered to the ground as enchanted words in the demonic language floated up to Titan's ears.

Magic casting.

Titan turned to Iron and Tung, who had joined him in the air. "I'm going to stun the apex. We can't get close to the chamber with him hovering," Titan roared as he loosed an arrow into the chest of an elite near the chamber.

"When the apex is down, I'll blow out the window. Then we grab and go," Tung shouted.

They all nodded in agreement as Tung gripped a silver baseball grenade in one hand and his chrome-plated, tungsten-infused 9mm in the other. When Titan turned back to Iron, the angel had already begun clearing a path to the chamber. The giant flew low to the floor and, with his massive arms spread out on either side of him, clotheslined every charmer that came in contact with his ax and mace. The tactic was brutal, yet highly effective.

"You're too late, you know."

The unknown origin of the words, spoken in an icy hiss,

flustered Titan and nearly broke his concentration as he let loose another arrow at a mystic muttering a spell under the table supporting Rose's sister. As bullets and blades laced with angel fire found their marks, the room quickly filled with the smokeless scent of charred flesh and boiling blood. Bodies writhed under Titan's feet as he rolled his shoulders back and grabbed another arrow from his quiver. The table with Tammy was largely empty now. Most of the demons had fled to other parts of the mill or jumped through the few remaining open portals, the mystics especially. But one remained.

And apparently, the nasty motherfucker liked to talk some good game.

The apex reached behind his neck, grabbed fistfuls of his robes, and yanked them over his head. Three gleaming gold bands sat snuggly around his neck and biceps, culminating with solid gold cuffs at his wrists. Eyes of saturated, glinting yellow swirled with magic as the apex's tattoos, moving rivers of teal and gold against a wall of muscled translucence, rippled like snakes slithering over desert rocks. The markings ended against the belted waistband of black tailored slacks that hugged powerful, braced legs.

"You'll never save this one. Cyro made sure of it." The remarks were delivered with a menacing sneer as golden and teal flames bloomed up from the apex's tattoos and engulfed the charmer in crackling electrified magic. "And I'll make sure you don't even try."

Titan read the maneuver and cursed. As soon as the muscles in the apex's arms gave way to the barest hint of bunching and straining, Titan yelled to his brothers, "Get down!"

Before the last word left his lips, he dropped and flattened himself against the black blood-soaked stone. With his cheek to the floor, he watched as the others did the same. At least the ones he could see in front of him. He exhaled a brief sigh of relief at the sound of metal thuds on his opposite side, what he presumed were the other angels hitting the deck. But dammit, had they all heard him? He couldn't tell for sure.

A deafening clap shook the building. As pulsing teal and gold light shot through the mill, hunks of stone crumbled from the wall, though not enough to allow in the final wisps of daylight. Electrified tendrils fanned out in a great lashing arc at waist height, decimating anything it touched that was not of the dark realm. Had it not been for their metallic forms, the heat of the caustic fire would have singed them all from the proximity overhead, never mind the instant cauterization that would have befallen them had the blast been a direct hit.

Titan winced against the lingering heat as he struggled to raise his head. The apex still stood on the opposite side of the table, arms bunched and hands clasped in front of him. If they stayed down too long, the charmers would regroup. Since the demons were unaffected by the dark magic, they were no doubt doing so already.

Titan squinted at the chamber. At Tammy. For as close as she was, she may as well have been a million miles away. She was close enough for Titan to make out the rise of her cheek through the barrier and how much like Rose's it was. Yet too damn far to reach. Too far to protect from all the darkness that had befallen her and Rose's family.

Rose.

The simple stamp of her name in his mind reinvigorated his grit. Rose, his petal, was hunkered down in the woods outside this putrid den of disgrace while he promised he'd bring her sister back. The sister he'd failed to protect and whose life and light he was ultimately responsible for.

That realization was all the ignition he needed.

A great roar thundered through Titan's gritted teeth as his angel fire consumed his metal form. Blue flames of celestial power thrummed over his body as he shot into the air, wings spread and scorching.

"Now!" The bellowed war cry left his throat as he angled his body parallel to the floor and fucking flew. As he launched himself across the room, flaming fists were punched out in front of him in a classic Superman pose.

The impact of the titanium missile of his body against the apex's bare chest sent the charmer flying into the opposing wall. As the impact reverberated down his spine, Titan roared through clenched teeth. The apex's residual electrified magic still swirled around the behemoth's pale body and latched onto Titan where it connected. Titan's eyes flew open in pain, but his hands never left the stunned charmer beneath him. Instead, grunted pants of agony left his throat as he moved his hands from the center of the magic user's chest to the bald shell of his head and slammed that thing down against the stone once . . . twice . . . a third time . . .

An explosion off to Titan's left threw him off balance, causing him to fall even more into the hold of the apex's magic. A deafening cry erupted through him as flames licked and engulfed his form. But then light, barely glowing and desperately seeping through the stone in a trickle, settled over him and the charmer.

Daylight.

Raging cries rang in Titan's ears. They were no longer his own, however, but belonged to the apex beneath Titan. The charmer was covering his face and thrashing around in the sun's muted glow.

Titan's gaze shot to the wall, which sported a sizable hole in its more-than-a-century-old shell. Beside it stood Tung, leg propped up on a pile of rubble and his chest sucking wind like he needed recycled carbon dioxide from a paper lunch bag. Titan's hazy vision finally slid into place as Tung jumped down and ran toward him.

"Grenades are highly effective at relocating stone, my brother, but less effective at relocating this chamber. C'mon, we need to move now. The daylight is almost gone. We don't have much time. Minutes at best." Tung waited for Titan's angel fire to recede before he put his hands under the angel's arm and got him to his feet.

Iron was already at the chamber, assessing the best way to transport it and completely ignoring the writhing bodies of charmers who were doing their best to scramble away from the sun's meager rays. Loud pops and sharp slices quickly followed as Chrome, Brass, and Bronze knocked off as many of the sitting ducks as they could.

"You each take an end and get her airborne. Once she's up, I'll fly under her and keep the thing steady," Iron said.

Titan forced his legs to get with the program and jogged over to Tammy's head, with Tung at her feet. The chamber was beyond clumsy to grip, let alone fly with, but their choices were sort of shit at the moment. He spared only the barest of seconds to glance down at Tammy before they got her up in the air. By the mages, she hadn't aged a day. Her hair, her clothes, her complexion . . . It all looked like a time capsule from six months ago.

Images are deceiving. She's been imprisoned by demon magic. Don't think for a second things are all hunky-dory inside the shiny shell.

As they awkwardly lifted the capsule out of the mill, with his brothers flying behind them, he should have been relieved. The mission had been a success, and he could return Rose's sister to her as promised.

But as Steel joined their flock, with Rose clinging to the angel's neck and worry etched on her face as she looked at the chamber, Titan wasn't sure what he was returning to her.

Or whether any of them were prepared for what the chamber really held.

CHAPTER 21

If Rose ever wondered whether it was possible to feel more helpless than she had the past six months, she'd just gotten her answer. Turns out, yes, it was completely possible to feel as useless as a Band-Aid on a severed limb. Especially when seven hulking metallic angels were standing around her preserved long-lost sister with more blood oozing out of them than in them.

The hard circular rim of the stool bit into her butt as the angels all mulled around the den in various states of healing (or was it seeping?). Rose sat next to Tammy's head with her arm draped over the top of the chamber. She peered through the transparent barrier for the third time in ten seconds and tried to dissect all that had happened.

The whole battle had taken no more than fifteen minutes, not even long enough for her butt to fall asleep on the log she'd occupied in the woods, but hell, had it seemed like a lifetime. One moment, she had her hand over her eyes like a visor as she squinted at the glinting light reflecting off the angels flying toward the mill. The next, a huge explosion rocked the scraggly stone structure and out popped a coffin-like capsule held in suspension by said angels. Who, putting it mildly, looked like shit. Once they all made it home and their metal forms receded, all manner of acid burns and corrosive pitting marred their formerly smooth flesh. And no amount of aloe vera was going to make a dent in that type of healing.

And then there was Tammy. The long fall of her sister's voluminous chestnut hair lay cushioned against the floor of the chamber. Unlike Rose's hair, Tammy's locks still retained the vitality and color of health, despite her long imprisonment. The warm lushness of her sister's complexion still radiated off her full cheeks and the softly angled slope of her nose and chin. There were no hollow planes or sunken bags to speak of. Even her clothes sported the crisp seams and lint-free trademarks of her prior profession at the marketing agency. The light blue button-down blouse, black slacks, and leopard-print ballet flats Tammy had donned six months ago were still as work ready as Tammy looked.

Except for the whole unconscious thing.

Still, she was alive. Miraculously, Titan had kept his word and brought Tammy back to her. Every time Tammy's chest rose and fell with steady respirations, Rose's breathing did the same. And though they hadn't yet managed to open the chamber to assess things with all certainty, the healthy glow to her twin's complexion proved adequate oxygenation and blood flow.

And since that news was more than she'd had to go on all these months, she would take that as the biggest freaking win.

Heavy footsteps scraped along the stone in front of her. Chrome shuffled up to the chamber, his gait much slower and less confident than she was used to seeing. And, boy, did he look like he'd been squeezed through a meat grinder. Angry red blisters bloomed over the angel's right eyebrow and forehead, stopping just short of his closely cropped hairline. Singed skin along his forearms was stretched so taut, a quick flex of muscle looked like that would be all it would take to sever the fragile protective epidermis wide open. All along his legs, chest, and back were holes in his clothing. Denim, leather, and cotton had been melted to his skin in patches, while in other spots, burn marks left wide gaping holes that exposed blistering flesh. All injuries sustained from acid bombs, ammonia, and other corrosive materials to his metal. The same injuries that the others were tending to, though none nearly as bad as what Steel had endured earlier. Rose had been assured they'd be fine. And since she had no basis to protest their claims and was far too emotionally exhausted to argue, she let the statement lie.

"How do we get her out? Can we use your angel fire to get through the chamber's barrier somehow?" Rose winced at the desperation in her voice, but she was all out of pride at the moment. More like bordering on hesitant joy at having her sister back, but shame at feeling relief when the breathtakingly powerful men around her were so battered. And all for her, a woman they'd known less than a day.

"Not tonight. Out of juice," Chrome rasped before clearing his throat in what Rose suspected was an unnecessary attempt to regain more of the natural gruffness to his voice.

"Juice?"

He nodded. "We need to recharge."

"Oh, the hyperbaric chamber again, like you did for Steel?"

"Nah. Not this time." He gripped the back of his neck as he bent over to inspect the seams of the chamber, squinting and grazing his fingers along the seal. He shook his head and grimaced before straightening again. "Little downside to being a fallen angel relegated to the mortal realm? Our angel fire doesn't last beyond a day if we don't recharge our bodies each night. Our metals, our fire, they're all connected to the elements of the earth somehow. Part of the mages' gift, we think. So, each night, by resting within the earth, by living and breathing in the sediments and stones around us, we restore the flames of our angel fire. It's why our den is largely underground and built near the mountains. Whole lot of metallic bits and pieces tucked into these nooks and crannies, let me tell you."

"So you just rest and recharge each night? And that's enough to heal you? To restore your fire?"

Chrome's head bobbed heavily on a nod. The weight of the day and the toll of his injuries were clearly dragging him down.

"When we fell, our chemistry changed and took on the traits of the metals in the stone around us. As best as we can guess, each night, the earth's elemental energy—which our new makeups share, kind of like a symbiotic osmosis of energy and elements—calls to our forms and refuels our bodies and our fire. Think of it as a celestial battery, with enough energy stores to last the day. The more fire we call on each day, the more we need to recharge each night." He shrugged a great meaty shoulder, as if the explanation was so basic, so nonchalant that even a preschooler would accept the reasoning without question.

"Look, there's nothing we went through here that can't be healed with some R and R." He turned to Rose and softened his expression as he rested one hand on top of Tammy's chamber. "As far as I can tell, your sister's safe in there. Tomorrow morning, when I'm up to full speed, I'll work on cracking this puppy open and getting your girl back to you. But in there, in whatever magical stasis the bastards put her in, she's at least alive and physically safe. That's got to be enough of a comfort for tonight."

Rose didn't miss his emphasis on the word *physically*. It was the great elephant in the room. Because anyone with two eyes in their head could see Tammy was *physically* in pristine condition. Her chip-and-growth-free nails still had the same manicure from six months ago and happily sported the latest spring colors of the time.

It was all the stuff underneath the pretty package that weighed the room down and gave voice to nightmares Rose wasn't sure she could process yet. She'd heard stories of prisoners of war, hijack victims, and children abducted by cults. The emotional and mental devastation was oftentimes far worse than the physical. And Rose had no freaking clue what kind of sick magical torture the charmers were capable of, especially if Tammy supposedly held some spark they'd been on a manhunt for since she shuttered to think how long.

Still, she was grateful. No, not grateful. Ecstatic. Elated. Voluminously joyful to the point of shaking. Because at least she had her sister back. There would be no next step, no cause to worry about the unknown, without Tammy physically by her side.

As pungent fumes began wafting through the room, Rose wrinkled her nose. She glanced around Chrome at the other angels squeezing oils onto cloths and spraying aerosols into rags. The freaking men practically had chunks hanging off them, yet they were gearing up for some fall cleaning?

Chrome caught her eye and turned his head to follow her gaze. "Ah, yeah. Weapons maintenance. Various gun and knife oils. The shit smells like some sick combination of gasoline and bananas, but it keeps our gear in tip-top shape. Gotta clean it right away, though, or you'll never get the blood out."

Rose squinted against the stench and covered her nose and mouth with her forearm. "I bet," she mumbled. She turned to face the kitchen—to be blissfully upwind from the chemical warfare—and froze.

Titan's strong profile filled her vision. His haggard expression sat mournfully on his features as he leaned against his fists planted firmly on the kitchen counter. The familiar pale green of his Henley had been cut away after being badly burned, along with his khakis. He'd managed to throw on a pair of black athletic pants, which sat low on his hips, but that was all. His eyes were pinched at the corners, and she realized that surprisingly she'd been so overwhelmed with her sister's return, she hadn't sought him out yet. Though, to be fair, neither had he sought her out.

He had no burn marks, no corrosive pitting or charred patches along his skin, despite his clothing being nearly seared off. From what Tung had described of the rescue, Titan's angel fire had protected him against his attack with the apex, though they weren't entirely sure how. All of his injuries were superficial, when they otherwise shouldn't be.

It didn't matter. None of it mattered. Because this man, her angel, had fought a freaking demon and brought her missing sister back to her. There wasn't a bucket big enough to fit every ounce of gratitude and admiration she had for him.

The barest prickle at the back of her mind whispered of something more as well, but she shooed it away like one would a housefly.

"Excuse me," Rose whispered absently, and her feet carried her in leaping sprints across the room. Titan barely lifted his head in time before she launched herself at him.

He didn't even have time to suck in a breath before her mouth was on his.

CHAPTER 22

The warm woodsy scent of scorched earth and campfires filled Rose's senses as she wrapped her legs around Titan's waist, clinging to him like some kind of wanton barnacle. Yet, as she moved her lips against his, relishing the soft prickles of his beard, his essence had changed slightly. His scent was sweeter, like burnt marshmallows mixed with oils from freshly trodden pine needles. It was new and intoxicating and exactly what she wanted from the man she utterly needed.

The iron bars of his arms bracketed her instantly, finding their home in the dip of her waist. Warmth radiated from his bare skin like a furnace and wrapped her in a soothing balm of comfort and relief.

And something else she wasn't quite sure she could name.

Rose broke away from the kiss and held Titan's head between her trembling hands. His stunned expression only added to the vibrating energy skittering over her skin and through her bloodstream.

"Thank you." She let her head drop to his forehead with a heavy weight. His warm hand settled against the back of her head, clutching her impossibly closer to him. Her eyes fell closed. "I just . . . Fuck, Titan. Thank you sounds so paltry. So woefully inadequate. It's what you say to a waiter for bringing you your food order or what you weakly mumble to the stranger in the coffee shop for complimenting your dress. Those two tiny words can't begin to cover the gratitude I have for you. For getting my sister back. For just . . . everything."

They were moving now. As he held her, Titan's hips brushed along the underside of Rose's thighs with each stride he took. She had no interest in opening her eyes, though. Didn't need to.

There was only one place she wanted to be, one place where they could be alone. Where she *needed* to be alone. With him.

Once the door to Titan's suite clicked open and closed shut behind them, Rose opened her eyelids and looked up. Espresso brown irises set in weary eyes stared back at her as he let her feet fall to the floor.

"You don't have to say a word, petal." But the smile that spread across his face was pained and offered a half-truth kiddie sparkler to Rose's explosive declaration of honesty. "But who knows how long Tammy's been in that thing, what they've done to her, or if they've found a way to—"

"Shhh." Rose's hands never left the sides of his face. She used her thumbs to massage away the tension in his brow. "For right now, for tonight, I'm choosing to hang my hat on the positive. She's here, thanks to you. Chrome believes she's physically alive and well. I have to trust that." Rose paused, and her fingers curled around the hard muscles of Titan's shoulders. She watched as her fingernails, which had been chewed and gnawed down to the quick over the months, traced every contour of his form. Once her hands had mapped each valley thoroughly, they moved on to the thick column of his throat.

Even though they were her hands, fingers she controlled with her brain, they moved on a magnetic path she didn't intend. She just hung there in Titan's solid grasp and allowed her brain to shut down as her fingers literally did the walking.

The relief at not forcing herself to think, to make one more damn decision, was practically cosmic. Tonight, she'd give herself over to her body's need for language and give her exhausted mind the rest it deserved.

Her fingers began their journey near his shoulders, where the stern ridges of his collarbones jutted out like protective battlements over a fortress of stone. Her light touches fluttered softly up to the hollow at the base of his neck. They lingered there with a soft dip, the barest of caressing kisses, as they inched higher. As he exhaled with a shudder, Rose's lashes fluttered briefly under Titan's warm breath. But still, he didn't move beyond the simple act of letting her feet settle to the floor. She glanced down and took in the white knuckles on his fists balled at the dip of her waist. The image was striking. And sexy as hell.

Because this man was giving himself to her. Allowing her to trust that, whatever was to happen, it would be on her terms. No more unknowns, unless she wanted it. The thrill of the choice, of the enormous trust, was so potently powerful, she nearly combusted from the heat of it all.

Rose bit her bottom lip as her fingers crept higher. She reversed her hands so the backs of her short nails scored against the stubble blooming on the delicate skin of his neck. He sucked in a breath. Hungry eyes latched onto her mouth. Titan sealed his lips as his throat bobbed under her touch. A flick of her gaze down revealed the thickness behind his soft athletic pants. Pride mixed with her arousal and feminine strength heated her flushed cheeks. She brought her stare slowly higher, relishing in her newfound seduction. Titan's dark nipples pebbled, and goose bumps under trimmed chest hair rose in response to her dainty ministrations farther north. The large pads of his pectorals expanded, seemingly pumping with power as Titan leaned down slightly and took larger inhales of her breaths and scent.

Her fingers were in his beard now. Titan growled lowly in his throat as he stepped closer and glided the backs of his rough hands up the length of her thighs. Rose switched her hands' positioning again and, curling her fingers around his chin, burrowed her trim nails deep into his beard. His groans vibrated through the thin skin at his throat and shot directly through her body until they reached her deepest core and settled in the V of her legs.

They were both panting. Hot breaths swirled from open mouths with dry lips as they worked in tandem to consume each other's essences, their very life forces.

But it wasn't enough.

Rose extended the fingers of one hand to Titan's parted mouth, brazenly curled them into the inviting warm wet pocket, and pulled gently. As soon as his bearded lips were parted to her liking, she attacked his mouth with her own. Hungry, consuming pulls and greedy sweeps of her tongue claimed him. The maneuver was so unlike her, so foreign to the woman others knew her as.

To the woman she knew herself to be.

But was it, though? Over these months, she had grown into a fiery ball of opposition, despite her demure appearance. She'd given the stiff middle finger to every law enforcement agency, family member, and coworker who had told her to give up. And still, despite a veritable mountain of you-shall-not-pass that was placed in front of her at every turn, time and time again, she'd grown a bigger set of lady balls and got to trekking.

No, she wasn't a different woman. Merely a stronger one. And it was the fiercely empowering man in her arms who was making her see that.

A low rumble erupted into her mouth as large, solid hands palmed the backs of her thighs and lifted her off the floor again. Even though her eyes were closed, the sensation of spinning gave her all the directional information she needed. The cushioned mattress met her back in a whoosh as Titan settled his weight against her. He was large but lithe, and to have all of him on top of her, protected in the embrace of her eager arms, was a balm to her beaten-down soul.

Titan broke away from her mouth. Rose moaned and pouted her kiss-swollen lips at the loss until the scorching softness and languid heat of his mouth and tongue coasted up the side of her sensitive neck. When he reached the delicate flesh of her earlobe, he nuzzled behind it and laved delicious attention on a hidden treasure trove of sensation. Her toes curled under, and her hips bucked against the rigid length of his arousal behind his pants. An arousal so noticeably warm that it matched the rising heat of need spreading throughout her body.

Rose gently pushed at Titan's shoulders. His massive body resisted at first, his moan of disapproval getting caught in the crook behind her ear. But when she pushed again, a little more firmly this time, her upper body rose as well. Titan was forced to relinquish command of the helm. He huffed a brief breath of annoyance before softening under Rose's insistent touch as she pushed his wide shoulders back into the mattress, her coy smile hidden under the fall of her hair.

With Titan sprawled out beneath her, bare from the waist up and his muscular form flushed with passion, she straddled his hips. Holy hell, the man was a vision. A celestial entity who had descended from heaven and could command one of the strongest metals on the planet. And here he was, open and vulnerable beneath her. Completely at her mercy. With nothing but passion, pride, and hunger staring back at her.

"Titan, everything you've done, everything you are—"

"Is yours."

Rose's brow wrinkled in confusion. "What?"

Titan took her hands and settled them over his bare chest. The intensity in his eyes glowed silver as his gaze bore into her own. "Everything I am, everything I've come to be or will ever be, is yours, petal. Even if I had never touched you, even if I had never learned of you or your sister or any connection to the eternal flame, I would have been yours. Never in my agonizingly long existence has another soul tethered me so solidly to itself. I have saved countless souls, hunted the charmers in unfathomable numbers. But none of it has affected me as deeply as you have. None of it has altered my core so profoundly as you have. And damn . . . it has never felt so good to be so shaken as when your hands are on me."

Rose's lungs had been robbed of all breath. Every last puff had escaped and fled the room, along with any words that may have been circulating in Rose's mind.

Never had anyone spoken to her like that. Believed in her like that. Trusted her in such a soul-shattering way. Not since Tammy. But even still, her sister's love and their twin connection were unique, sure, but oh so different. This? Whatever this was with Titan? It flew far past family bonds and shot straight into the orbit of life-altering circumstances.

There were no words. They all seemed insufficient and colorless. To even attempt to reciprocate them in simple language was an exercise in futility.

No, she would have to show him.

Rose wriggled her trembling hands free of their warm cocoon against Titan's chest. She reversed their holds, grabbed his hands, and brought them to her lips. There, she imparted all her emotion, gratitude, and overwhelming adoration for this man into a chaste kiss against his rough skin. Then she pulled away but never let go of his hands.

Instead, she guided them to the hem of her shirt. A slight tug upward was all the nudging he needed before, ever the good student, he took over, stripping her of her T-shirt. As soon as the cool air of the cavernous suite kissed her bare skin, her craving for heat—*his* heat—flushed through her as if a dam had broken. She rocked her hips against his as she wriggled out of his still-borrowed sweatpants. Socks, bra, undies, everything. All of it was ripped away and tossed onto the floor in a frantically impatient dance.

Rose tucked her fingers under the waistband of Titan's pants and wrenched them off his legs. Titan's cock bobbed free of its confines and stood erect against her belly button. She sucked in a quick breath as the fiery heat of the smooth head slid against her sweat-slick skin. Rose glanced up at Titan and gripped his member firmly in her pale hand. She was so much smaller than him. Yet, as her lithe fingers offered the gentlest of squeezes from base to tip, she pulled a rasping sigh from the great and powerful angel at her mercy.

"Fuck, petal. Your touch, your heat. I could die right here. That's it, I'm done. Pure fucking heaven." Every short phrase came out in a strained pant as his head fell back against the mattress.

"Don't do that. I'm not done with you yet," she teased as she stroked him once, twice, and again before scooching her hips forward.

"Oh, you have me. All of me. Don't ever forget that."

As each word that came out of him was more pinched than the last, she smiled and offered up a silent thank-you to Tammy for encouraging her to get an IUD. With her knees firmly planted on either side of his hips, she rose up, centered his weeping head at her core, and slowly consumed him. Her thighs shook as she settled her full weight on top of him. Once Rose was seated, she and Titan groaned in unison, a dual exhale of ecstasy that she chased as he placed his wide hands on her hips, gently guiding and softly urging her to move.

But she hardly needed any urging. The heat was everywhere. It flared vibrantly deep in her core, burned hot against the strain of her legs, and bubbled up along every nerve ending. Cool air kissed her bare breasts as they swayed with the rhythm she set. If she didn't move, she would die. She was sure of it.

Smolder into a ball of fading embers like abandoned coals at a community campsite grill. But she needed to burn. Chase the spark inside her until every molecule in her body ignited in a fireball of universe-beginning proportions.

Rose moved harder, faster, and jockeyed against Titan so frantically that she had to fall forward and brace herself against the tense muscles of his lower abdomen. Heat from his skin bloomed beneath her palms as he gripped her hips so firmly she expected to see his fingerprints branded on her. But when she lifted her head and tossed damp hair out of her face, her breath nearly died in her throat.

The telltale incandescent rainbow shimmered briefly in his eyes before they settled into the startling silver of his metal. The swirling spark within Rose burned hotter as fluid titanium rippled down and over every muscled plane and hulking curve of Titan's body. It cascaded over him in a scorching wave and didn't stop until every inch of him was coated in the protective armor. But in spite of the change, he didn't relent. The transformation only urged him harder. His eyes pinched closed as he gritted out pants through clenched teeth, pumping his cock into her from beneath. Once his celestial metal reached its pinnacle, extending to his cock buried in her body, a pulsing white light erupted from within them.

Rose cried out. Her orgasm shattered through her. Her body trembled with delicious wave after wave of ecstasy as Titan roared his release. Heat, light, and metal surrounded Rose. She gasped from a power she couldn't comprehend, but damn sure wanted to. Beneath and inside her, warm smooth metal rubbed against her. She fought to gain her bearings against Titan's altered body.

Yet, like a tidal wave, the intensity receded as soon as it appeared, though all who were caught in its grip were definitely worse for wear. Titan snatched Rose to his chest in a bear hug as his metal retreated. She whimpered softly into the crook of his neck. He slid out of her and repositioned them so she was tucked into his side with her arm draped over his chest. The light was gone, the heat—no, the *inferno*—had faded. As far as Rose could tell, there were no singed sheets. No flaming holes in the mattress.

Just a whole lot of sucking oxygen.

Titan peppered moist kisses across her sweaty forehead.

"What . . . what was that? I've never experienced anything like that before." Rose struggled to get the words out. Exhaustion—the flip side to amazing sex—came creeping in like sharks to blood in the water.

But Titan didn't respond. She was expecting him to make a flippant joke about his stamina or something, but there was nothing. Just eerie silence. And didn't that make her feel about as comfortable as sitting on the pointy end of a bee's butt.

Rose willed enough energy into her muscles to at least get upright. When they blessedly complied, she rested her weight on her elbow and looked at Titan. His head was flat against the pillow, and his expression was stern. Almost worried. His eye color had returned to that rich chocolate tone she adored, except she adored it a whole lot less when said eyes were roaming back and forth incoherently, as if he were doing an internal assessment of something.

"Hey. Are you okay?" Rose placed a palm on his chest and rubbed soft soothing circles to get his attention.

His eyes flipped to hers. And then those full lips she loved so much turned up into the biggest, brightest smile she'd ever seen. He practically glowed at her as he sat up and gripped her shoulders.

"I have my fire back. I can feel it. Every bit of my full angel fire is back." He shook his head in disbelief. "It's not humming with stored energy like it usually does. There's no sense of loss or urge to recharge like I normally feel. No, this is different.

This is . . . normal. Right. Holy shit, Rose! My fire is back! Just like it was when I was in the Empyrean!"

Rose laughed a wide smile back at him and basked in his exuberant joy. Jeez, he was like a kid who had just been told he was having ice cream for dinner instead of tuna noodle surprise.

"This is you. This is all you, Rose." He grabbed her and roamed his hungry mouth over her still-smiling lips. She playfully tried to push him away, and he only relented at the pinch she gave his ribs that caused him to yelp.

"Wait a minute. Just hold your horses there. Are you telling me you think I'm so good in the sack that all it takes is one lay and I can literally restore you to your former glory? Do you have any idea what kind of power that could give a woman?"

"I already told you. You've got all the power over me already. The sex is just a bonus." That damn gorgeous man winked at her and it was all she could do to resist leaning forward and biting his lower lip in retaliation.

Those freaking winks would be the death of her.

Rose opened her mouth to quip out a response, but her words were cut off by a yawn to end all yawns. She barely had time to do the polite frantically-cover-her-mouth thing before Titan got an eyeful of the back of her throat. Before her gaping jaw had time to rehinge, the bed dipped and the soft weight of the down comforter settled over her skin.

"Easy, petal. You can yell at me all you'd like tomorrow. For now, you need to rest. And so do I, frankly." Rose was about to argue, and even had a mind to remind him about *his* apparent burst of newfound energy, but when he settled her against the firm cushion of his bicep, the fight went out of her like helium in a balloon. Besides, he was more than right. Gosh, when was the last time he had even slept?

She snuggled closer against his side, even going so far as to hook a leg around his toned thigh. She was rewarded with a light chuckle and the soft caress of his lips on her forehead.

"Don't worry. I'm not going anywhere. Everything I need is right here," he teased.

"Flatterer," she mumbled and gave herself over to the most contented sleep of her life.

"Always."

CHAPTER 23

The metal doors in the den definitely had pluses and minuses. Plus side? Ain't no sound getting through. Titan didn't have to worry about anyone hearing Rose's delicious cries he had greedily coaxed out of her or the deafening roar he had tried to suppress as his full angel fire flooded through every part of him. Like, *every* part of him. That was a shock to the system as well.

The best shock of his life.

Downside, though? Creaking metal, especially the reinforced heavy shit Iron had built the den's doors with, was really fucking loud. And given the size and weight of the metal entrance to his living quarters, it'd take a football field's worth of WD-40 to grease the squeak out of it.

Titan heaved his shoulder against the rough metallic grain of the door. He'd never had to pussyfoot around his own pad before, so the action was foreign. Especially when he had the most beautiful of all sleeping beauties in his bed and a tray in his arms laden with every possible breakfast food he could whip up.

He didn't even bother to fight back his smile as memories of the night before came flooding back to him. Of her anything-but-delicate hips filling his hands as she rode his cock with unrelenting determination. Of her gorgeously perfect tits bouncing inches from his mouth with each thrust he gave her. Of his whole freaking body, cock included, transforming to solid titanium underneath her touch and inside her as they erupted together.

Fucking paradise.

Titan quickly shuttled the tray over to the dresser, his haste tamping down his prior need to be silent, and leaned his hips forward against the hard side of the furniture. He groaned in frustration as the pressure against his already aroused cock did jack shit to satisfy his craving.

Thoughts of appetites had him turning to Rose, who still—miraculously, given the noise he was making—slept in his bed.

His fucking bed!

He had never ever had a woman in his bed—here, at his cabin, or any of the other myriad dwellings he stayed at from time to time. Of course, he had hardly been the good angel mortal lore would like to believe. He and his brothers had needs like any other being, and as long as they kept things temporary and one-off, no one was the wiser.

So to see Rose's mahogany locks wrapping around *his* pillow, her long bare legs tangled around *his* sheets . . . he'd never wanted to be a bedspread so badly in his life. Seriously, he'd be more than content for the mages to stuff him full of cotton and make him as wide as he was tall if it meant he could cocoon every glorious inch of the woman warming his mattress.

He stepped over to the bed and slowly settled his weight against the edge, just enough so his ass had sufficient meat under it that he wouldn't slide off and sink to the floor. Still, Rose didn't stir. If it wasn't for the steady rise and fall of her pale shoulder and the lightest of light snores floating out of her parted lips, he might be worried.

Titan inhaled everything into his lungs. Despite her adorable name, Rose's fragrance was anything but floral and was about as no-nonsense as she was. Without the barriers of clothing, he was finally able to indulge in the subtle notes of the earth that clung to her. Like the slight bite of the sea's breeze mellowed by a damp forest rain. Nothing fake or fruity there, absolutely as real and honest as the woman who wore them.

A slight twitch caught the corner of his eye.

Rose's bare foot poked out from beneath the comforter. Her delicate toes inched toward him just a tad, as if they were seeking him out, though a glance pillow-ward at their still-sleeping owner confirmed the movement was involuntary.

Involuntary or unconscious attraction? Could her body sense my nearness before her mind?

The thought burrowed its way into his chest and warmed him from the inside out. He didn't even bother to hide his grin . . . or the way his lips settled into a newfound position of comfort, an action he hadn't done a whole lot of in his long existence.

Until Rose.

Titan reached for Rose's blindly searching foot without another thought and settled it within his palms. Between the span of two breaths, Titan's hands warmed with the pure energy of his angel fire. His *full* angel fire. Hell, he still couldn't believe it and couldn't even come close to explaining it. But his connection to the woman in his bed brought back a part of him he hadn't even realized he'd missed so dearly. For the first time since he'd been in the mortal plane, his fire didn't need to be recharged. There was no regeneration needed, no elemental energy being harnessed from the rock and metals around him. His strongest offensive weapon didn't need to rely on the most basic of defensive maneuvers.

He had finally—*finally!*—been able to rest. Solely and completely rest. All because of this woman.

The slightly chilled skin of Rose's exposed toes warmed instantly under his encompassing touch. With both palms and fingers working in tandem, he wrapped her foot snuggly and radiated his fire's muted heat into her as he deftly massaged her foot. Titan pulled on each toe gently and firmly pressed the pads of his thumbs into the ball of her foot. Still, she barely moved. Though the slight hitch of her breath was definitely the progress he was hoping for. It wasn't until he slid his thumb through the center of her arch, leaving a trail of tickling tingling heat, that she finally jerked her foot out of his hold.

Aaaand I just found a new favorite way to wake up in the morning: playing footsie with Sleeping Beauty.

"You know you're giving a whole new meaning to the phrase 'magic fingers,' right?"

Hell, even her morning voice was sexy.

"Morning, petal." Titan's hand settled against the rise of her hip as she tucked her foot back under the covers—ouch—and snuggled back into his bed.

"I'm not quite ready to wake up yet."

"Oh, no? That foot massage wasn't doing it for you?"

"Well, that depends. Was it a one-off thing? Do I have to schedule another appointment? Is the quick-dry gel included? I mean, you obviously no longer need the hot stones— *Uf!*"

The navy-blue comforter crumpled to the floor as Titan exposed every perfect inch of Rose's nude body beneath him. He surged over her and caged her huddled frame within the protection of his taller one. Once she was completely blanketed by him and him alone, he breathed deeply and radiated the low warmth of his angel fire into Rose's chilled skin. Her initial resistant gasps and shrieks quickly melted away as he brushed his lips over hers.

Nope, he was wrong. So completely wrong.

This was his new favorite way to wake up in the morning.

With lighthearted teasing, Rose's warm curves filling his hands, and her intoxicating flavor on his tongue.

"Petal, if it's heat you want, I've got it in spades."

"Oh, I have no doubt of that." Rose smiled widely as she squirmed and repositioned her hips beneath his. "Nope. No complaints here."

Her head fell back against the pillow as he trailed a line of kisses down the side of her neck until he settled on the ridge of her collarbone. His hands had already been busy at work elsewhere, caressing the underside of her arms and smoothing them out at her sides toward the edges of the bed. More soft murmurs coasted through her lips as he let his tongue slide over the soft delicate skin of her bicep, only pausing to tease her further.

"Well, that's very good to hear. Wouldn't want to do anything to offend."

"You're . . . talking . . . a lot," Rose panted out as she anchored her shoulders into the mattress and used the leverage to press her breasts against his chest. And wouldn't you know? The maneuver worked just fine. The rigid tips of her nipples caught against the cotton of his shirt and slowly dragged against the fibers. It was abrasive and distracting on all accounts. But as much as he wanted to strip off his clothes and answer every one of her tempting squirms and thrusts, he would see her fed first and properly reunited with her sister.

But by the mages, she tested him, though. Put his honor up in front of a jury of very hardened and very willing peers and waited for it to choose the warm and wet low-hanging fruit.

He'd never intended any sort of morning activities beyond breakfast and a rehashing of recent events, despite his cock wanting otherwise. He'd walked into his suite with a clear and present game plan: to see her fed, see to her well-being, and support her when she visited with her sister.

Apparently, he also chose to spell dumbass as T-I-T-A-N.

With a groan, he sat back up, but he still couldn't bring himself to remove his palms from her wrists. He couldn't help it. The cad in him rather liked the look of her all sprawled out before him, even if acting on the vision was a giant no-go. He could not, *would not* take advantage of Rose's sexy-as-sin body while her sister lay unconscious rooms away, suspended in whatever dark magic the charmers had infected her with.

"I brought you breakfast."

At the mention of food, Rose looked over to the dresser where he'd placed the tray. As if on cue, her stomach chose that moment to voice its protest of any activity other than taking in calories. At the intrusion of her body's grumbling, Rose scrunched up her nose and turned her head.

"Ugh, sorry about that. Human bodies can be so gross."

He chuckled at both the noise and her reaction. Because, frankly, he hadn't found anything about the noise off-putting. On the contrary, it was rather endearing. A physical sign of her need that he could easily interpret and fulfill without a second thought.

The caring act hit him on an instinctual level. To care for Rose, specifically, had become as innate as blinking. To his surprise, he hadn't even balked at the fact. Or that her stomach's gurgling was oddly pleasant to him. Even sexy.

And who in the actual hell found stomach noises sexy?

He did, apparently. There wasn't a single thing about her he didn't find sexy. From her acts of service and selflessness to her intelligence and awe-inspiring bravery.

"Human bodies are human." He shrugged his shoulder and smiled. "And most bodily functions aren't exactly species specific. Hell, you should hear some of the noises that come out of Chrome after taco night. Like, whoa." He shook his head in a mock shiver.

"Aaand we're done here. I don't really want to be thinking about him or any other man while I'm naked under you and talking about bodily functions." She squirmed against his hold slightly, silently voicing her intent to get up, but he didn't relent. Not just yet. Titan quickly dropped his head down and stole one more passionate kiss before freeing her right wrist.

Damn, he couldn't get enough of her.

"Believe me, petal, I don't want you talking about anyone but me when you're naked. Or ever, for that matter." The predatory growl that vibrated through him surprised even himself.

Crap. Had she heard that? And where the hell did that come from?

"Deal," she said with a final peck on the tip of his nose. "Now feed me, you big goober. I'd hate for the food you made to get cold."

"If it's cold, I'll make you more."

"Oh, please. I live my life on cold food." She waved her hand dismissively before she had a chance to self-edit her words and remove the implications of her statement. Ignoring the fact that she'd neglected her own needs for so long, even forgoing something as simple as a hot meal.

Never again.

Rose made to get up, but Titan tensed his body over hers to draw her attention. Once her questioning eyes found his, a resigned understanding saddened her gaze. He refused to let her tear her eyes away from him.

"You will never want for a good meal, a warm and safe bed, or even so much as a fucking tissue ever again. Do you hear me, Rose? You fell into hell because of me and have given more light and love of yourself than anyone has a right to. Yet you do it selflessly and tirelessly." Titan cupped the side of her cheek and poised his thumb into position to catch the single tear that— despite her pushed-out bottom lip and defiantly raised chin— welled up in the corner of her eye. He'd catch and cradle every single tear that Rose would cry and make damn sure she'd never shed any again. "You deserve so much more than the shit end of the deal you've been dealt. And by the mages, nothing would make my heart soar as high as ensuring you'll never have to fight that hard again. Because I'm here, with more grit and gun oil than anyone has a right to have, and I'm throwing it all in your corner, petal."

Warmth pressed into the pads of his thumbs. His left hand was coated in a steady stream of hot tears as he swiped at each drop running down Rose's cheek. His right thumb, however, was dry as a bone and still cradling her wrist against the bed . . . far away from any source of sudden warmth.

Curious, Titan removed his thumb from Rose's pulse point on her wrist, looked down at her arm, and gasped.

The pale skin covering her delicate veins was flushed red. The spot was no bigger than a quarter. But against her warm flesh, however, was a pattern of gold swooping marks that were nearly undetectable unless caught in the light.

His breath froze in his lungs as he leaned closer to inspect the marking.

"What? What is it?" Rose sat up, regardless of his weight against hers. He sank back onto his knees next to her as he cradled her wrist close to his face. "Oh my gosh . . . is that a tattoo?"

He couldn't move. Couldn't breathe.

Because the markings staring back at him were as familiar as his own mind.

They weren't just markings but symbols. A single symbol, one he hadn't seen since before the fall.

"*Malthoran* . . ." The word left his mouth on the barest of whispers, almost hesitantly, as if he wasn't sure his tongue remembered how to pronounce it.

Rose looked up at him with brows scrunched into a deep questioning peak. "What? What is that? And how come it's not coming off?" She frantically rubbed her palm over the symbol as one would wipe off a coating of crumbs or powdered sugar, but it had no effect on the tattoo.

"That's my name. My Empyrean name, written in the symbolic language of the celestial mages." He traced his fingers over the swoops and dips of the symbol in reverence before settling her worried hands against the bed and shaking his head in disbelief. "A name I haven't spoken or seen written since my time in the Empyrean."

"And what the hell is it doing on my wrist?" Alarm replaced all the flirtatious timbres in her voice.

He couldn't answer her. Couldn't even begin to form a thought on the subject. Because, not for the first time since Rose had come into his life, he was low on intel and just as baffled about his world as she was.

Screw the French press. He'd have to pull out Chrome's fancy specialty espresso machine for this one.

Because he was going to need high-test caffeine by the bucket. Pronto.

CHAPTER 24

Not even the mellow herbaceous steam of the peppermint tea Titan plunked down in front of Rose could calm her frazzled nerves. Oh sure, her skin still hummed with the reverberatory effects of her angel's touch and the glorious press of his heat against her body as he slowly teased and tickled her sleeping form back to consciousness—

Wait. My angel? No, he isn't my angel.

But then her worried eyes fell on the small gold symbol etched delicately on her wrist. A wrist that lay shakily in Tung's hand as he carefully examined it under the light of a desk lamp. The slight heat from the spot had stopped burning some time ago, but that was hardly enough of a consolation to convince her ping-ponging mind to chill the heck out.

Rose wrapped her free hand tightly around the ceramic mug. As soon as her fingertips made contact, heat from a different source settled over her other shoulder. Titan's comforting hold gripped her protectively around the cap of her arm and gently urged her to lean against him.

Like she would ever argue.

Tung's golden head, which ironically looked as if it possessed a halo under the lamp's incandescent light, rose from his examination of Rose's wrist. Once her arm was freed, she quickly brought it back into the shelter of her body, where she cradled and caressed her appendage like a mother would a newborn baby.

Which was utterly ridiculous. It was a tattoo. Albeit, apparently a celestial tattoo that carried the name of her lover, which had coincidentally popped up the very morning after the most amazing night of sex and intimacy she'd ever had.

Like, ever, ever.

But as her body settled in snuggly to Titan's, her eyes intent on Tung's perusal of her wrist, she tried to dissect her emotions. Fear and worry were certainly there, of course. Plenty of that crap to go around. Yet, surprisingly, they weren't all-consuming. Wonder, trepidation, excitement, guilt, confusion, and something far weightier than adoration and compassion all swirled around in her gut. If she was forced to put things on a scale and see where the proverbial chips stacked up . . .

Well, she wasn't quite willing to bet on anything just yet.

Tung rocked back on his hind chair legs as he took in questioning eyes. "I . . ." Tung's thought petered out as he pressed his lips together and shook his head in disbelief. "I never thought this could be possible."

"That *what* could be possible?" Titan asked, reining in the edge to his voice, despite his obvious urgent worry. She had to hand it to him, because she was about a million miles away from being able to display any kind of cool outward demeanor. And especially not to any sort of commanding leader like Tungsten. The realization of yet another one of Titan's awe-inspiring qualities lifted her esteem of him higher. If that was even possible.

"The mark of your name on another. It's something I've seen

before, among some of the mages." His words cut off again as his charcoal-gray eyes volleyed between Titan and Rose. "Among their soul bonds."

Titan's breath caught in his chest. His heartbeat tapped out a rapid pulse beneath her ear as she leaned against him.

"What's a soul bond?" Rose asked when a cat had apparently caught the tongue of the two suddenly silent angels in the room.

Tung shook his head. Then a quick laugh escaped him, followed by a beamingly radiant smile. At her side, Titan inched back away from her slightly and dragged a hand down his mouth and beard. She sat up fully.

Tung's deep, gentle voice broke through her piqued worry. "It's the connection of the eternal flame's light in two individuals. It's incredibly rare. I hadn't thought it was possible for us, and especially not for a mortal, to bear the mark. I've seen the soul bond occur only among a very small handful of mages. But, I suppose, the logic stands regardless of commonality. Titan's angel fire and the eternal flame's spark in you, Rose, must both fit the bill."

"Wait. Just wait a second." Rose flew her hands up and leaned her head down. "But why is this symbol on my skin? This . . . you said this is your name?" She turned to Titan.

Titan's hand fell from his face, and with it went the exuberant sparkle in his teasing eyes and the vibrant flush under his tanned skin. The man looked wan and had all the telltale enthusiasm of a new father watching his wife give birth to their first child . . . and growing queasy at all the blood and guts that came with it.

Shit, that isn't a good look.

"Hey, it's okay." Despite her own damn confusion, Rose couldn't bear seeing Titan in such a compromised state. A state that was clearly about as alien to him as, well, metallic angels had been to her just a few short days ago. She cupped the sides of his face and gently rubbed her thumbs down over his lightly furred cheeks. She'd learned, surprisingly, that it was somewhat of a weakness of his. A soothing comfort that she'd picked up on when he'd settled his head on her chest the night before, after they were both still sweaty and flushed from their lovemaking and the gesture had coaxed him into a deep, rumbling sleep.

There was no time, however, to examine why knowing that trick made her stomach turn cartwheels. While she cooed and fussed over the angel in her arms, a resonating laugh floated up behind her and she half turned to face it.

"The names you know us by were of our own choosing once we fell from the Empyrean. Our celestial names"—Tung nodded slightly toward her wrist—"have been away from our vernacular for some time. But to find your soul's bond in another, to have the eternal flame's light call out among both of you. Well . . ." Tung smiled widely at the thought and stood from the table. "It is a gift. A true gift."

"A gift? A gift of what? I still don't understand." Rose shook her head in confusion as Tung rounded the table to stand next to Titan, whose breathing had leveled out but who had still never taken his eyes from hers.

"Mate." Titan croaked the word out through slightly trembling lips. "I believe mortals may refer to the anomaly as a soul mate."

Rose whipped her head around to face him. Come again?

Because she sure as hell knew that phrase. It was as fantastical in its existence as it was in its meaning. A concept relegated to fairy tales and romance novels. A perverted notion that, by the sole function of it being spouted, somehow magically tethered two people to each other under the guise of some predetermined fate.

Rose placed as much stock in soul mates as she did cheap pink women's razors that guaranteed a nicked-free smooth finish.

Suffice it to say, not a lot.

Tung's meaty hand dropped down onto Titan's shoulder. "I believe you have your answer as to why your full angel fire has returned." Tung glanced between her and Titan. Despite her shock, Rose didn't miss the downturned glance of the prime sentinel's eyes or the slight tightness in his lips before they spread, seemingly forced, into that easygoing grin from moments before. "Treat her well, brother." After a slight pump of Titan's shoulder, Tung took his hand back and left them alone.

Soul bond.

The words rattled around in Titan's skull like bullet shells bouncing on the ground after a rapid-fire discharge.

How could this be?

Surely, there was some other explanation. Some other reason for all the changes. Changes he had no damn business wishing for in all the years of his agonizingly long existence. Why him? It wasn't as if he and his brothers had nullified the charmer threat. Those fuckers were still out there, still amassing power and wreaking havoc on any source of light they could. Sparks of the eternal flame had only just been found in Rose and—they suspected—her sister, and he was sure to put a big fat *allegedly* at the beginning of that sentence. As far as he knew, he and his brothers were still locked out of the Empyrean. Of their home.

But he could not ignore what was right in front of him.

He turned his head, which was still cradled between Rose's palms, slightly to the left and stared down at his name on her slender wrist.

Malthoran.

Rose stroked her thumbs over his beard as he quietly examined his name tattooed on her skin. And fuck, did he like it. That and the soft petting of her thumbs as they pressed soothing, massaging touches down his face. Touches that, all through Tung dropping this Titanic-sized bombshell, she had never stopped doing. He slowly moved his face from side to side, leaning into her soft strokes, nestling into the feel of her like one snuggles into their favorite pillow. He allowed his eyes to close for a mere second of private stolen bliss before his lids shuttered open to meet the confused pools of Rose's sage eyes staring back at him.

He took her hands from the sides of his face and held them in his lap. "My name, my celestial name, is Malthoran. Our language is one of symbols. A logographic language, you'd probably call it here." He absently stroked his thumb over his name on her wrist, as if he were drawing courage from the mere connection to it, to her. "If you had any doubt before of just how freaking special you are, Rose—of how special you are to *me*—this should surely put it to rest. Not because of me or my name specifically, but because there is an amazingly strong and powerful spark in you. A spark that—"

"Is connected to yours." Her words cut off his rambling at the knees.

"Yeah." He swallowed down the heavy truth of the circumstances. "But it doesn't mean anything. I mean, it does, but it doesn't have to. This isn't your world. You never asked to be dragged into our mess. And I've done an utterly shittastic job of fucking up your life." Titan's pulse thundered in his ears as his brain spun out on shaky ground. There was no way Rose could stay in his life. Not after he was responsible for her sister's abduction. Not after his actions had all but put a giant target on her back.

He gritted his teeth as he glanced over to Tammy, who still lay unconscious in the chamber on the other side of the room. It was early in the morning still, and after the beating they'd all taken—again, because of his insistence on finding Rose's sister —Chrome and the others hadn't yet risen to investigate Tammy's state.

"I don't have any answers for you. Only promises. A promise that this won't change anything." He gripped the sides of her face, all but trapping her wavy tendrils against her nape. By the mages, she was a vision. His petal. His soul bond, whose misty-green eyes and slim winged brows pleaded with him to . . . what? Save her sister? Return both women to a life and time without angels and demons breathing down their door, even though they all knew that was no longer possible?

Titan swallowed audibly and threw his shoulders back. A shaky breath slowly sputtered out of him as he steeled himself in the same manner he would were he issuing tactical mission procedures to his brothers.

And then he sliced his heart open in front of her. Because despite all the fear and logic smacking him upside the head, he couldn't ignore the deeper pain that lanced through him at the thought of not breathing in her heady scent every day.

"I want you, Rose. Not for the gifts you've returned to me and damn sure not because my name magically appeared on your wrist. Not because fate says your mine or because my fire recognizes yours."

He dropped his hands to the sides of her biceps and inched closer to her. "I want you because of your stalwart devotion and loyalty to family. Loyalty that's so fierce, it sings in harmony with my own. I want you because yours is the first face I see when I think of compassion and light and all I have been fighting for these long years. I want to care for you, feed you, and take every one of your burdens into my own body so your stunning beauty and soul would never be marred with the weight of exhaustion again. I want you because I can't think of a damn thing I'd rather do each morning than slide into your body and capture every single cry for my own."

Titan grabbed Rose as the weight of his words left him. He brushed his lips gently to her temple before lowering his mouth to the shell of her ear. Heat rushed out of him with each predatory pant he tried to keep in check. "And I've wanted all of these things since the moment I had you alone in my cabin . . . and you were more interested in interrupting a mama black bear's mealtime than eating more of my spaghetti."

A light laugh made Rose's shoulders bounce.

A laugh was good. He'd take a laugh. Better than a punch or a cry. Still, though, not the response he was expecting. Titan pulled back to face her and lifted one questioning eyebrow.

Rose's lashes blinked fiercely for a moment, as if she were shooing away something she didn't wish him to see. Then her eyes settled on his, and one corner of her lush mouth rose in a tenuous smile.

"It was the salt." Her words were tense with emotion, but he heard them clear enough. But still, they made little sense.

"Salt?"

Rose nodded and shrugged as if her statement was a foregone conclusion he was too dense to realize.

And no way in hell would he acknowledge just how accurate that supposition was at the moment.

"Yeah. Your marinara sauce was too salty. Almost inedible, really. I figured I'd have better luck with the bears. At least they'd have access to more variety, what with the mama having no doubt picky-eater bear cubs and all."

Joking. She was joking with him. He'd just flayed his insides open for her examination, and she was flinging jokes.

By the mages, his woman was infuriating. And the most adorable challenge he'd ever encountered.

But he could volley as well, if that was what she wished.

"Is that why you had two bowls of it? And apologies, but I

hadn't exactly planned on hosting guests. Hence the jarred stuff. In the future, I will, of course, endeavor to have the appropriate San Marzano tomatoes on hand. And sea salt only. Or perhaps the pink Himalayan stuff. I'll freaking carve it out of the salt mine myself if you want."

"Good. Because I'll be expecting the good stuff. In the future." She nodded her emphasis on the last sentence, and Titan's breath caught in his throat.

Future. She definitely said "future."

Before his head could fully spin out into analysis paralysis, Rose's hands were on his face again. Her thumbs smoothed down the crisp hairs of his beard in her calming, reassuring way. Her soft lips brushed gentle caresses back and forth over his stammering lips.

"Yes, Titan. I said future." Once her caresses had ensured the resuscitation of his normal breathing pattern, she delivered one peck on his lips and sat back. Her face was beaming all kinds of happiness he was sure he had no right to be thrown his way, but he could hardly give a fuck.

"I want those things, too. Now, don't get me wrong, I'm still not sure how I feel about all that soul bond stuff. It's more than a little overwhelming. But," she hedged, lifting a shoulder, "I'm a different person around you. Less bitter, less sad. I've been on my own for so long, with my only focus on getting my sister back. And even though I know you feel responsible about the circumstances that brought us all together, I don't hold it against you. In fact, you brought her back to me. When everyone in my life had given up the fight, I stumbled onto you. You, who had, like me, never given up searching for her. For a woman you didn't even know but who still needed help." She paused to take a deep breath before continuing. "And that's loyalty I can get behind. That's the kind of selflessness you don't find every day, and I'd be a complete fool to turn my back on it out of fear."

Titan chuckled. "I've never known you to be afraid of anything, petal. Simply refer to my previous example of said bears."

She smiled and nodded. "You're damn right, and I'm not afraid of you or further exploring what this connection is between us. And if I'm being completely honest, I've always wanted a tattoo." Rose bit her bottom lip coyly as she stared at him under hooded lashes.

"Oh yeah?" And holy hell, why did the thought of it make his abs and cock jump a little?

"I mean, I never thought it'd be an angel's name in a mystical symbolic language I had never heard of before, but I did have an idea for one."

"And what was this idea?"

"A truck."

Titan sat up straighter and cocked his head to the side. "A truck?"

"Mm-hmm. Something like a semi-truck with a six-cylinder diesel engine. Red and blue paint, of course."

"You mean . . ."

Rose nodded smugly. "I think I kind of have a thing for Optimus Prime. He is one of the greatest leaders of all time, after all. Level-headed, logical, confident, trustworthy . . . all things my favorite angel has in common. Oh, and sexy. We absolutely can't forget sexy."

Titan couldn't help himself. The laugh that erupted out of him was so loud and boisterous, he didn't give a rat's ass who he woke up. Because Rose was in his arms and wasn't going anywhere anytime soon.

"Hey, can you keep it down? Some of us haven't gotten our caffeine in yet." Bronze's raspy voice was barely heard over the clanging of ceramic mugs and the faucet's running water. The lumbering angel clamored about the kitchen still half asleep.

But it was all just background noise to Titan, like chirping birds or water sluicing through pipes.

Titan captured Rose's smiling mouth as the angel behind them grumbled around the kitchen, muttering something about shitty timing and no consideration for roommates.

CHAPTER 25

Metal clanged against the stone floor as Chrome threw down another useless tool in frustration. The iron crowbar this time. The sad piece of metal bounced slightly at his feet before he went back to rummaging in the bin at his side.

"There's got to be something in here that could pry this puppy open." The comments were muttered more to himself than Rose or Titan, who both stood over Tammy's chamber. They had been at it all morning. At first, Chrome had used his angel fire on the capsule. But there wasn't so much as a crack in the plexiglass. Then more of them tried. Chalk it up to a post-breakfast team-building exercise. Chrome, Titan, Steel, and Tung stood at four points around the chamber and put as much of their fire into the thing as they dared to.

Zilch.

Even Titan on his own, who was the only one of them back to full strength, couldn't bust through whatever magical barrier was floating around inside that thing. And Rose couldn't do anything but watch as her angel strained and pushed himself to near exhaustion.

Finally, after two hours of good angel fire wasted, she

chimed in and suggested more traditional tools of the trade. As in, items used for good, old-fashioned breaking and entering.

Still nothing. Which was so infuriating! The chamber was just another hyperbaric oxygen chamber similar to the one they were used to, though a bit beefier and more highfalutin than the one the angels had. It wasn't anything otherworldly or celestial. It had screws, metal feet, and even freaking creaky casters and wheels just like any modern-day piece of medical equipment. But none of it mattered. The angels even tried to use their metallurgic talents to loosen first—and then melt—the screws, smash the glass, incinerate the seals. Anything to gain entry and get Tammy out.

But still, they came away with a whole lot of nada.

Rose shuffled from one foot to the other. Her hands worried an utterly useless screwdriver. She tried to find comfort in the grooves. Closed her eyes and tried to focus on the side of her thumb stroking up and down the smooth, slim valley of the fiberglass handle. But the exercise was about as comforting as sitting on a pile of pine cones.

"I'm trying again. Rose, you up for trying with me this time?" Titan clinked his glass down on the table behind them and cupped her elbow as he drew her in close. Soft notes of fermented apples from his brandy mingled with the assertive peppermint from Chrome's chewing gum. And boy, did the two of those things not jive. But Rose had quickly realized that stress manifested in different ways for these two men. For Chrome, he went hard and heavy on the Ice Breakers, even though she suspected he probably preferred his cigars to drug store gum but was choosing sides for her sake. Angels couldn't die from second-hand carcinogens, after all, but she and Tammy were different stories. Titan, on the other hand, had turned to his favorite apple brandy, even though it was barely lunchtime and he was on his third glass of the stuff.

Figures angels would have a stellar metabolism.

"Sure. Not certain it'll work, but I trust you. What have we got to lose?" Her affirmation was more resigned than eager beaver. Because this light inside her had very little to do with her control or wishes and everything to do with some sporadic energy within her reading the room and playing favorites, apparently. It worked for Steel, but it hadn't worked for Tammy.

Yet, she told herself.

Titan dropped his head low to her ear. "She's safe in there, petal. At least physically. Chrome's sure of it. But we *will* get her out. We just haven't found the right key yet. Every lock has one, though. It's just a matter of finding it." His whispered words of encouragement mingled with his reassuring touch at her elbow. The combination was like a warm blanket in winter. Despite the uncertainty and worry laid out before her, she allowed herself to settle into his strength. To try this newfound partnership on for size. And boy, did it feel good not to have to go this alone. Around Titan, her worry was lighter in its harshness, as if the weight she was carrying had two handles instead of one. She on one side, and him on the other. Still heavy, still cumbersome, but far more manageable.

Her throat tightened with emotion. Rather than risking shaky words, which would no doubt lead to more worried glances from the peanut gallery, she simply cleared her throat and took her place at Tammy's head. And just as she had done with Steel, she placed her spread palms on the clear barrier to the left and right of her sister's face. Titan took his place at the foot of the chamber and assumed a similar stance.

"All right, you two. Have at it. While you work your magic, I'll examine the seams again. Check for weaknesses or fissures. That's got to be where we can gain access." Chrome squatted down and positioned himself at eye level with the seams that connected the top portion of the chamber to the bottom.

Rose exhaled a shaky breath as she stared at Titan. Then her breath hitched. His stern gaze bored into her. Downcast brows.

Clenched jaw. Eyes of liquid silver that signaled his fire simmering below the surface. Fierce determination practically radiated off him in menacing waves. His biceps bunched under the tight caps of his T-shirt. The veins in his forearms distended as he prepared to expel a power not of this world. Not at her. Never at her. But *for* her.

Rose's feelings for this man had long passed fluttery butterflies and shy smiles. When he looked at her—*really* looked at her, like she was the sun in his solar system and he lived and died by her light—he stole more than her breath. He stole every vibrant, vital part of her and claimed it as his own. Under his protection. Under his care.

And in his heart as well? Because she was most definitely trending in that direction. Bad.

She closed her eyes and gave herself over to the increasingly familiar thrum of warmth that blossomed in her chest. A warmth that signified her connection to the eternal flame's spark within her—which had definitely increased in its coolness factor, despite her confusion about its intentions. The sensation crept throughout her body, swimming through her bloodstream and racing along every nerve and electrical impulse. When the heat crested, Rose opened her eyes and moaned as white light leaped off her body, traveled all along the perimeter of the chamber, and immediately crashed into the electric blue of Titan's fire. There was no sparking, no explosion of incompatible elements. Just a coming together of like energies as bolts and beams danced around them, encasing the chamber in a loving embrace of dual power.

Rose gasped slightly at the profoundness of it and willed everything she had into the connection. Chrome's dark head bobbed around her as he scooted along the perimeter of the chamber. Titan never looked down. Never soaked in the awesome glory of their intermingling lights. Never checked to make sure Chrome didn't miss something. No. Those breathtaking silver eyes, which intermittently flashed that incandescent rainbow she loved so much, stayed glued to hers the entire time, commanding her to do the same.

Like she could look away from him if she wanted to. Because this angel had captured pieces of her she hadn't known were scattered and broken and lovingly stitched them back together. As if she were a patchwork quilt, made better by the sum of its parts that were carefully handled and arranged by a man who wanted to see her whole.

"All right, kill it," Chrome yelled, more to get their attention than to be heard over any sort of noise.

Rose lifted her hands from the chamber. Her light receded instantly, but it was some time before she could tear her gaze away from Titan. Damn, she had it bad for this man.

And is that so terrible?

Chrome's boisterous voice jarred her out of her thoughts. She quickly glanced down at Tammy and sighed regrettably when her sister's appearance and the chamber remained exactly the same.

Chrome settled into a chair near the chamber. The old wood groaned under the angel's massively built body, but it stood strong, as if the thing knew that failing the angel by not supporting him in his time of need and frustration was a fate worse than being fed to the wood chipper.

Talk about your A for effort.

"I saw cracks." Chrome held up his hands to silence them just as Rose's chin dropped and Titan jumped from his seat. "Not physical cracks in the structure of the chamber. Ain't no busting through that thing at this point."

"Then what cracks are you talking about?" Titan barked before raising a few fingers dismissively in an apparent brotherly form of an apology.

Chrome nodded his quiet all-good-brother before elaborating. "Cracks in the magic, as if it's arcing toward something it needs, but it's not there. I think the problem might be that there's magic inside that thing that's allowing Tammy to sit pretty, but nothing on the other side to balance it out."

Titan mused over Chrome's words for a moment. "When I first saw the chamber, it was glowing. Then that apex touched it and seemed to call the magic back into himself. Right after that was when we attacked and I jumped him."

"Bingo and Bob's your uncle!" Chrome pointed to Titan. "I need that chamber in a complete state of homeostasis. Then I can open up the sucker."

"I'm sorry. Can you go back a bit? High school biology and I were not exactly tight. Homeostasis is an equilibrium thing, right?" Rose asked.

"Essentially. Think of it as a state of steady living conditions all around. You see, I'm willing to bet that the chamber is run by magic inside and out. The magic on the inside of that thing is still working just fine, leaving Tammy all comfy cozy. But outside, there's nothing. No counterforce to keep it in balance with itself and work the way it's supposed to. To be in homeostasis, both environments need to be blended and work in harmony." Chrome brought out the hand gestures at this point and held up his right palm and then his left as if he were balancing scales. "Outside magic plus inside magic equals a whole lot of wakey wakey."

"Fuck," Titan growled out. Tense hands flew to his hips as he turned away from them.

"My thoughts exactly. That apex you pole-axed? I'm willing to bet my new wood-fired pizza oven that we need his magic. He's your ticket to opening this thing."

Rose swallowed down her anxiety as she eyed her sister, lying there all coiffed and primped like she always was when she went to work, looking for all the world like some moronic princess waiting for her prince to come and kiss her.

But in Rose's upside-down world, Tammy's prince was a vile

demon. And the kiss was the very magic that had ripped Tammy out of Rose's life for six excruciatingly long months.

"No. Absolutely not. There's no way. No way!" Rose shrugged and threw her hands in the air like it was a foregone conclusion before turning her back and walking over to Titan's bed. But even once she plopped down on his mattress, the fight hadn't left her.

Any other time, Titan would have laughed, stalked toward her, and taken her delicious motormouth against his own to swallow down her protests. But not now. No, after Chrome's little bombshell revelation, his mood had soured into all shades of piss yellow.

"You can rail on me all you want, petal, but if going after that apex is the only way to save your sister, no amount of denials coming through that pretty mouth of yours is going to change my mind. I'm going."

Rose threw her hands up in exasperation and looked toward the ceiling. "Why are men so fucking pigheaded?"

"One," he held his finger up to her, "I'm not a man, technically, so try again. And two, why are you poo pooing this? For the first time in twenty-four hours, we've got a solid lead. I'd call that progress."

Rose's finger delicately tapped out an impatient rhythm against her chin. "Oh, gee, let me think. Because I don't want anyone else getting hurt over me and my family!"

Titan was nearly blown back by the rage emanating out of her. A bright flush crept up Rose's cheeks as her chest heaved in exertion. But the blush wasn't the good kind, the kind he'd learned to coax up and over her sweet skin as he trailed his lips around every dip and bend of her body. No, this was the furious kind that caused his tongue to lodge in his throat and his feet to stick to the floor.

Like a five-year-old being scolded by its mother for eating too many cookies before dinner. Talk about a takedown.

"I refuse—absolutely *refuse*, Titan—to have a single person's soul and life lessened in any way in order for mine to be raised up. Period. End of story. Tung and Chrome both told me about those things, about that apex or whatever. I saw how you all barely got out of that charmer den and how chewed up you were. I literally saw pieces hanging off Chrome. You think I want to see that again? On you? You think I could live with myself for even a single minute if—"

Titan flew across the room and dropped to his knees at her feet. His kneecaps cracked at the impact, but he was too focused on the woman falling apart in front of him to care. "Hey, stop it. Just stop that. And listen." He grabbed her thighs and squeezed them for emphasis before shaking her a little to get her attention. But despite her obvious fury being thrown his way, the barest tremble of her lower lip spoke of just how shattering the whole situation was for her.

A situation she would never have found herself in if it wasn't for him.

"Do not, for one second, think you are worth less than anyone else. And especially not to me. I clearly haven't been doing a good enough job of showing you that. It's a mistake I intend to rectify immediately, I assure you, because you live here permanently." He tapped out two fingers on his temple. "Your soft snoring and exuberant laugh are the soundtracks on my favorite channel. I couldn't turn you off if I wanted to. Which I don't." He lifted his eyebrows and glared at her, silently urging her to argue because he could shut her down in an instant.

But when her hot breath fanned across his face and her shoulders deflated, the fight had clearly gone out of her. "There has to be another way. There just has to be. I didn't come this far just to hit some magical roadblock that I can't bust through because I'm mortal and I don't want the people I care about to get hurt."

She cares about me. About my family.

Titan swallowed down the emotion that trembled in his throat. "I know. And you didn't. But let this be plan A, all right? I'll go in quietly during the day tomorrow. I've got my full fire, something the others don't have and something I didn't have the last time. It's a recovery operation. Plain and simple. In and out."

She snorted at the words *recovery operation.*

When Chrome had mentioned the need for the apex's power, the lot of them had put their heads together on that one, because it wasn't like they could capture the bastard and risk bringing him back to the den. And none of them wanted Tammy moved.

But then Brass had brought up the gold cuffs each charmer wore around their wrists. At first, they had all just stared at the angel, unsure where he was going with the revelation. But then he expanded on the time he and Bronze had had a run-in with a group of mystics who had used weaponized magnetic energy against them. The dark rays thrown their way had attracted zinc from Brass's metallic form, leaving behind weakened porous holes in his skin. The clarification Brass offered had been brief and succinct and more words Titan had heard the man mention to Rose since she'd arrived in their den. But he was grateful and acknowledged what speaking up about the fight may have cost Brass. Zinc wasn't normally magnetic and was a key component in the angel's metallic makeup. For the charmers to corrupt it and use it against him was wholly unsettling. A violation. But it was a story Brass thought to share in that moment nonetheless, despite what it cost him to admit it.

Because gold was porous as well. Even more so when the stuff came in contact with acid, which the charmers had been weaponizing in abundance. Pores, regardless of the material in which they formed, loved to play host to all kinds of things. Magic included.

"Ah, yes. Brass's 'gold is like a sponge' theory and that the apex somehow left magical residue in his jewelry." Rose rolled her eyes and grunted.

"I'm sorry, but I didn't hear quite enough disdain coming through. Want to try that again?"

Rose tossed him a deadly leer, but it quickly faded into contrition when he stood and sat next to her on the bed and one-armed her to his side.

"If you need any more proof that magic can live in metal, I'm sitting right beside you. Every night, my brothers leech properties from the metals in the stone around us. They wake recharged, reenergized, and ready to slay the day. We have no reason to believe gold would behave any differently, especially for beings from different realms."

Rose eased into his hold and rested her head on his shoulder. Titan swallowed down the enormity of the gesture. Even in her extreme agitation, she'd still turn to him for comfort. "And let me guess. Your idea of a simple extraction would be to find the apex during daylight hours, slip the cuff off his wrist somehow, and scram with none the wiser?"

"Pretty much." He held in a shoulder shrug for fear it would disturb her warmth and weight against him. But he damn well wanted her to know he could do this. No, not could. *Would.* Had to. With one hundred percent certainty and success. Titan would spoon-feed her his confidence all day long until she had no choice but to believe in him.

"Not alone. If this has to happen, you don't go alone." Her tone was firm. Unshakable.

"If that's what you want, I'll take a team. We'll do this right. For Tammy."

Rose's head gently brushed against his chest as she nodded her quiet acceptance.

"Tomorrow, we'll head out. But tonight . . . tonight is for us. For you."

She leaned back and raised one sly brow at him. "Oh yeah?"

"Definitely." Titan skimmed his thumb over the soft thin skin below her eyes. Brilliant green eyes that had been haunted and empty when they first met now glowed back at him with vitality. The dark gray under her lower lashes had begun to fade, along with the sunken hollows of her cheeks. Her health and safety had become a private charge in his world. He'd taken up the mantle of that cause with both hands and would forever hold it sacred.

For his soul bond.

"You've invaded every single thought that flits through my meathead brain. And I'm stronger for it. More determined. Keener. More resolute in my will and precise with my targets. All because of that teasing smile of yours that's plastered on the back of my lids each time I blink. I'll never be able to thank you and worship you as fully as you deserve, but I'm nothing if not motivated. Scout's honor."

Titan raised three fingers in the air and flashed a smile that was all teeth and excitement before dipping those fingers under the hem of Rose's sweatshirt.

CHAPTER 26

Never in Rose's life would she have thought that cotton—freaking *cotton*—would be too abrasive. Not only abrasive, but constrictive, prohibitive, itchy. Hell, for all she was concerned, it was the devil's fabric. She wanted nothing more than to be free of the stuff. Because the moment Titan's fingers skimmed under her shirt, her skin trembled with fiery goose bumps. Her lower lip fell as hot breaths, Titan's breaths, sawed in and out of her. She was consumed and utterly lit aflame with his nearness.

Was this the soul bond thing? Was their connection somehow stronger, more intense than before? Because, as his curious fingers expanded in their search, swirling tempting circles around her navel, she couldn't remember their intimacy being this heady. This mix of being all-encompassing and volatile. With every touch of his skin, another part of her body responded. No, not responded. Recognized him, was pulled toward him, like a new bloom stretching toward the first warm rays of the springtime sun.

"Do you feel this, too? This . . . I don't even know how to describe it. It just feels . . ." Rose closed her eyes and tried to concentrate on all that was wrapped around her, devouring her like a forest fire and crawling over her skin until her most sensitive places trembled with unshakable need.

"It feels right. Like home," he murmured against her lips.

Her eyes sprang open. *Home.* She'd never considered it. Had never even given an ounce of credence to the notion that home could include anyone other than her sister. She had long ago dismissed her parents as factoring into that equation. In recent months, she had relegated them to the ranks of uninterested bystanders who had no more association with her than the neighborhood school crossing guard or the pushy congresswoman always hounding Rose for her vote.

But Titan was none of those things. He had never looked at her with those enough-already and time-to-move-on glances that everyone else threw her way. He had seen her for her. For the plight she'd been through and for her longing to see it corrected. He'd never rushed her through her grief or even hinted that she should no longer feel it.

In Titan, she'd found a partner. A like-minded individual who believed in her goals because they were his own, who cared for her without needing a reason why. He just did. End of story. Not because his care would result in her getting over her loss faster or would hopefully encourage her to interact more fully with people again.

She let the feeling wash over her and blanket her in its intensity as he skimmed his fingers up the sides of her torso, leaving scorching prickles in their wake. Her arms stretched to the ceiling, quickly obeying his touch. A brief tug over her head and her shirt fell to the floor, freeing her hair. Cool air kissed her bare skin and teased her already tormented nipples beneath her sports bra.

Rose swept her mussed hair out of her eyes and took him in. The man who had become more of a true home to her than even what she'd known with her sister. Oh, she loved Tammy.

Fiercely. But her love for her twin sister was exactly that. A deeply personal connection with another soul who had often walked the same path as Rose had. With Titan, however, the connection was deeper and on an inconsummate scale. Like the spark of their journey had been lit but not yet traveled.

And it was a road her body ached to discover, because every thrumming pulse and electrified nerve ending called to him like a beacon.

Rose lilted forward and brought her chest against his, which was still annoyingly clothed. What was not annoying, however, was the sharp cut of his pectorals that defined the ridges of his shirt's soft fabric. Or the clenching jump of his abs against her fingers as she repeated the same maneuver on him that he had on her. When his erection strained in his jeans, the denim rasping against the underside of her forearm, she withdrew her hands and flicked at the shirt.

"Off. I need to see you. All of you." But just as he grabbed the hem of his shirt and was about to raise it over his head, her hands stilled on his balled fists clenching the fabric. He raised a confused eyebrow at her.

All or nothing, girl. He's shown you his cards. Time to show him yours.

Rose exhaled a deep breath as her eyes mapped the contoured angles of Titan's face. The deep-set brow that could be both stern and playful. The high angle of his beard that painted his visage with masculine ferocity. And those eyes. Eyes of endless molten dark chocolate that could give way to flashes of a glistening spectrum before solidifying into swirling pools of gleaming silver.

A face that was hers. A face that she desperately needed to look upon every morning and night. As profoundly and indisputably as blood cells needed oxygen.

"Show me what coming home to you looks like. Because I don't think I want to live anywhere else." Rose whispered the words resolutely, without a hint of fear, doubt, or even guilt. They had been the truest and most freely given words she'd spoken in six months.

A low growl rumbled through Titan's chest as he frantically whipped his shirt off. The act would have been comical, like a raccoon trying to free itself from a burlap sack, if not for the ferocity that poured off his body in scorching waves.

His mouth claimed hers before his shirt even had time to hit the floor.

A heartbeat later, she had her answer. She was home.

Whatever tether that normally reined Titan in, that held his frenzied, feverish ass in check and prevented him from attacking Rose's perfect mouth, had snapped. Just, poof! Like a little girl's hair elastic attached to a little boy's slingshot.

Because she was it for him. And as soon as she said those words, spoken softly yet unwaveringly through lips that were as petal-soft as they were full, he was done. Wrecked. Claimed. His Rose. His soul bond.

Titan took her mouth in a rush and wasted no time devouring every flavor he could. The spicy cinnamon she insisted on sprinkling in her coffee, the richness of the vanilla cream she swirled into it. All mixed with her earthy sultriness that had long ago—or did it just seem that way?—become an aphrodisiac.

His tongue dipped and swirled into the cavern of her mouth. He no longer needed to learn the shape of her or how she'd offer her bottom lip to him on a whimper whenever he stroked over it with his wet heat. She did so now as he palmed her back, lifted her bra free, and pressed her breasts against his chest.

"I have many favorite parts of you, but this . . ." he said softly before tasting her lower lip with the tip of his tongue, "is a particular fan favorite. Delicate as a flower's petal and just as beautiful." Still holding her to his chest, he laid her down against the mattress with her head nearly dangling over the foot of it. He rose up on his forearms and dipped his head to her breast.

Her chest rose to meet his mouth with each frustrating exhale. "If you think going with a cliché flower reference is going to work in your favor, you've got some more work to do. My parents named me after a freaking flower. You're not exactly trying your best here."

"Impossible." He smiled at the hitch in her breath as he squeezed one nipple between his teeth, then the other. By the mages, he'd never tire of her soft pants of pleasure. The way her neck elongated as her breaths fluttered up her throat and how her chest rose closer to his hungry mouth with each heightened breath. "I'm an A student. I always go for extra credit."

"Oh, shut up and fuck me." Rose dropped her head back over the edge of the bed and slung a limp arm over her eyes. They'd hardly touched and yet her skin was already glowing with exertion. Damn, he'd never get enough of her. Never tire of the banter, the need, the all-consuming passion that just being near her stirred. If she wanted a home, he'd lay himself down as the foundation and build her a house so sturdy, not even her misguided self-doubt could breach the walls. He'd build her a paradise. Brick by fucking brick.

"Anything, petal. Whatever you want, it's yours. Along with this." He removed his hand from her breast and grasped her wrist, the one dangling precariously over her closed eyes. Quickly, without hesitation, he placed her hand in the center of his chest. She raised her head and glanced up at him. There was no tell in those subtle green eyes of hers. No giveaway that he was treading on presumptuous ground and he should turn back, get to loving her like she'd asked, and keep his mouth shut. She hadn't nodded or cried or done anything to affirm the enormity of his statement. Because it was enormous. Never had he felt for a woman even an iota of what he felt for Rose. She was his breath, his fire, his very life force. And yet she lay there, still silent.

Until her slender fingers curled around his and pumped a loving squeeze against his chest. He looked down at their joined hands, just to confirm all senses were on board and sending signals to the same place.

"I'll take it," she murmured.

His head shot up, and Rose's brilliant smile melted away every final remaining uncertainty he had.

She was his.

Game on.

Titan pulled away every stitch of clothing still covering Rose's body and then his own. He lowered himself over her, protecting and worshiping every inch. He feathered heated kisses down the underside of her arms, along her collarbone, and peppered a delicate trail through the valley between her breasts. A moan rumbled through his lips as his cock dragged up the spun silk of her inner thigh until it glanced the heated wetness of her core. The tempting caress was torture as his muscles strained with the restraint to plunder further, a restraint he knew himself capable of. Because this wasn't, and would never be, about his pleasure.

But before he could give it another thought, Rose's firm hands gripped his cock, gave it a firm tug, and guided it home into her waiting body.

"Fuck!" Titan's fire ignited within him as his little vixen writhed beneath. She wasted no time bucking her hips against his, scoring his back with her trimmed nails. And he'd take it all, coax every little feral act out of his woman and accept them like brands of honor tattooed across his chest. And back. And ass, apparently, as she urged him on. Like he cared. Everything he was belonged to Rose now.

I will never tire of this woman.

Titan pulled out of her slowly, eliciting soft murmured breaths through those lips he loved, and stroked back into her. Heat emanated off her skin as she met every one of his thrusts. Their movements were frantic, hurried, as if they were racing against an unknown opponent. He dropped on top of her, holding her, caging her as he gave over every part of himself to her pleasure. And when her grip tightened on his shoulders and her open lips settled into the crook of his neck as she cried out her release, he came on a shot. His hips slammed into her. Every jerk of his body inched her head just a hair farther over the edge of the bed, until the column of her long neck was right at his mouth.

He kissed her throat softly as the last tremors of their passion shuddered through him. Her body trembled with the remnants of her release and he huddled her close before scooching her down more securely on the bed. Titan peppered a tender kiss along her forehead. Rose sighed and snuggled into his warmth.

He chuckled as her body shimmied against his. "Cold?" he teased.

"Nah. I've got the best space heater right here." She patted his flank. And then looked up at him with exhausted, satisfied eyes.

"That you do. And I'm not going anywhere," he murmured into her ear.

"Good, because I like it here just fine." The sentence drifted off as Rose curled into him further. He grabbed the opposite end of the comforter and whirled it up over both of them. Once he was satisfied that no part of her was exposed to the air, then, and only then, did he allow himself to rest his head. He resettled her higher against his chest and threw his leg over hers.

He wasn't taking any chances on risking her discomfort. Rose was his world, his light, and he would protect that sacred bond fiercely, doing anything to keep her happy.

But despite their connection, the truth sat heavily on his heart. Because Rose would never truly be happy as long as her sister was still a prisoner. And by the mages, he couldn't stand by and witness her anguish if it was within his power to end it. Every longing look Rose threw at her sister's prone form and every tear she attempted to hide but couldn't were constant reminders of the months' long suffering she'd endured.

Suffering he should have prevented.

Titan exhaled as Rose's soft snores vibrated against his heart. A safe, peaceful sleep.

He would see to it that all her remaining nights were as such. Yes, he had the power to end her anguish. To heal his soul bond's suffering and course correct his fuck-up.

He only hoped she wouldn't hate him for it.

CHAPTER 27

The aromas of smoky bacon and French press coffee pulled Rose from the best sleep she'd had in the past six months, possibly her life. No, definitely her life. She was quickly learning all her new favorite ways to wake up in the morning.

And her new favorite ways to fall asleep.

And to wake up in the middle of the night. Twice. From different angles on the bed.

God, her muscles ached with a soreness she didn't know was possible. It wasn't a strain or general fatigue. Nothing like the cramps and charley horses of her high school track and field days. No, this was different. More thorough in its reach, as if even her tendons pulsated from painfully pleasurable exertion. Hell, she was pretty sure her toes needed a good stretch after their constant strenuous state of curling into the mattress.

Could one get repetitive stress injuries in their toes?

Rose let the notion simmer as she stretched out and reached her hand over to where she'd left Titan sprawled out at her side.

Except warm jersey cotton sheets kissed her palms instead of the crisp hairs that dusted Titan's forearm. With a groan, she cracked her eyes and stared at the expanse of empty bed. A bed she really frickin' wished had a naked angel in it.

But then she remembered the smells of bacon and coffee and her temper cooled slightly.

This was Titan's way, she had learned. Oh, she'd make damn certain he got on board the stay-in-bed-and-snuggle train real quick, but honestly . . . how could a girl complain when her lover had a knack for cooking elaborate meals and was jack-rabbit quick to bring her some hot and fresh at the first rumble of her tummy?

Wait . . . lover?

Rose paused in her stretching and let her head sink back into the pillow.

Lover . . .

She turned the word over in her mind, testing out its flavor and significance. When the word didn't taste off, a tight smile threatened to poke free.

Yes. Yes, I suppose he is.

A larger, fonder smile and lightness—true lightness—spread through her as she jumped out of bed and all but skipped to Titan's closet, where she turned to the right side, *her* side, and yanked down a shirt. Her fingers made short work of the flannel button-down Titan had given her. She rather liked snuggling into the balsam, woodsy scent of him. The action instantly smoothed every one of her frayed edges and went a long way toward coaxing out those held breaths and relaxing those tense muscles.

He'd assured her that they'd return to her home to pick up any clothing and other items she needed. Under his protection, of course. He had tried to temper the sternness of that last warning with a slight head bow and arms clasped behind his back, as if he were some Secret Service agent protecting the First Family. But she had seen the gesture for what it was. That she'd be returning to stay with him. But protection—once the primary reason for his nearness—occupied only a fraction of his motivations now.

He simply wanted her and made sure to show it.

Talk about acts of service being someone's love language.

Rose threw her sneakers on and heel-toed it down the hall as she made a beeline for the kitchen, doing her best to tone down the goofy smile straining her cheeks. If she pranced in there beaming like a kid who had just been handed a king-sized candy bar on Halloween instead of those vile yellow peanut things, Bronze would rib her to no end.

And she hated to admit it, but she was really beginning to like the shaggy potty-mouthed redhead. He was sort of like the older brother she had never asked for and never really wanted but wound up having anyway, and once there, she couldn't imagine shaking him. It made her wonder how she ever made it through the day without him in the first place.

All of the angels had begun to feel like family, actually. Even Brass, whose stern politeness and regal respect hit her with all the awe she normally reserved for swooning over members of the British royal family on television. He was kind, yet quiet and always helpful, like how she imagined a significantly older sibling must be to a younger one. All annoyed patience mixed with a hefty dose of reluctant team player.

And then there was Iron. Granted, the angel certainly kept his distance from her, and she was bursting to know why. But if the traumatic ordeal of losing her sister had taught her anything, it was that healing wasn't a one-size-fits-all situation.

The angel clearly suffered. But still, he stayed and did his best to help her and Tammy, despite his obvious struggles. Rose loved him for it. She loved all of them.

A family.

She slowed her pace as she neared the end of the hall and did her best to tamp down her giddy excitement. Her whole body itched to sling herself on top of her angel's broad shoulders as she imagined him working his culinary magic at the stove.

That hardly seemed safe, what with hot bacon grease and all. But some part of her wanted to see his reaction. Would he change to metal to protect himself from the splattering fat? Would he sense her coming and turn around to nab her before she even got close?

Man, she had it bad for him.

My soul bond.

Rose raised her shirt sleeve and admired the gold tattoo painted on the inside of her wrist. She couldn't help but smile as she turned her wrist from side to side to catch the golden glow of the otherwise imperceptible symbol. It may not have made sense to someone who wasn't a twin, but for Rose, the brand was perfect. She had always been used to being part of a pair. That was one of many reasons why her sister's disappearance had been so awful. A vital part of her had been ripped away.

So Titan's name, a name he'd never shared with any other woman—any other mortal for that matter—being branded on her skin hummed with all sorts of just right.

Rose shook out her sleeve, turned the corner from the hallway, and walked into the dark granite kitchen.

And stopped.

Because a mop of shaggy blond hair stood over the stove. Not dark brown. And void of the lush, yet neatly groomed beard she had looked forward to nuzzling.

Steel's hand flicked off the burner as he set a pan of bacon aside, grabbed his kitchen towel, and reached into the oven to retrieve a sheet pan of biscuits. She mentally rolled her eyes at her disappointment and chastised her insipid thinking that, of all the men in this house—well, underground den—Titan was the only one capable of cooking bacon.

"Oh, hey, Rose." Steel nodded a friendly greeting at her as he moved the sheet pan to a cooling rack and slung the kitchen towel over his shoulder. "You hungry?"

"Definitely." She walked over to the stove and dipped two intently searching fingers into the pan to retrieve a choice slice of the porky goodness. She blew on it for a moment before crunching down on a slice. "Have you seen Titan?" she asked, her mouth already full but her head not really caring.

"Nah. Not yet. Wait . . ." After pulling a spatula from a drawer, Steel turned. "He's not with you? Well, that's surprising. Would have thought he'd, um, well . . . let's just say I'm surprised, is all." He leaned his tall frame back against the lip of the counter and crossed his toned arms over his chest. His blond head cocked to the side. He seemingly did his best to appear sheepish while also mulling over the absence of his bonded brother from the woman said brother was bonded to.

Rose turned her attention back to the bacon and nibbled another piece, doing her best to shrink down into the shirt's collar and avoid the flush of embarrassment that had begun heating her cheeks. Steel sized up the gesture immediately.

"Hey, nothing to be shy over. We're all grown here."

"So, I guess privacy isn't really a thing among you guys."

"Pffsh!" Steel waved his hand at the notion. "When you've lived the lives we have, privacy becomes a fallacy real quick. It's best left feeding false confidence to the mortals who use incognito browsers to watch porn, thinking no one will ever know. Boy, I'd kill to see the looks on their faces when they learn that nothing's truly private on the internet."

"Okay, first off . . . ew. And second—"

"Titan's gone."

Rose and Steel turned to take in a veritably pissed-off Tung stalking toward them, with Chrome and the others hot on his heels.

"What?" Rose asked.

"He left. He's not in the den. And he is not without weapons."

"Okay, is that uncommon, though? Are you all on house arrest or something? I figured you guys always carried weapons on you."

Tung's boots ate up the expanse of the great room's stone floor before he stopped in front of her. His nostrils flared, and his lips were pulled in with agitation. Rose took in his hands, the fingers of which had curled around the lip of the dark granite countertop. She held her breath as the great rocky slab held its own against the aggressive pressure emanating from the prime sentinel's vice-like grip.

"I did not say he had taken only his." Each word was spoken with slow precision, clearly eliminating any possibility that Rose wouldn't catch the severity of the situation.

"I don't understand." She made her confusion clear, despite Tung's tone.

Chrome stepped around Tung and laid a placating hand on his leader's tense shoulder. "Titan's weapons are gone from the armory, that's true. But so are several of our others. Weapons he, of course, knows how to use expertly but are not ones he favors." Chrome's expression was grim as he fished into his back pocket to withdraw a piece of gum. Once he threw the small square into his mouth, he leveled sad eyes at Rose. "A number of the gun cases were cleaned out. Tung's reinforced Desert Eagle was swiped, along with several other firearms, scope rings, optics, you name it. The man racked up like he's about to take out everyone who'd ever looked at him funny and their mothers to boot. And let me be clear, he ain't a gun guy. He'll use 'em if needed, sure, but he's too much of a Boy Scout, always waxing poetic about his preference for his bow and blades. If he took that kind of heavy artillery, he means to deal out some nasty business."

Cold dread squeezed around Rose's throat as she met the eyes of the angels around her. But just as the feeling eased and she recalled that Titan was trained and far more experienced with things that wanted to kill him than she was even aware of, the tension returned. Like a tidal wave that slowly left you dry and safe on the shore before crashing down in a torrent on top of you. This time, however, as the dread receded, it was quickly replaced with the stabbing agony of betrayal.

"No. No no no . . . he said he wouldn't do this. He promised me!" Blood pounded in her head so loudly that she wasn't sure whether she whispered the words or yelled them. But judging from the looks around her, it had been a mix of both.

"What did he promise you, Rose? Be specific." Tung's tone was authoritative, commanding, but not unkind or without compassion. She could see why they trusted him to lead.

A raspy sigh escaped her as she collapsed into a chair in front of the nearby dining table. "He wanted to go after the apex. To try and steal its cuff. Something based on what Brass had told him about gold being porous enough to hold magic. He thought if he could get the cuff, the magic would still be there and it would help get Tammy out somehow. But I told him no. Not alone. That it was too dangerous. And he agreed. He said, and I quote, 'I'll take a team.'" Each word was slowly enunciated, not for emphasis, but because her lungs were refusing to draw in the proper breaths she needed to rage against the table in front of her.

Muttered curses swam around Rose, but she was too enraged and heartbroken to distinguish who said what. Somewhere in the background, she faintly registered Tung barking orders and metal weapons being swept off mounted brackets. But all the clangs and buckling and general scrambling of Titan's brothers were like the barest whispers of butterfly wings in a hurricane.

Because Titan had lied to her. A lie that was nestled between sweet words and fiery embraces. And she didn't know what hurt worse. The fact that he was probably going to get himself killed in a suicide mission that didn't need to be one.

Or the fact that she had so easily come to love a man who could hurt her so easily in return.

CHAPTER 28

Titan dropped his right shoulder and ducked low so the fletching of his arrows wouldn't get snagged on the crumbling stone of the mill's wall as he crawled through. His boots on the dilapidated structure were nearly silent as he slowly advanced on the same stairwell as last time.

Last time. When he'd had his brothers at his back and his muscles weren't weighed down with more firearms, magazines, and Ka-Bars than was comfortable on his frame. Hell, he'd even managed to strap down an ax or two. Admittedly, a tad overkill. Especially for what was, for all intents and purposes, a recovery mission.

Then why did his conscience continue to tap out a tune of if-you're-foolish-and-you-know-it-grab-more-ammo? It was a story as old as he was. Motivation versus discipline. Motivation may get you to the starting block, but it doesn't mean shit without the discipline to carry you the rest of the way. And over time, when motivation fell to the wayside and your grocery list of reasons faded to the background, it was the muscle memory of discipline that finished races and achieved goals.

All lessons he had learned and, hell, taught his brothers as second to the prime sentinel.

And yet, despite his well-honed discipline, he couldn't deny the powerful pull of his motivations as the tread of his boots ghosted over the few remaining stairs to the higher floor.

Rose.

Images of her brown hair sprawled out on his forearm, of her long limbs and warm smoothness wrapped around him as she murmured in her sleep. She was all manner of perfection. And for those few fleeting moments, he imagined that the grandiose flood of peace and light that flushed through him when he looked at her was something akin to what the souls felt when they entered heaven's realm. What the other soul-bonded mages in the Empyrean must have known and celebrated each day.

Love. Without boundaries or borders. Without restrictions or limits. Just expansive, soul-searing, endless love.

His fire heated with the knowledge of his bond with Rose and threatened to overtake his current metallic form with blue flames. Titan closed his eyes briefly and willed away the temptation. The last thing he needed was to announce himself like some sort of enraged tiki torch.

Because, while care and compassion for his soul bond fueled the flames of his motivation, rage stoked them until they were honed lasers of molten fury for the charmer who had imprisoned Rose's twin.

Rose would never be free of her anguish until Tammy was free of hers. And that was more than enough motivation for Titan to end this and leave with a gleaming gold cuff as a souvenir.

His finely sharpened discipline would carry him the rest of the way. The whole practice-what-you-preach model could be revisited when everyone under his protection was finally safe and no longer suffering from his mistakes.

Titan nocked his arrow and, for a moment, regretted that he was in his metallic form. He wanted to feel the bite of his bowstring as it pulled across his cheek. Needed to feel the straining tension in the valley of his knuckles as the string dug into the underside of his drawing hand. But the remorse was fleeting as he turned his body and slowly crested the lip of the short wall covering him.

"Shit." Titan spat out the soft curse as he scanned the barren factory floor.

Tables and chairs had been left in various states of toppled and snapped in half from their last foray. Broken glass littered the expansive floor and offered an illuminating contrast to the larger chunks of shattered ceramic and porcelain vessels that no doubt housed some especially nasty experiments lovingly prepared for the benefit of him and his brothers.

Seriously. Why couldn't people just regift a scented candle if they didn't like you and be done with it?

He sighed. All signs around him pointed to vacancy.

Titan loosened some of the tension in his shoulders but never dropped his aim as he swung his arrowhead around the room in slow sweeps. Down at his feet, a rat scurried across his path. Titan halted and let the thing by, ever the man of manners. The rat wandered over to a broken beaker in the far corner of the room and danced its curious nose and whiskers all over the thing. When a remnant of some liquid dripped onto its seeking nose, the rat licked its snout clean and began lapping up the remaining liquid from the broken shards in front of it. It didn't take long for the poor thing to sneeze violently and shake its head like it was caught in a tether.

"Wrong thing to drink, little man."

Titan pulled his bowstring taut and slowly, sadly aimed it at the struggling creature, intent on cutting short its suffering. But before he could loose his arrow, the rat flopped over on its side.

After a few heavy pants and frightened squeaks, the poor rodent's belly descended on a great exhale.

And didn't rise again.

Titan lowered his bow and sighed with a weariness that went soul deep. Because that poisonous liquid, whatever it was, had surely been crafted specifically for him and his brothers. Even vermin, it seemed, weren't immune from getting stuck in the crosshairs of Titan's messes.

He wanted to scream and nearly vibrated with the urge to do so. His foot itched to kick over every fucking piece of broken wood and toppled Bunsen burner in this heap. To call forth his fire and lay waste to this entire mill. He threw his arrow back in its quiver and grabbed the knife from the small of his back. With a great scream, he heaved the thing at the only target that would still give him a modicum of pleasure, no longer caring about making his presence known in a thoroughly abandoned hellhole.

The table on top of which Tammy's chamber had lain. The thing was still there, although toppled over, with the length of its six-foot top staring straight at him.

Mocking him.

The blade landed with a thud that was louder than it should have been given the soft wood of its target. Titan stood there, chest heaving and throwing arm still extended. His eyes darted around the mill. The thud quickly turned into a hum. A growling hum that Titan knew would crescendo into a screeching roar.

Right before a portal would open up.

Titan didn't even have time to curse before he dove behind the nearest downed piece of furniture—a cabinet—and froze. His hand took advantage of the portal's din behind him and quickly swiped an arrow free before nocking it. Titan yanked the bowstring back just as the roaring of the portal's magic hissed and faded into silence.

And then he waited.

Echoes of heavy boots thumping against the wood floor resounded in the abandoned cavernous space. A single stride, slow and purposeful.

Titan inched toward the edge of the cabinet, not even daring to breathe. The tip of his nose cleared the side of the cabinet's panel first, then his eyes and arrowhead. That was all he would risk showing, as it was all that was needed. Chrome had more of a knack for grand entrances. Titan far preferred stealth.

Titan twisted his frame and caught the sight of an inky black robe trailing behind a lone pair of boots that gave way to a charmer of tremendous height and stature, one who soared a full head above the mystic class of demons, as well as most of the elite.

The apex.

The black robe smoothly skirted along the floor of the mill behind the apex, as if even the broken glass knew to give the draping garment a wide berth. The charmer's focused stride led him down a back hallway Titan hadn't realized was there, so he hadn't yet explored it. Original offices of some kind, he presumed. But as the apex moved with deadly confidence, he lifted one heavily muscled pale arm to grab something from inside his robe.

When he did that, the sleeve fell away slightly, revealing one gleaming gold cuff.

A cuff that might as well have had Titan's name engraved on it in big fat letters.

Because that fucker was as good as his.

Titan forced himself to wait a full five minutes before rising from his location to make sure the apex was alone. Patience never came naturally to him. It was an annoying byproduct of his metal. One didn't get to take on the amazing properties of one of the strongest metals on earth without falling prey to the cons as well, namely a lack of patience and an abundance of stubbornness. He was too hard, too set in his ways once molded to tolerate thumb twiddling.

So, yeah . . . that five-minute buffer was all he could offer.

He sprang to his feet, arrowhead out and imbued with his fire as he moved swiftly across the room, careful not to step in something that could potentially sear off his foot. When his tiptoe procession finally got him across the booby-trapped landscape, he huddled next to the wall near the hallway and listened.

Soft clanks mixed with the telltale whirring of magic. Not so loud as the portal had been but on a smaller scale, like an ominous casting or tinkering.

On light feet, Titan moved. The dark, moldy stone of the main mill fell away as short, neat rows of ruddy bricks and a single inoperable gas lamp took up the length of the truncated hallway. A few strides of his long legs took him to the only entryway.

An entryway missing its door, with a whole lot of movement behind it.

Titan called forth his metal, unfurled his wings, and curved them around the sides of his body in a protective titanium cocoon. The only sliver visible was enough space in front of him to aim his arrow. Inside the room, murmurings were drifting about. Some he understood, some he recognized as spell casting. All of it was not good.

It's time to end this. Rose needs her sister. And you need her. Get the cuff and get out.

Titan whirled into the room, arrow raised, and . . . stalled out.

The apex's massive frame was towering over an oak office desk, looking down at two swirling green pools of magic and whispering words Titan couldn't make out. Within each pool, however, was the visage of a woman.

Both with matching brown hair. Both with vibrant green eyes. Yet one had more pallor to her complexion, with heavy bags under her eyes and hollowed cheekbones. The other had warmly flushed skin, with a light brush of makeup painting her lashes and the apples of her cheeks.

Rose and Tammy. What the fuck?

Pain lanced up the back of Titan's right wing and threw the women's images from his mind. His fingers released the arrow as the impact of another hit sent him slamming back into the hallway and against the hard brick. Chunks of clay and mortar gave way under Titan's metallic weight and crumbled around his feet.

"Back for more? Let me guess, Sleeping Beauty still sleeping?" The apex's mocking words were smooth and fluid. Not an ounce of flinch in them as he stood and picked up Titan's arrow, mindful of the angel fire, which had fallen haphazardly on the desk.

As in *not* sticking out of the bastard's neck where Titan had shot it. And Titan rarely missed.

The charmer raised the arrow and dangled it tauntingly between his thumb and index finger. "I do believe you missed me with this little toy. The thing to remember when going for my jugular is that, unlike some of my brethren, the trappings of my station are far more elaborate. And for good reason."

Titan clenched his molars together as the charmer snapped his arrow in two.

"Here, let me give you a better target."

Black velvet whirled over the charmer's head and puddled to the floor, revealing seven feet of ashen gray skin pulled taut over massive power and enormous strength, as well as the three gold bands collaring the apex's throat.

Not one or two like on the charmers Titan was used to battling. Three gold bands that went higher up his neck.

Titan's aim hadn't been off when he'd gone for his usual positioning on the neck. It had been wrong altogether.

Fuck.

Titan retracted his wings, wincing slightly as his singed wing protested, shouldered his bow, and pulled Tung's gun from his holster. The tungsten-reinforced butt of the gun smoothed over his titanium palms as he let the bullets fly.

He really did hate talking during a fight, especially when he was quickly realizing he was singularly outmatched.

Remember: this is a recovery mission. Get in, get the cuff, and get out. You're no good to Rose if you're dead.

Titan got two bullets in, one in the pec and one in the ribs, before the bastard got wise to the program and deflected the rest with a magical shield that emanated from his gold bicep bands.

But two was all it took. Especially two bullets laced with angel fire.

The apex's sneer grew tight and a low grumble bubbled up through surprised pants as the fire began to take root.

That's all the distraction you'll get. Now!

Titan dropped the Desert Eagle and charged toward the apex. His roar was deafening and threatened to crumble the very stone around them. Blood pounded in his ears as he leaped onto the table and plunged his hands into the deflective magic surrounding the apex's meaty arm.

Titan screamed. Part blinding pain, part war cry. His titanium fingers began to curl in on themselves, fighting through the onslaught and banding his grip more tightly around the apex's bicep just below the gold band. Titan glanced at the spread of his fire as it danced and licked across the nearly translucent landscape of its victim. The apex writhed and muttered more magic Titan had no interest in.

Because his focus was on the meaty wrist in front of him and the glinting gold cuff encasing it.

Titan dropped his right hand to his hip and, with clumsy shaking fingers, freed Iron's ax from its holster. *Thank you, brother.*

The ax arced through the air, singing its battle cry as it sliced cleanly through the apex's skin, muscle, and bone just below its gold bands. Not a single snag.

The apex threw his head back and erupted in fury and pain. Titan glanced at the charmer's chest and was horrified to see his fire had slowed. It no longer crept and charred the flesh as it spread. Instead, it had stalled out. Not yet extinguished, but no longer taking over the body that played host to its base appetite. Like a fireworks display that fizzled in the rain.

The revelation was chilling and stopped Titan short. Impossible.

But the growing puddle of black blood oozing around his knees deserved his immediate attention. He needed to stay on task and not borrow tomorrow's trouble.

Once the arm was severed, the magic painfully paralyzing Titan had been severed as well. He grabbed the arm by the—well, arm, released his wings, and erupted through the partially collapsed window of the office, which had previously been boarded up. Once he was free of the structure, the morning's early sunlight burst through the gaping hole he left and bathed its rays all over the small office.

Including the apex.

Cries of terror rose behind Titan as his wings carried him higher away from the mill. He risked a glance back and couldn't help but smile.

The sun's rays were working their magic on the charmer as its remaining healthy flesh tightened and curled in on itself. Pale translucence gave way to flaking black char as the bullets laced with Titan's previously stalled angel fire were reignited with a vengeance. Electric blue flames grew out of the ammo's points of origin and slowly overtook any and all available flesh.

Still grinning, Titan turned his head forward and banked left over the Ellis River as he set his course for home.

Home. To Rose.

The weight of the sentiment made his heart both heavy and light. Was that even possible? And when did he start waxing poetically?

Titan glanced down at the blood-soaked severed arm in his hands and thought better of the gift he'd give to his soul bond. Red didn't seem like it was her color. After a few tugs and some fiddling, Titan coerced the gold cuff free of its prior host and dropped the arm into the river—

A sharp impact clipped the back of his right wing, his injured wing, and Titan swerved mid-air. Once steady, he turned back and saw the mostly charred body of the apex hanging out of the mill's dilapidated window with his remaining arm dangling lifelessly against the side of the stone, as if it had just thrown something.

No sooner had Titan looked at the apex did the angel fire fully engulf the charmer's body in a bright blue conflagration before dimming into nothingness and ashes.

Confused, Titan lowered his wing slightly to inspect it. But it didn't move.

Cold tightness spread out from the impact zone of his wing, creeping along the silver expanse of his wingspan, back, and legs. Once both wings were immobilized, Titan dropped from the sky like a stone. There was no time to panic, no time to strategize or problem-solve. He couldn't shift form, couldn't use his wings, couldn't fucking *breathe* as whatever magic had been hurled at him quickly worked over his legs, hips, and chest, pushing out every remaining ounce of air in his lungs.

Titan's vision was the last to fade as the dark magic skated over his eyes, sealing him into a tomb of frozen titanium.

His metallic body splashed into the active river below and sank until it found a new home nestled among the muck and river weed of the mighty Ellis.

The last thought Titan had before he was imprisoned in his own metal was of Rose and how foolish he was for not listening to her. For not trusting his soul bond when every word of her caution and logic had been for his benefit alone, despite her desperation to free her sister.

Again, he had failed her. Though this time, his failure was permanent.

Rose hated the feel of Steel's arms around her. Oh, it had nothing to do with the angel himself. He was sweet as pie and had a damn fine knack in the kitchen to boot. And ever since she helped heal him following his run-in with the charmers and their acid bombs, they'd shared an unspoken easiness that smoothed her interactions with the others.

But now his arms encircling her waist clamped around her like rusted iron bars. Her skin itched and prickled as if metal filings had embedded themselves within every open pore and around every delicate hair follicle.

Because they weren't Titan's arms. It wasn't Titan who held her close to his taut body as massive silver wings—steel, not titanium—soared higher through the treetops. Oh, Steel's grip was chaste and necessary, one of safety and security, but still, it grated at her. The touch was foreign, far too intimate, and utterly miserable to endure.

She may as well have been held by barbed wire. And didn't that just suck donkey balls? Because Titan had lied to her. Trampled all over her trust and discounted her concerns.

And yet, her stupidly stupid body quaked with the loss of his touch and revolted against anyone else's. *Traitor.*

"It's just up ahead."

Chrome's booming voice had her turning her gaze toward him. His high-polished chrome form flew at the head of the pack, urging them on toward the old mill, the last known place of the apex and the only possible lead they had on where Titan went.

Rose turned her head and resumed her backward gazing as Steel flew them forward. He was gracious, despite the awkward way he had to fly while holding her. It was a more vertical position than he was used to, she presumed. But he never said a word of complaint or even balked when, despite the clawing betrayal shredding her heart, she still insisted on coming to look for Titan. And since it was daylight, the threat of charmers was nullified, so none of the angels had much of an argument against it.

Even if her head said otherwise.

Why do you care what happens to him? He lied to you. You trusted him not to do something foolish and he agreed. To your face. Before he turned around and did the exact opposite.

He dismissed your concerns in one fell swoop, just like everyone else had when Tammy had gone missing.

Rose's throat quivered and ached against the sob she struggled to hold back. But as soon as it threatened to appear, she swallowed that fucker right back down.

She would *not* find herself buried under the weight of her circumstances again. During the flight, she'd had plenty of time to modify her mission objectives: get the cuff from Titan, free Tammy, get out of Dodge.

All this soul-bond-eternal-flame nonsense could settle right back into the bookstore's bargain bin fantasy novel it'd bubbled up from.

Steel slowed his descent and gracefully landed with the

others. Once Rose's legs had steadied, she glanced around and was slightly surprised they weren't in the same thicket of trees she and Steel had hunkered down in before.

"Where are we?" Rose asked.

Chrome retracted his wings as the gleaming silver of his metal receded, revealing tanned flesh and the sourest of sour pusses. He nodded his angular chin in a direction through the trees. "Mill's that way."

Tung stepped forward and laid a heavy hand on Rose's shoulder. The heat from the contact was welcome and inviting and instantly chased away the chill that had crept in once she had left Steel's hold.

"Rose, I think it's best if you stay here." Tung's insistent gaze held all the weight of his words and the unspoken expectation of his request.

Oh, damn, he's good.

"Yeah, yeah, I know." She waved her hand dismissively in his direction and glanced around at the others, who had all suddenly found every crumpled leaf and snapped twig under their feet the most interesting things since streaming television services. The great outdoors' version of the proverbial eggshells.

Well, she'd just about had it. She shook out of Tung's hold and pointed her finger at him before sweeping it around at the rest of the angels. "No. You know what? You don't know what's best for me. Chrome doesn't know what's best for me. Neither does Steel, Bronze, or anyone else here. But you know who does? *Me.*"

Rose drew out the last word long and slow. "Look, I will never be able to thank you all enough. But this"—she frantically waved her arms around her—"is not for me. I don't belong in this world any more than you all belong in mine. Whatever you think I am, whatever's happened, I refuse to carry into my future. My sister needs me, and as soon as I get her out of that *thing*, I need to get back to my own life. We both do."

Rose didn't miss the pained pinch at the corners of Tung's lips or the downcast droop of his eyes. But she wasn't in the mood to placate them either. And she sure as shit didn't need Tung's bedraggled tone and sour words making her feel worse for showering him with her emotional and churlish remarks.

"You know you can't go back to the life you had before. The charmers know about you, know about your sister. Do you think they will stop searching for you just because you profess stubborn ignorance at not having what they've spent eons trying to find?" Tung's smooth delivery did little to pacify the sting when the truth bomb landed. His heavy sigh suggested as much as he took a step toward her and braced his arms behind his back. "If you want to return to your home, to collect anything you'd like, even live there under our watch, you're certainly welcome to. You are not a prisoner, Rose. In fact," he spared a glance at Bronze and Steel before returning those pewter eyes to her, "you have become a welcome addition to our family. But you will do well to remember why we are here. What we, and Titan, have all sacrificed our lives for."

"To protect whatever celestial flame is inside me. Collect them all and you win a prize. I get it."

He bristled at the jibe, as did the part of her who'd come to care for and respect these angels. She was the first one to acknowledge her petulance, but her wounded pride wouldn't let her care. Hurt people hurt people, and all that. And hell, did she *hurt.* "Look, I need to go for a walk."

Rose barely stuck around long enough to see Tung's tense nod before she stomped off toward the sound of running water. Once she made it to the river's edge—making damn sure to kick every stick, rock, and moss-riddled log in her way—she was only further miffed when her ire hadn't cooled in the slightest.

Because Tung was right. They all were.

And that was why Titan's actions were so hurtful. With one callous lie, he'd effectively severed her tie to a group of men who had accepted and welcomed her. The sense of community she'd been filled with had gone above and beyond Carla's occasional meals or the sad look of condolence thrown her way by the café owner in town who, since Tammy had disappeared, refused to accept Rose's coffee money.

She ambled over to a giant boulder settled next to the river bank. She couldn't sit on the massive thing. So, instead, she leaned against it, let the sharp angles of the stone knead out the ache between her shoulder blades, and blankly stared out into the rushing river.

Crunching leaves pulled her from her morose thoughts. Rose glanced down in time to see a gray squirrel scamper off with two acorns massively disproportionate to the size of the poor thing's cheeks.

Then she froze.

Trapped under a tree branch that had fallen in the river was a long, pale swath of teal-and-gold tattooed flesh. Flesh so transparent that Rose was able to make out every vein and artery beneath the thin surface, right up to where they diverged in a delta feeding five thick fingers.

Fingers that appeared human.

Rose flattened herself against the boulder and screamed.

By the time Rose finished her second blood-curdling cry, Tung, Chrome, and the others had burst through the trees. She whirled around and, this time, had zero freaking problem staying close to them.

"There!" Rose pointed toward the river bank while her feet continued to carry her away from the scene.

Chrome ran ahead first, followed closely by Tung. The others landed somewhere in the middle, with Steel and Bronze staying closer to her. Brass and Iron quickly followed the others. Confusion and tension dotted their features. All manner of weapons were out and proud as uncertain gazes swung left and right, searching for a target.

A low whistle wove through the lapping river water as Chrome holstered his gun, dropped to one knee, and reached in his back pocket for the gum he kept there before popping a piece into his mouth.

"Damn," Chrome remarked in between chews. "I'm impressed."

At what the others clearly considered Chrome's all-clear, they scrambled closer to the river bank. Bronze was the first to clamor into the river, not at all concerned about the water sloshing up to his ankles around his boots. He leaned down and grabbed the severed arm by the wrist. Water sluiced off the thing in great rivulets. Rose shuddered as Bronze dangled it for everyone to see, like salami on a rope being subjected to the close inspection of an expertly picky Italian grandmother who knew her way around dried meat.

"Would you look at that? You know, I can't say I've ever seen such fine work of charmer dismemberment before. It's usually such a hack job, but the lines here are so clean." Bronze awed at the gaping end, which would have eventually led to a shoulder had it obviously not met with something sharper. "I don't often admit this, but I'm with Chrome. A solid ten out of ten. I'm definitely impressed."

"Where's the cuff?" Tung's voice of reason chased away the chuckles and groans. The prime sentinel stood in front of Bronze, arms crossed and jaw clenched as he eyed the appendage. The question had everyone's attention.

"Don't know. You thinkin' it's an elite? Mystics don't usually have this much muscle." Chrome mulled over his question as he scratched the underside of his chin with the backs of his fingers.

"It's an apex."

Rose and the others turned at the softly spoken bass of Iron's voice. But the giant angel didn't immediately address any questioning looks. He merely stepped toward Bronze and took the severed arm from him as if it was a baby in need of swaddling. Iron laid out the length of it perpendicularly across his forearms and began examining the juicy gruesome end.

"Are you sure?" Tung asked.

Iron nodded grimly. And not for the first time, Rose's concern for the quiet giant flirted just beyond curiosity and had begun its gradual left turn toward worried territory.

"The elite always have trim nails. Better for hand-to-hand. But the apex often keep their thumbnails long. It helps them cast their magic. Easier to swipe out a spark on the fly by catching it on an abrasive surface so they can quickly funnel their magic to it." Iron's gaze, as well as the others, fell on the long thumbnail that extended three-quarters of an inch off the nail bed and crested with a rounded-off point. It reminded Rose of lead guitarists in rock bands who chose to keep their thumbnail long to use in place of a guitar pick.

"Do mystics keep all their nails long, then? Those are the magic users, right?" Rose winced at how squeaky and quivering her voice sounded, but then she remembered she was well within her right to show a little discomfort. Because, hello, severed arm.

Iron lifted his gaze to Rose and pinned her with those dual-colored eyes. "Yes. They typically engage from a distance, so there's no need for them to worry much about maneuverability or—"

Those hazel and brown eyes dropped from Rose's gaze and flew to the severed end of the arm. Though she'd have to take Bronze's word on the whole clean-slice thing, her stomach still threatened to revolt at the exposed tissue and muscle wrapped around severed bone.

Impatient boots shuffled nearer to Iron as he brought his head down closer to inspect the cut end of the arm.

"What is it?" Tung asked, stepping alongside the giant and peering down at what Iron was inspecting.

"Iron. Iron filings left behind, wedged between the muscle and bone. From one of my axes." Iron whipped his head around and stared off at the choppy Ellis River behind him. As his angel fire bloomed high, a glowing sheen of topaz brightened within Iron's eyes before he dropped the arm. The giant angel took two long strides, then leaped into the air, flesh shimmering into menacing iron, and spread his wings. That hungry topaz gaze swept back and forth over the small white caps that licked and crashed along the craggy landscape of the water. Rose ran to the edge of the water while the others took to the air in the same fashion, obviously unsure why but never doubting their brother.

A flick of Iron's wing was all the warning Rose got before the angel took off like a pelican dive-bombing for a fish. His massive frame broke through the water's surface until his boots were the last thing to be swallowed up.

"Wait! What's going on?" Rose hollered to the others, but no one even so much as looked her way. One by one, they all followed suit, diving into the water.

And then, nothing.

The Ellis River had been a significant resource for this region back when the mill was first established. And rightly so. The waterway was a far cry from a sleepy creek or babbling brook. The Ellis could be as lively as she was long. Rose recalled some of the local fishermen in Aurora bragging about their catches during the height of the fishing season. She could give a fig about fish at the moment, but she wasn't so quick to dismiss the memory.

Because that conversation had also told her the depth of the river. About ten to twelve feet.

Shit. What the hell is going on?

Rose paced a mean streak into the bracken along the river

bank. But while her feet moved frantically, her mind kept a different measure. One minute . . . Two minutes . . . Five minutes . . .

A whole *seven freaking minutes* later and the water finally broke. Flapping wing tips of varying silvers and tawny browns poked through the river. As the water cleared and the metallic forms of men gleamed before her, grunts and bellows replaced the sounds of the river's ramblings.

The six angels rose above the river. Anguish was etched along all their faces as they struggled to lift something that was huddled in the center of their cluster. But what, exactly, she couldn't tell.

Rose ambled up and down the river's edge to get a better look as the mass of them slowly, agonizingly descended toward the bank. When they finally touched down, the effort was met with groans and full-body exhaustion. Tung and Chrome slid to the ground instantly, their metallic chests heaving as if they'd just run back-to-back triathlons. Steel and the others looked just as bad, reaching out to grip anything and everything for support.

But as the angels fell away one by one, the cause of their strain—and the reason for Iron's swan dive into the river—glared back at Rose.

Titan.

The angel was in his titanium state. His wings, usually glorious in their span, were splayed haphazardly in awkward directions, as if they hadn't been able to deploy fully in flight. His face—that handsome and alluring face, which had somehow always managed to calm Rose, yet still take her breath away—was twisted into an expression of panic. Eyes wide, lips strained. The whole picture spoke of sheer terror.

A bright glint in the morning light had Rose's eyes dragging down his frame farther, until they landed on the object responsible for the reflection.

A single shining gold cuff. The very one she was willing to bet her mediocre savings on belonged to the apex who was currently missing a very significant appendage.

And her heart broke.

Oh, Titan. What have you done?

She flew toward him on shaky legs. As soon as she was within reach, she jumped and threw her arms around his solid neck. God, he was so *cold.* So lifeless. Like a frozen statue that had once been a vivacious, molten element but had been quenched and cooled for the pleasure of others.

"What happened to you? Oh, Titan . . ." The worry and fear in her words made her voice unrecognizable to her own ears. She gripped his neck more tightly and waited for the edges of his wings to curl around her, for the rasp of his beard to turn into her and tickle her cheek.

Nothing. Just cold harsh metal biting into every point of contact along her body.

"Hang on, baby. Just hang on. I can do this."

Rose clenched her arms more tightly around the statue of Titan's body, closed her eyes, and reached down to access that secret warmth within her. As the familiar heat spread from toe to fingertip, she willed every single beam of light into Titan's body. The bright energy pulsed and danced around them until it encased them both in blazing torrents of healing energy. In the background, Rose vaguely registered crunching leaves under shuffling feet as the others no doubt scrambled away from her light show. But she quickly refocused her attention on the angel in her arms and deepened her concentration. Willed every ounce of her soul into the angel who had once claimed hers.

A great breath rushed out of Rose as the light around her receded back into her before dimming entirely. Her limbs shook and her core shivered slightly at the loss. But she had done it and was beyond grateful the others had taken her with them to find Titan. If not, she would have been too late. Would never have been able to heal him or return him to his brothers.

To her.

She leaned back to look into his smiling face . . . and froze. Wide and unmoving terrified eyes still stared back at her. Nothing on Titan had changed. His chest didn't rise and fall with new breath, nor did his arms and wings relax with released tension.

Nothing.

Her light, the one thing she had been prized for and the only thing that could save him, hadn't worked.

They were all utterly helpless.

CHAPTER 30

"I don't know why it didn't work. I did everything the same. I thought we were supposed to have this amazing magical bond. This connection. Surely, that would have brought him back. Broken the spell of whatever happened to him, right?" Rose addressed her rambling, frantic questions to no one in particular. No, that wasn't true. She aimed the words at the tense backs of Chrome, Tung, and the others as they dipped their heads in hushed conversation, trying in vain to find a way to free their brother.

It had taken most of the day, but they had finally managed to get Titan back to the den. The sheer bulk of his solid titanium was clumsy and agonizingly heavy to fly with, from what Rose had gathered. Especially with Steel being unable to help his brothers, as he had Rose to carry.

She had never felt like more of a burden in her life. A literal cause of strife and an unwelcome load.

The great room of the den had been cleared of bulky furniture. At least she had made herself useful in that regard. Her spark may have been useless in healing her soul bond, but she could sure as shit still push a table out of the way.

Titan had been settled alongside Tammy's chamber, with a four-foot aisle separating the two, as if they were in some sort of celestial sick bay. The angels hovered frantically around their brother. The energy in the room was one of utter exhaustion and painful worry mixed with the frustrating inability to change a single circumstance.

It was Rose's definition of fear, one she had lived with for far too long.

Chrome and Iron were crouched down in front of Titan, all manner of tools in hand as they worked to free the cuff from Titan's solid grip. Tung and Brass, meanwhile, hovered at Titan's back and were analyzing a mark on his right wing.

"No one's blaming you, Rose." Chrome bit the words out but never met her eyes as he tried to jockey the gold cuff from Titan's frozen fingers. Iron kept his head down, adding more oil to every crease and crevice as Chrome pulled. All gentle maneuvers. None of them were willing to risk harming Titan's frame in any way.

Tung dragged weary eyes up from Titan's wing to address her. "You are his soul bond. That has nothing to do with what's at work here. Your spark is irrefutable." The words were spoken with no small amount of reverence. Almost a painful admiration. "No, there's more at play here. Come see."

Rose walked with lead feet around to Titan's back. The gleaming silver feathers of her angel's wings stuck out at odd angles, each one frozen in time in its own individual metallic shell.

"Here." Tung traced a finger along a patch of Titan's wing near the center of his back and just slightly to the right of where his quiver and arrows lay.

It pained her greatly that she couldn't even remove his weapons, for they had been encased in titanium against him. Couldn't even lighten the bulk of his frame by stripping him of the weight of numerous guns, knives, and even Iron's ax. The ax whose metal origins, despite its titanium coating, had called to its maker and alerted Iron and the others to Titan's location.

The angels' weapons never took the form of their owners' metals. The weapons were too altered and reinforced already to have their elemental structures changed further. And yet here, they were nothing more than titanium artifacts encased against Titan's cold metallic frame. The only stand out was the cuff. That stupid, vile, tainted gold cuff that mocked Rose with its gleaming contrast against Titan's body.

But as Rose squinted more closely at the skewed feathers Tung directed her to, a slightly off-color sheen danced in the muted light. Curious, she cocked her head. It was a one-of-these-things-is-not-like-the-other situation. The oil slick, for that was the first thing that came to mind, dressed the small patch on Titan's back in tones of light sepia, a stark disparity to his metal's natural color.

"What is that?" Rose whispered, itching to touch it but knowing better.

"Magic. Dark magic. Another enchanted projectile of some sort. I believe it is responsible for Titan's frozen state and why the cuff was not affected by whatever caused the transformation, unlike his weapons. It is . . . not a weapon we've encountered before. No, this is new." Tung's sigh dripped heavily with fury.

"Anyone willing to bet who threw the damn thing? I'll give you one hint. They won't be doing the arm movements to the YMCA dance anymore. Hokey Pokey's out, too—" A sharp slice rang through the cavernous great hall. Chrome's colorful dance commentary was cut short as the angel fell backward with a grunt and landed on his ass.

With a shining gold cuff in his hand.

"Got it!"

As Chrome got to his feet, Rose scrambled around Titan. "The cuff looks like the one I found at the park. The one I was holding when Titan found me. I had dropped it, though. Left it in the grass somewhere."

"This one's different. This," Chrome said, waving the cuff in the air like a captured flag, "is the money one. The apex wore it when he imprisoned your sister. Brass is confident there's still some of the asshole's magical juice in here. Let's stir the pot and see if we can't at least spring your sister. Have some good come of this nightmare."

"I believe it's your best chance to open that chamber. You have nothing to lose." Brass crossed his arms over his chest and nodded solemnly. He was a man of few words, but they were always chosen carefully. Rose respected that. False hope wasn't Brass's style or any of theirs.

"OK. I'll try. But let me try on my own first. You're all gassed enough as it is."

Tung gave a silent nod of appreciation as Chrome handed her the cuff, though she didn't miss the tense cut of Tung's shoulders or the pained worry that briefly danced across his face. She had to fight back a cringe to grip the thing. But grip it she did, despite her revolting stomach and the guilt hammering beneath her breastbone.

They've lost their brother, and still they're devoted to helping you.

Rose's throat clogged against the enormity of a gesture she'd done absolutely nothing to deserve. But for the moment, she put the weight of her inner turmoil from her mind as she laid the gold cuff on top of the chamber, just below the plexiglass.

She dropped her shoulders, placed her hands on either side of the barrier over Tammy's face, and concentrated. Rose's body had fallen into the routine of calling on the spark within her. The spark that was connected to all things light and life. The spark that, up until this morning, had connected her to the frozen angel to her left.

Warmth filled her body, kissing every spare inch of her with gentle and caressing heat, from the backs of her eyelids to the bottoms of her feet. But she didn't open her eyes. Didn't look to see what was happening to the cuff or whether her light had been powerful enough to seep out the apex's magic and penetrate the chamber's seal. She didn't need the proven or unproven potential efficacy of her efforts to cloud her goals. Rose kept her eyes shut and just continued to will everything she had into her twin's body.

If she could offer nothing else to these men, she could at least try her hardest in this one thing.

Rose exhaled as the heated flush flared brightly before receding back into her body. The spark drained away from her as quickly as it had risen, until all that was left was the creeping chill trapped by the den's stone walls and deafening silence.

Her lashes fluttered open and her eyes scrambled to adjust to the scene in front of her.

Which was that of a limp, sagging Tammy no longer lying in a perfect Sleeping Beauty position within the chamber. And the obvious absence of a magical glow emanating from within.

"Holy shit!" Rose dropped her hands and curled her fingers around the rim of the chamber's lid. Chrome, Brass, and Tung joined her as, together, they heaved the lid of the chamber open, not caring a whiff about the gold cuff that fell tinkling to the floor. The hinges groaned with disuse, but they were no match for the combined resistance prying them open. Once the lid was fully open, Rose swung around and grabbed her twin by the shoulders, crushing the delicate sleeves of her sister's crisp blue button-down shirt.

"Tammy! Oh, God, Tammy! Wake up. You're safe." Rose continued her gentle but insistent jostling, running a hand over Tammy's pulse point. A strong, even thrum tapped out a regular healthy beat against Rose's fingers. She was near tears and frantic with exuberance.

Soft, mascara-slick lashes lazily flipped open. A dazed,

uncertain expression flitted over Tammy's face before recognition dawned in her matching jade eyes.

"Rose." The name came out in a whisper through vocal cords tense and groggy from disuse. But it held every bit of her sister's compassion and love that had been missing from Rose's life for the past six months.

Tammy clasped shaky, weak arms around Rose's shoulders. They were more than strong enough to hold Rose through every sob that burst through the floodgates.

Floodgates that had been locked shut for far too long.

<hr>

Tammy and Rose sat nestled in every manner of quilt, blanket, and comforter on the stone floor of Titan's bedroom. Rose had raided what she could find on her own and then asked the others for more. If they had any questions about her request, they were smart enough to keep their thoughts to themselves. Thank goodness. Besides, they had their grief to process. They had lost a brother, after all. So even the smallest kindness of being given a blanket was more than Rose could stomach.

Or the betraying gnaw of guilt that consumed her whenever one of them looked at her with weary, forlorn eyes. As if she was responsible for Titan's state because she couldn't heal him this time, despite everyone's faith and awe surrounding her.

The confusion, pressure, and heartache had sent her running to Titan's bathroom, where she promptly vomited up everything swimming within.

And man, what she wouldn't give to have that stupid spark erupt out of her so she could flush it down the toilet along with everything else.

She'd never wanted any of this. She was no one's savior. No one's except her sister's.

And at long last, she had Tammy back. After six months of agony, she'd finally found her twin.

Then why do you feel like half of you is still missing?

As soon as Tammy awakened, Rose had asked the others to leave the great hall. There was so much to say, so much to explain, and so much to check on. Tammy had seemed well enough physically. Even though she hadn't eaten, drunk, or gone to the bathroom in half a year.

Mentally, however, was a different story. And the last thing Rose wanted was to have six hulking metal angels standing over a woman who had been abducted and was being told the whys and wherefores of her circumstances.

Hard freaking pass.

So Rose quietly asked Steel to prepare some food, leave it in the hallway outside of the door to Titan's suite, and Rose would fill Tammy in on the state of affairs.

But not in a damn bed. The woman had been lying still for six months. So they were kicking it like they had when they were in high school, all crisscross applesauce amid a bed of blankets spread out on the floor.

And they had been that way for the past three hours. It was nearing eight o'clock in the evening, but the snacks had held up, and Rose had finally gotten everything off her chest. Literally everything, from what Rose's life had been like the past six months to their parents' growing distance. From her run-in with the charmers to Titan's rescue. Which, of course, led her to spilling her guts on the whole spark-of-the-eternal-flame-soul-bonded-to-an-angel thing. And then there was the part about how Titan had lied to her. Made her promises, bedded her, then left her. And now, he was gone, frozen in his own metal because she wasn't worth listening to.

It was a lot. But once the final words had tumbled free, her lungs filled with a pervasive lightness she hadn't realized she'd been missing. Utter and complete relief.

But it hadn't all been a happy reunion with French braids and friendship bracelets.

Tammy was . . . different. When Rose would speak for a long clip, Tammy's attention would lapse and wane every so often. Her sea-glass eyes would grow glassy and far off. Her words, the few she spoke during Rose's long-winded spiel, would sometimes come out stilted or garbled. Like Tammy was trying hard to remember how to form sentences or respond accordingly. But the comments did flow eventually, fitting snugly into the bizarre context of the conversation. Rose had to pack her patience and remember that, despite appearances, there was no telling what trauma the charmers did to Tammy internally, especially when her sister had no memory of any of it.

It was a battle for another day.

"Angels, huh? Metal ones?" Tammy asked, her tone having gone from disbelieving over the past few hours to more playful, though still stilted in its delivery.

"Yeah. Pretty crazy, right?"

Tammy nodded, then settled her gaze absently on the floor. "Angels and demons are real. And you and I have some parts to play, from what you're telling me."

"Hey . . ." Rose laid her hand on Tammy's forearm and tried to smooth away her sister's blank stare. "Don't worry about that. About any of it. I'm taking care of it all. You're sleeping here with me tonight. No one will bother you. Tomorrow morning, I can introduce you to the others, if you'd like. But if not, that's perfectly fine. We'll grab some food for the road and head home. Your room's just the way you left it, by the way. Well, except for your clothes hamper. I had to wash your dirty laundry at one point—"

"What on earth are you rambling about? Why would we leave? If we're safe here and those things are out there, why would we leave?"

Rose blinked in confusion. "You want to stay? No, there's no reason to. The apex is dead. And the longer we stay around here, the more we'll be targeted by association. No, we'll go home. The charmers don't know where we live. We've been given this second chance for a fresh start, and we need to take it. Trust me, Tam, it's better to leave this world far behind. Nothing good has come out of it, and nothing will."

Liar, liar, borrowed pants on fire.

Rose's throat clamped down on the sermon she was feeding to Tammy. The words had sounded logical and authoritative. They were words any key decision-maker who was responsible for others would say, even if the speaker had doubts about the validity.

"Nothing?"

The lilt to the word said it all, and Rose internally winced at Tammy's incredibly inconvenient time to flare up their Wonder Twins' powers of sensing each other's bullshit and firmly calling them out on it.

Yeah, Rosey. I'm going to question the premise of that one.

Rose just bit her lip and nodded, unsure she trusted her voice to be the backbone she needed.

Because going home *was* the right thing to do. She'd gotten nothing but a face full of heartache and pain ever since Tammy's abduction. And she'd had enough of that, thank you very much. She was better off the way it always had been.

Just her and her sister.

A great sigh filled the room as Tammy picked up her tumbler of hot apple cider, which was now mostly lukewarm murky apple juice. After a few sips, she set it down on the tray next to her and stood. "Introduce me to him."

Rose looked up with uncertainty. "Who?"

Tammy rolled her eyes. "If you're asking *me* what your soul bond's name is, then we're in big trouble. But if you want me to just nab the first wall of muscle I see and start shaking hands, I can do that, too."

"No, not necessary." Rose got up quickly. "But I told you, he's frozen. Or something. Transformed into his metallic state permanently. I've tried. We've all tried. He's lost, Tam. He's gone." She shook her head as tears threatened to well up. But Tammy would see through Rose's tough-gal act. She always did.

"He's not gone, honey. No one's truly gone until they're bones in the ground or ashes in the sea." Tammy swept Rose into the warmest of sisterly hugs, despite their unsteadiness after months of disuse. "And if he's all you say he is, then, at the very least, you need to introduce him to your sister."

Fuck.

"Can't . . . hurts . . ." Rose's throat threatened to collapse in on itself as the emotional tide threatened to burst through her tightly packed dam. "He hurt me. Even before . . ."

Tammy's arms tensed around Rose's shoulders at the word *hurt.* Rose rushed to clarify before her sister jumped to untrue conclusions.

"I meant he lied to me. I didn't want him to go off alone, knew I couldn't bear it if something happened to him. I don't give a fig about grand gestures. Just that everyone I love is safe. He said he'd take a team with him. But he didn't. And . . ."

Everyone I love . . .

The tears flowed hot and fierce down Rose's cheeks, dotting the collar of Tammy's button-down shirt with dark blue clusters of pent-up anguish. And the gut-punch realization that Titan had somehow weaseled his way into the micro-short list of people she loved.

Truly loved.

"He knew I'd lost you. Knew what it did to me . . ."

"Shhh. I know. But people make mistakes. And sometimes, they're made for the stupidest of stupid reasons, especially when the male brain is involved. But seriously, if you knew half the stupid things I did to protect you when we were growing up, especially in high school, you'd never speak to me again.

And I'm sure it hasn't been easy for you while I was gone, Rosey, but I'm telling you this." Tammy pulled back and met Rose's teary eyes. "Our parents fell apart at the seams. They were slow to unravel at first. But small things snowballed into bigger things until we all got stuck under the avalanche and it was too late to get out safely. So ask yourself whether you're willing to work through and mend the small things, if you can. Because you and I both know what's on the other side of that tear, whether it's a rip in the fabric or a crack in the stone. And she ain't pretty."

Rose erupted into racking cries over her sister's shoulder as the truth she didn't want to acknowledge crashed over her in waves.

"I love him, Tam! I love him. And he's gone," Rose wailed.

Tammy just kept stroking Rose's back through the sorrow that threatened to drown her.

Because she was about to introduce her twin sister to the man she loved and he'd never be alive to see it.

CHAPTER 31

It was nearly midnight when Rose had finally worked up the courage to bring Tammy back to the great hall. God, did she hate that name. It held all the ominous pretension of a boarding school mess hall, complete with visions of a long dais and even longer bankrolls.

None of it fit the vibe of the room she escorted her sister into, which its inhabitants simply referred to as great because of its size and nothing else. They were warrior angels, after all. Not interior decorators.

But the space loomed with all sorts of greatness as Rose woodenly walked into it, the cold stone kissing the bottoms of her bare feet. Her eyes swept the scene—flitting over the large television, pool table, and gigantic sectional sofas—and for the first time since she arrived, she admired the height and breadth of the room. The cavernous space had been carved into the earth and made to function with amenities befitting a palace, brimming with love and kinship through every fleck of shale and glint of mica. Walking in from the main entrance, to the far right, racks upon racks of various weapons were stacked neatly and pristinely, a proud testament to the angels' skills and service. And that was only the selection of stock they chose to keep here for easy access, never mind what was in their armory. To the left, just next to one of the main hallways, was the hub of the kitchen filled with state-of-the-art everything and, more often than not, an angel of one form or another who cooked and fed his family the best of the best.

Because these men—angels—were a family. And this was their home. A home that she and her sister had been welcomed into with open arms by angels who offered the protection of their services.

A home that was missing its most beloved brother and leader.

Hot breath rushed out of Rose as her stiff legs guided her and Tammy toward where Titan was situated. The chamber housing Tammy had been removed, thank goodness, hopefully incinerated along with the cuff. The long farmhouse table had been returned to its place just outside and to the right of the kitchen, along with the chairs.

The only thing out of place was Titan, who stood erect and panicked in immobilized titanium at the head of the table like some terrifying statue of an angel's scion coming to meet their reckoning. Rose bit down on her tongue to keep from screaming.

At the head of the table, right next to Titan, was a dusty blond head bowed over fisted hands.

"I didn't think you'd still be up," Rose whispered, knowing full well Tung could still hear every word.

The great prime sentinel's golden head rose from its position at a sluggish pace. Saddened eyes of tarnished pewter brimming with fatigue settled on Rose. "I could not sleep. The others are . . . grieving as well. In their own ways."

Rose sucked in her bottom lip as she nodded past the pain. "I'm so sorry, Tungsten. So incredibly sorry."

"I know." The simple words were not meant to coddle or accuse but were merely said to acknowledge the state they found themselves in.

We are all grieving and we are not ourselves. Perhaps we never will be.

Rose nodded as Tung's gaze settled on Tammy, who had stood silently at Rose's side. Tung, as if remembering himself, pushed his brawny frame back from the table and stood as the women walked toward Titan. "Forgive me. I am Tungsten—Tung, if you wish." The introduction stopped there, Rose realized, because she suspected Tung didn't know how much Rose had revealed to Tammy about the angels.

And like a buffoon, Rose just stood there in silence because, despite the past few days, she had never formally introduced Tammy to anyone. Oh, everyone was well aware there was a new body walking around, but the guys were letting her take the lead on this one. It was her sister, after all.

So it also figured that manners flew out the window. Because, you know, family.

Nothing says family like showing your assy side. Jesus.

"Crap. Sorry. Tung, this is Tammy. My twin. But I guess you knew that already. Tammy, Tung is the prime sentinel. The leader of the other angels."

At the mention of *leader*, Tung offered a soft correction. "More like the eldest brother. We are as much a family as we are a team. And it's wonderful to finally meet you." The side of his full lips inched slightly higher as he settled his steely gaze on her sister. His arms were clasped behind his back, revealing the breadth of his chest in the way monarchs often posed without even realizing it.

"It's nice to meet you, too. And I understand. I'm the oldest as well." Tammy laughed lightly and flitted fingers in Rose's direction.

"By four minutes. Four freaking minutes, Tam. It's not like

you were already potty-trained and reading *Goodnight Moon* by the time I was born." Rose huffed her annoyance at their age-old gripe, but there was no real malice in it. For so long, she wasn't sure she'd ever be able to make those types of jokes again.

So, she'd happily take the ribbings and then some.

Tammy smiled at Rose's obvious jibe, but her focus remained on Tung a moment longer. The angel's wide shoulders bobbed on a slight chuckle before his eyes followed Tammy's gaze as it shifted to Titan's solid form.

"Wow. I take it this is Titan," Tammy breathed out, craning her neck up and around to take in the angel's metallic state.

Up until that point, Rose had managed to look at every possible place except at him. It was foolish and cowardly. He deserved so much more. Infinitely more.

"Yup," Rose squeaked. It was all she could manage.

But Rose didn't need to say another thing. Tammy's warm hand was wrapped around Rose's trembling one, bolstering her with all the strength and support she'd been having to muster and shore up on her own these past six months.

Talk about pouring from an empty cup.

The three of them remained silent as they took in Titan's stoic form. Rose's glassy eyes danced along the angular frame of his bearded jaw, the sloping sweep of his shoulders, the long splayed fingers of one outstretched hand, and the painful clench of his other hand, which was tightly wrapped into a fist.

The fist that singularly held the gold cuff while his body turned to solid titanium. The anguish and terror of the moment were so clearly etched on his face. He was dying, and he knew it. And yet, he still held tightly to the one thing that would save her sister.

Tickles of a memory teased her mind. Memories of fear and uncertainty cocooned with the scents of lazy marinara and steaming peppermint. Of scorching fire and rustling leaves.

Of other promises. Promises Titan had made to her when it

had been just the two of them and they had known nothing of soul bonds or magic cuffs. Just whispered words and pseudo simple explanations, with no one else around to judge their pretense. It had been just the two of them . . . with the occasional black bear thrown in for fun.

Titan promised to find and save your sister.

He promised to get you somewhere safe after the charmer attacked you.

Promised to see you well-fed and rested.

One skewed promise against the backdrop of many fulfilled ones painted her angel with rays of softening light.

The dumb fool. Rose, not Titan. Because he had always lived up to his promises. Rose had just been too hurt and scared to see the larger picture.

"Oh, Titan . . ." The whispered words ghosted through her parched lips as she reached out and ran a soothing thumb over the clenched swell of Titan's ring finger.

The same finger that, in her culture, would have held a ring of promises. Just like his celestial name branded on the inside of her wrist held his promises.

Tung joined them in front of his brother. The sentinel's arms were still clasped behind his back. His resting pose for comfort and clarity, Rose had learned. But without saying anything, Tammy held out her free palm and looked up at him with sad imploring eyes. Tung studied her twin's hand for a moment and then settled the weight of his large grasp within hers.

Pulsing heat flooded through Rose's core as her spark lit, unbidden. Confused, she glanced down. Her left hand, the one still holding Tammy's right one, glowed with the pure white of the eternal flame she had grown used to calling upon.

But what she wasn't used to was the same glow coming from her sister's clasped hand and torso as well.

"Rose, what's happening?" Panic and fear erupted out of Tammy as she screamed.

"It's okay! It won't hurt you, Tammy. It just feels like—"

Tung gripped Tammy and Rose by their shoulders and quickly pulled them away from Titan. The three of them fell back, landing amid a set of dining chairs. Tung took the brunt of the fall, angling himself so his back hit the chair legs first. Tammy and Rose toppled against his torso, with their legs and bottoms taking the hard hits from the stone floor.

Groaning, Tammy sat up and crawled away from Tung on her hands and knees. Rose stumbled to a shaky upright position and turned to face the electric blue heat behind her.

Tungsten was lying on the floor, limbs scattered through various chair legs, and he was panting heavy breaths. His fists and teeth were clenched as if he were holding back something inevitable.

Blue flames licked up and over Tung's body until the entirety of his powerful frame pulsed with the roaring heat of his angel fire. His full angel fire. And judging by the shock and strain on his face, he hadn't been the one to summon it.

Rose cut her gaze to Tammy, who was scrambling to her feet and running over to a tapestry on the wall.

"He's on fire, Rose! Help me get this down. We need to put the flames out!" Tammy's fingers curled into the maroon and gold fabric as she yanked with all the uncoordinated panicked effort of a person trying to move an elephant that didn't want to be moved.

"I am fine, Tammy. By the mages, I am more than fine."

Rose and Tammy whipped around to Tung, who stood a good distance away from the dining table. His arms were held out before him, palms and fingers spread wide. His eyes were alight with wonder as he basked in the power of his fire.

He smiled. Not a demure grin, but a big shit-eating smile-for-the-camera toothy smile that was nearly as blinding as the flames engulfing him. And that smile was directed squarely at

Tammy, who still clung to the tapestry so tightly she looked as if she was about to climb it.

But before Rose could formulate a single thought about what her eyes were processing, a soft crackling pulled her in a different direction.

She turned her attention toward the noise coming from near the dining table and gasped.

All along Titan's form, stemming from the very spot on his ring finger where Rose had touched him, were electric blue fissures. Thin winding cracks snaked up his forearm, across his torso, over his hips, and down his legs. And they were moving at an insistent pace. Every time the tendril of one fissure intersected with another, the lines would cluster into a fragmented pool of titanium mosaic.

And then a tinny clang echoed throughout the not-so-great hall.

Rose crept closer, barely breathing around the lump in her throat as she kneeled to pick up what had made the sound.

A small fractured piece of titanium.

More of the metal's brothers joined the party on the floor as, piece by piece, hunks of titanium fell away from the entombed angel before her until the tanned skin of Titan's upper cheek, gleaming with a sheen of perspiration, glowed back at her.

She rushed over to him as larger expanses of his frozen, tense body gave way from cold unmoving metal to vibrant healthy flesh.

But it wasn't until the bright silver of Titan's eyes faded to rich chocolate brown that she dropped the metal from her hand and flung herself at him. Warm, flushed skin met the kiss of her lips as she dragged them over the column of his neck, which was now completely free of metal. Not romantic kisses, per se, but rather constant wellness nibbles. Proof of life kisses. As long as every spot she felt touched her back in some warm manner, she'd check that area off the list and move on to the next. Rose was frantic in her clinginess and wasn't taking any chances.

Solid arms circled her waist and back. The bottom forearm settled right into the dip of her hips, while the other curved around her torso just under her breasts. It was Titan's preferred way to hold her when they flew together. It was safe and secure for both of them.

But now, his arms around her in this way meant more to her than any proverbial safety harness.

"I never thought I'd feel this again, petal. Feel you against me, your heart beating against mine." The froggy rasp of Titan's voice vibrated against the unsettled crook of Rose's shoulder as she took on his tired, sagging weight. The tremor skated over her skin like a tectonic shift and she all but sobbed at the sensation of it knowing she had him back.

"You can't run off on me like that again. Ever," Rose said as firmly as her crippled voice would allow. "That's not how this works."

"I know. By the mages, I know," Titan said, resigned to any beating she would give him. "I was an utter fucking fool. I didn't want to risk you, didn't want to risk my brothers for my fuck-up—"

"No, that's not how this works because when the man I love makes a promise to me, I know he'll always keep it, come hell or high water." Rose pulled back to take in his stern, desperate features, his searching eyes, and nearly trembling lips. "But hell ain't got nothing on my stubborn will and determination. I love you, you silly foolish angel. And I can never thank you enough for saving my sister. All I can do is love you. And when I say I'm going to do something, I sure as shit follow through."

Titan held her face in his hands and, for a moment, just stood there staring at her. Staring at every feature and, no doubt, every worry line, pinched brow, and dark undereye circle. She never liked scrutiny, but with him, it was more than that. It was like he was scanning the deepest parts of her she never showed to anyone and was lovingly acknowledging them. Giving them their space to exist and silently vowing to protect and cherish them as well. His care was truly unrelenting, whether it be for her or anyone else.

And damn, did she love that. It had just taken a literal act of divine intervention for her to see it.

Titan dropped his forehead to Rose's and laughed against her lips. Then he ate up her sassy mouth with a searing kiss. Firm, clinging hands pressed into her lower back and pulled her to him more tightly until there was nothing individual or separate between them.

They were bonded far beyond any words or gestures. They were soul bonds. And that was pretty frickin' special.

Rose let her lips linger a moment longer against his before settling back. Titan groaned his protest, but the sentiment died in his throat once he eyed Tung, who looked a little worse for wear despite his gaping smile. Several feet away from him stood Tammy, who, though pale and tense, carried herself with health and happiness—and a torn scrap of the den's tapestry.

Her family. Together.

Titan softened his hold and slowly slid his palms up to cradle Rose's face. Brown eyes of immense depth twinkled with a knowing look as his full lips lifted in an exuberant smile.

"Rose, I've loved you since the moment I first held you against me and flew with you in my arms, figuring out where I could take you to keep you close to me. I've loved every laugh, every soft snore—and yes, you do snore, but it's adorable and I fucking love it so hush—and the bright light of your loyal, trusting soul. A soul that speaks to mine in the same language that no other will ever understand. I was such a fool, Rose," he said, closing his eyes and brushing his lips across hers.

"Yes, you were," she said, half teasing.

"But I'm not anymore." Firm lips pressed against hers in a peck.

"Mmm . . . No, I don't suppose you are."

"Well, that's a relief, petal. I don't imagine you suffer fools lightly." He rubbed his beard along the ridge of her jaw in a tender caress, one that had her curling into the hard shell of his strong chest again.

"Nope. Never have. Never will."

They held each other in silence for a few more moments. Too much had been said and misunderstood, and none of it mattered anymore.

At some point, the den woke up. Titan and Rose had separated reluctantly and were greeted with slaps on backs and a slew of side hugs. Steel had even brought out bowls of ice cream while the other angels introduced themselves properly to a much less frightened and far more animated Tammy. They all should have been exhausted, should have been dragging their sorry keisters around on fumes.

But they weren't. Because no good celebration should commence without utter jubilation of all parties involved, and they had that in spades.

Rose tugged on the fabric at Titan's shoulder, urging him to lean his ear close to her. "Ice cream is all well and good, but there's something else I want more, strangely enough."

"Oh? And what's that?"

Rose grinned. "Pasta with marinara sauce. With the *good stuff.*"

Titan chuckled as he held her to his side and escorted her into the kitchen. "I seem to remember a promise I made regarding San Marzano tomatoes and sea salt."

"Pink Himalayan salt, to be specific. And you did promise, yes," Rose teased.

Once they reached the kitchen, Titan spun Rose out of view and cradled her against the wall, not pressing or caging her but holding her close to him, one hand on her hip and the other clasping her hand to his chest. The embrace was all love and passion without words, like two dancers locked in a sensual tango.

"If there's one thing I excel at, petal, it's keeping my promises."

Rose didn't doubt him in the least.

EPILOGUE

The moment Rose's computer clock switched from 11:59 a.m. to 12:00 p.m., her handbag strap was around her shoulder and her butt was out of her desk chair.

"Bye, Carla. Headin' to lunch!"

"Take your time. Jimmy and Greg are out on service calls all afternoon, so if any emergencies come in, they'll have to wait until after-hours or tomorrow anyway."

Rose mouthed a quick thank-you to her boss and barreled out the front door. Before the bell chime above the door even had an opportunity to finish ringing, she was bounding down the three front steps and leaping into Titan's waiting arms. Warm hands settled around her as she clung around his neck, toying with the thick cabled wool collar of his emerald-green sweater.

He held her close and nuzzled his warm beard against her for a moment before kissing her. "Favorite part of my day, petal."

She smiled against his mouth as he slowly slid her down the front of him until her feet touched the ground. "Mine, too." She stood back and hitched her handbag higher on her shoulder. "So, what are we eating today?"

"Moroccan."

Rose clapped her hands together as they started walking down the street, not hurrying their gait in the slightest. "Oh, I love Moroccan! Those Moroccan cigars are addictive. The lamb tagine, too. And the honeyed mint tea, where the waiter tries to put on a show by pouring it really high from above his head and still gets it in the cup."

Titan scoffed. "Not sure pouring tea needs a production . . ."

"Oh, hush. It's fun. Besides, their mint tea doesn't hold a candle to yours. I *promise*. Eek!" Rose yelped at the mild sting of Titan's pinch against her hip.

"I don't take promises lightly." He looked down at her and smirked.

"I wouldn't have it any other way."

Rose smiled against Titan as he tucked her to his side. Together, they walked into town for their daily lunch date, a routine they had begun two weeks ago, once she and Tammy returned to their shared apartment. At the time, there had been a litany of questions about the next steps. Where did they go from there? Were the charmers still after them? What would happen with Rose's and Tammy's jobs?

Obviously, Rose's absence had been far less severe than Tammy's. And to Rose's great relief, she could explain her handful of missed days away by claiming she originally lost a battle with food poisoning, followed by "Oh, hey. My sister's back!"

But Tammy's life had been much harder to piece together, and it was something she and her sister were still working on. Probably would be for years. After all, one doesn't get to disappear for six months without answering a slew of hard questions, many of which Tammy couldn't answer because of secrecy or memory loss.

So, for the time being, Tammy was lying low.

"Tung's flying by today for patrol," Titan said.

Rose sighed. "Just make sure Tammy doesn't see him."

"He knows, petal. But I've got to tell you, it's killing him."

She winced. "She just needs more time. It's only been two weeks."

"Took you less time than that to accept me." He winked and smiled down at her playfully before contrition took over and sadness flitted through his eyes. "But I get it. Your sister's been through an unspeakable hell. And no one more than me wishes he could take that away from her, reverse the past. Doesn't mean I won't go to bat for my brother, though. I've never seen him so miserable. His fire's been unsteady, restless. And that's just what we've noticed in the field. What he won't show us worries the guys a hell of a lot more."

A nearby pedestrian crosswalk signal beeped out a tune that matched Rose's stride. The monotonous repetition was a metaphor for the frustrated failed attempts she'd had when talking to Tammy. Explaining how her sister most likely harbored a spark of the eternal flame within her. How, when Tung touched her skin that day in the den, the spark had called to his innate angel fire and given him the gift—well, more like a tempting taste—of the full force of his fire, which he had not felt since he and his brothers had lived in the Empyrean.

Not to mention the suspicion of the soul bond flapping around between those two.

When Tammy started connecting the pieces together, her formerly pleasant demeanor had spoiled like month-old milk.

"No!" Tammy had shouted. "Absolutely not. No way am I being bound to something against my will. Not again. Not ever!"

Rose bristled at the memory and the harsh coldness her sister spouted about Tung. It was unexpected and beyond unnerving. It was *not* her sister. Not the kind and loving woman she had shared her life with since birth.

"She's freaked, Titan. It was like Tung had turned into a charmer in her mind or something, even though she knew him and knew his goodness. Hell, she'd gotten along with him just fine in the beginning. More than fine, actually. Then something just flipped in her brain. I suspect some of her memories have started to return, but she still won't share them with me. The nightmares have kicked up, though. She hasn't had a full night's sleep since I brought her back home to our apartment. I'm worried. So the last thing I want to do is push Tung on her. Insist that she spend more time with him when something has triggered within her brain recently to form a negative association."

Titan shook his head and scoffed. "Absurd."

"I know that, and you know that, but Tammy doesn't. She just needs more time, I hope."

Titan hugged her more tightly to his side and sighed. "If there's one thing we're used to, it's the passage of time. It won't change the need for patrol, though. Now that we know for sure you both carry the flame within you, we'll need to think about moving you both to a more secure location."

"I can't leave my sister," Rose whispered heavily.

"Wouldn't dream of it, petal. Wouldn't dream of it."

They let the unspoken and uncertain settle thickly in the crisp air around them. For now, in the absence of anything productive or better to do, Rose swallowed the lump in her throat and pushed the worries aside.

When they arrived a few minutes later, Titan held the door to the restaurant open for her. Warm smells of toasted cumin and freshly ground cardamom soothed her frazzled nerves and reminded her of her own here and now.

The waiter led them to a table and handed them their menus. Rose settled back against the plush burgundy couch that was placed in front of a large gold circular tray that served as the table. She glanced at the menu while the waiter filled their water glasses. As soon as they were alone, she and Titan turned over their menus and smiled.

"Sultan's Table?" they asked each other at the same time before promptly bowing their heads together and chuckling. Seriously, who was this woman? And what the hell had she done with the dour, cynical Rose who refused to acknowledge the sun was shining even when she was standing right under it?

Damn, it felt good, this feeling. Being in love with Titan.

As Titan ordered the Sultan's Table, which was a two-person tasting course that ran the gamut from toasted pita with baba ganoush and hummus to beef kofta and baklava, Rose warmed at the sight of her angel.

She grew even warmer when the waiter left and Titan snatched up her hands in his.

"Now, I know you've got your mind focused on the fresh pita marching over here soon, but I'd like to borrow a sliver of that attention for a moment," Titan teased.

"Talk fast, pretty boy. Warm pita doesn't wait."

Titan held up his open hands to her and bowed his head, out of respect and reverence for the restaurant's amazing pita, she suspected, and began rolling up his sweater sleeves.

No, not sleeves. A single sleeve. On his right arm.

Humor and temptation danced in his eyes as a sly smile curled his mouth. It was beyond dangerous for him to flash skin around her, especially when the dim lighting of the restaurant was such that every slope of tendon and contoured muscle gave her body endless flutters in endless places.

And he fucking knew it.

The devil. I mean, devilish angel.

"Am I in for a show or something? Because, if so, you'll hear no complaints from me. A repeat of last night, perhaps?"

The light glinted in Titan's tempting gaze. What could she

say? It had been a fun two weeks. Turns out, soul bonds have a thing about not keeping their hands to themselves. Titan said that it was in the rule book, apparently. And Titan, ever the upstanding leader, was all about showing her the benefits of following the rules. She didn't hate it.

"I'm always up for a repeat performance. But first, I want to give you something."

"Oh, more than lunch? Because this is plenty special enough."

Titan nodded solemnly. No more laughing. No more teasing. Just a firm, serious nod.

Rose went still. "Titan, what is it?"

He cleared his throat and held out his right arm to her, the one with the rolled-up sleeve. Was he . . . *nervous?* He shifted slightly against the couch cushion as he turned his wrist palm up so the underside of his forearm was illuminated in the dance of the sequined light. Rose let out a breath.

A small delicate flower, about the size of a quarter, had been tattooed on his inner wrist. Wisps of soft pinks and hushed lavenders melded to form perfect interlocking swirls. Tight inner layers fanned out into larger, more lush beauty as the full image of the flower revealed itself, nestled against the backdrop of two simple green leaves that gave way to a long, slim stem with thorns.

A rose.

She shook her head, partly out of confusion and partly out of . . . well, she didn't know what, frankly. The man had stunned the words right out of her. So she did the only thing she could. She raised her head and settled imploring eyes on the face of the man she loved more than words.

"You have a part of me etched on you. I thought it only fair for a part of you to be etched on me. But it's not fair. Not in the least. Because I could never have just a part of you, Rose. This tattoo is a small representation of you, a mere reminder of your

soul's light that the universe has somehow given me guardian-
ship over."

Rose opened her mouth to speak, but Titan covered her
mouth with his free hand first. "Not as a burden. Never. But as
something that has gentled my anguish and lifted up my
purpose. You are so much more than my other half. You're my
everything. And I would happily wait countless millennia more
if I knew you'd be waiting for me at the end of the journey.
You're it for me, petal. And now the world knows that, too."

Titan slid his hand free of her mouth. The moment Rose's
lips were kissed by the warm air of the restaurant, she grabbed
his face and pressed her mouth to his. It wasn't pretty. Quite the
opposite. Tears blurred her vision, teeth clanked, and inco-
herent snuffles bubbled up as she tried to show her messy, all-
consuming love to the only man worthy of it.

"I love it. I love you!" she said against his lips. "I've never
been so happy to be stuck with someone before. And I mean
stuck in the best of ways."

"You can mean it however you like. There's a no-return
policy on the tattoo. And soul bonds, for that matter. It's an all-
sales-are-final type of situation."

Rose pulled back and beamed at her soul bond. "That sounds
like my kind of promise."

Find out what happens to our prime sentinel angel, Tungsten,
when he becomes Tammy's new bodyguard . . . and she wants
absolutely nothing to do with him. Can he convince her he's
more than the stuff of her nightmares? Start reading *Angel's
Duty!*

. . .

Can we keep in touch? Are you curious to see how Rose and Titan adjust to life post-demon attack? Claim your BONUS EPILOGUE when you sign up to my newsletter to read about these two love birds' most perilous journey yet: Hosting their first family dinner for all the angels! There will be shenanigans, people...SHENANIGANS.

Thank you so much for reading *Angel's Target!* If you loved seeing Titan and Rose's relationship grow, let your friends know. Help other readers fall in love with this couple, and all those hunky angels, by leaving a review.

Scan the QR code to start reading *Angel's Duty* and the BONUS EPILOGUE today!

ACKNOWLEDGMENTS

If there was one sentence that would sum up my life while writing this book, it would be this: BookTok made me do it. Fancy book clubs ain't got nothing on the power of that wonderful community. I have met amazing authors, learned invaluable career advice, and have been humbled and blown away by fierce content creators. Those amazing ladies love their books, love their authors more, and make talking shop about books and tropes a frickin' blast.

All hail, the queens of BookTok! Don't ever change.

A special thanks to my author bestie, Jessi Gage, who has no qualms about telling me when a chapter doesn't work . . . or when my foul-mouthed angels have just the right amount of potty in the mouth. No shrinking violets here. Thank you, my dear!

And, as always, many thanks to my husband, Ben.

My OG fated mate.

ABOUT THE AUTHOR

Aimee Robinson is a lover of romance novels in all forms. Her absolute favorites, though, are the ones that offer a little bit of something *extra*: time travel, guardian angels, good old-fashioned meddlesome grandmothers with a supernatural secret to hide, you name it.

She believes romance novels should transport you from the humdrum to the swoonworthy, preferably while being curled up on the couch with chocolate and tea (or a martini . . . or both!). Aimee's overactive imagination lends itself to fun tales with emotional adventures, sexy snark, and happily ever afters.

When not writing or reading, Aimee enjoys spending time with her husband and keeping up with her two young sons.